"Cam, don't take this the wrong way, but you look like a wild horse must look when he feels his first saddle. Your eyes are the size of half dollars, and I could swear I saw your nostrils flare!"

"Now, how could I take that the *wrong way?*" He sighed. "I look like a horse. Well, do I pass muster in whatever scratch and sniff survey you're taking?"

Mandy grinned. "Ask me no questions..."

"All right, all right."

She moved to the other side of the table. It was nice to be close to Cam, but it was awfully nice to look at him, too. And if truth be told, she was afraid she might lean so close she'd end up in a kiss he might not return with the enthusiasm she was feeling.

"What was I saying before I went on that brazen olfactory safari?"

"That you stayed in California so long because you and Oscar the mule have a gene in common."

She nodded. "Oh, yes. I used to be stubborn. But I'm thinking you already know that. Any questions?"

She stared into his eyes, expecting a teasing remark, but what she saw took her breath away. If eyes could eat, his would devour her. She blushed and dropped her gaze to her lap.

In little more than the time it took to swallow, he stood and slid around to her side of the table and took her in his arms.

"This is not a question," he said in a deep voice.

Before she had time to think about it, his lips were on hers. It wasn't any butterfly kiss, either. More like Clark Gable saying, "Kiss me, Scarlett." She turned her head to the side and opened her mouth a fraction to his tongue, then happily surrendered to a delicious sensation.

She wriggled her arms free from her sides and put them around his shoulders. She heard him groan and wound her fingers in his hair. When they broke for air, her heart was racing.

Second place winner of the Golden Pen Award for Short Contemporary ["Mandy, Remembered"] and finalist in both Emerald City Opener and Knock Our Socks Off.

"From the first page Lynnette Baughman proves she's destined to be a star. LOVE WITH A WELCOME STRANGER is the perfect blend of outstanding characterization and page-turning pacing. I hated to put it down. I can't wait to read more from this wonderful new talent."
~Pamela Britton, bestselling author of "Total Control"

Love With A Welcome Stranger

by

Lynnette Baughman

Love With A Welcome Stranger

Cover Art by *Rae Monet*

The Wild Rose Press
PO Box 708
Adams Basin, NY 14410-0706
Visit us at www.thewildrosepress.com

Publishing History
First Yellow Rose Edition, 2008
Print ISBN 1-60154-314-X

Published in the United States of America

Dedication

To Sophia Joy Beal,
a little girl who spreads joy
everywhere she goes.

Chapter 1

Campbell West felt blue eyes focus on his face, eyes the color of a glacier but so hot they singed his skin like sunlight through a magnifying glass. A smile, a dimple. Suddenly, a change—blue eyes wide in terror.

The sound of a single gunshot jerked Cam to his feet. *Mandy!*

No, no. *No.* His heart pounded and adrenaline gushed through his body as he reconciled his dream with the sound, so like a gunshot. He leaned stiff-armed against the pine beside him. The slim crescent of shade he'd claimed half an hour ago had given way to the broiling Montana sun.

There was no gunshot. Just a backfire from the old bus coming to collect his exhausted crew of firefighters.

Get a grip, West!

He listened to the bus grind its gears as the driver tried to find one that would pull it up the steep hill. Rubbing his hand over his two-week growth of beard, he surveyed his hotshots. The fifteen men, who equaled or surpassed him in soot, grime, and beards, lay around him like volunteers at a disaster drill. Fully clothed except for their yellow jackets, they had no visible wounds but all appeared to be dead. Only their walrus-like snores were proof of life. They smelled worse than walruses, alive or dead.

"The bus is coming," he called. "Let's haul." He went down on one knee to gather his supplies into his pack.

Fifteen groans and muttered oaths rose with the dust about how freaking hot it was, how late the bus was, and how hungry they all were.

"Rib eye steak!" one called out. That first mention of food was like the opening bid in a poor man's poker game.

"Rib eye steak and three eggs."

"I'll see your steak and eggs and raise you cream gravy on biscuits."

Cam zipped all the pockets on his pack and stood, glad that the clamor for food covered the sounds of his knees creaking. Long marches on tough terrain carrying heavy tools made his thirty-six years feel like forty-six to his knees and back.

Rodeo hadn't done his body any favors, either.

His assistant crew chief stopped on his way toward the bus. Coated with soot, and lacking the eyebrows he'd had the day before, Vic Tunney still had his good humor. "Are you sure you want to bail?"

"As of today, Vic, you're the man. You knew I was just in for this fire."

"I guess we were damn lucky you were available, with Otto laid up."

Cam didn't comment on that luck. He'd finished his seasonal firefighting career more than a year ago and was blissfully happy to be a full time horse rancher. But three weeks ago, when the Mill Hill Hotshots arrived to fight the Grail Fire and their crew chief broke his leg, the fire commanders had to get someone experienced on the job without delay. How could he say no?

True, the fire was close to his ranch and the outskirts of Bitter Falls, eighty miles away before they'd turned it, but when he answered the call, it wasn't for his ranch. It was for his Montana.

Fighting fires had been a way to make his grubstake. That and rodeos. Now he had all the trappings of success, but he wasn't the kind of man to turn his back.

He could hear his grandfather's deep voice. "We pitch in, Cam. That's what we do in Montana. What if everyone said, 'I'll fight fire, or crime, or injustice at my fence line, but not beyond it'?"

"Glad you were there yesterday," Vic said.

Cam heard the catch in the young man's voice.

"It was ugly." Vic laughed. "Now, I'm ugly."

"Your eyebrows were too bushy, anyway." He shook Vic's outstretched hand, careful to avoid the raw tips of his fingers. "You'd better get your skinny butt to the medical tent."

"Will do, as soon as that bucket of bolts gets us off this hill. Where did they get that thing, a museum?"

"Low bid, I guess." Cam watched Vic and the others move out toward the bus. He would miss the camaraderie and the adrenaline rush, but the sole fire he wanted to see from now on was flames in the grate of his cozy new house—while he looked out on acres of fluffy Montana snow.

For today, however, he had the sweltering heat and smoke of August, a month that usually brought cooling. Instead of fall and harvests, all anybody talked about was the god-awful heat and drought. The Grail Fire was seventy percent contained, but the damn thing would fester in stumps and logs, giving off smoke for at least another month.

A silver SUV with dark tinted windows moved up the road from their left, ahead of the battered green U.S. Forest Service bus with "Mill Hill Hotshots" on the side. Cam felt an old thump like a fist in his chest when he recognized the logo of McCay Enterprises on the SUV. He watched the sheriff's deputy, responsible for keeping civilians out of the forest, stop the car and go around to the driver's side.

Well, well, well. Out stepped Ford McCay himself. Tall, with a chiseled jaw, he looked as confident as he had on the cover of *Forbes Magazine*. Only McCay's white hair made him appear older than Cam remembered him.

He watched McCay gesture dismissively at the sawhorses blocking the road. The deputy shook his head; McCay persisted. *No, yes.* More gestures. *Hell no, hell yes.*

Cam's money was on McCay. He must have made it past other roadblocks to get this far. The front passenger door opened and an attractive young brunette stepped out. She opened the back door and held out her hand to help someone down.

His heart hit his rib cage and ricocheted against his backbone. For a moment he had more trouble breathing than he'd had back in the inferno he'd come through the day before.

Mandy McCay. Home at last.

She glanced around. For a long moment, her blue eyes met his but he saw no flicker of recognition in her gaze. Part of him grasped at the feeble hope that her blank expression was due to his unintentional disguise. He looked more like a cross between a black bear and a raccoon than the cowboy she used to know, especially in his yellow overalls and suspenders, goggle-rings around his eyes.

The rest of him didn't care what Mandy McCay thought. *That* was the part of him that mattered, that needed to be fed by the dark spring of cold indifference deep inside him. She was nothing to him now. The same way he'd been nothing to her for twelve long years.

But no man could look at Mandy McCay and quickly look away. After all she'd been through—the kidnapping by a deranged fan, the shooting, the long, painful months of physical therapy—it defied all odds, and yet, there she was. More gorgeous than he remembered.

He'd seen pictures of her in the hospital, when her face was swollen beyond recognition. Later, photos on a website devoted to her progress showed improvement. He wouldn't admit it under torture, but, yes, he'd looked at the site.

All the announcements of excellent progress were accompanied by the X-ray of the bullet lodged in her brain for a week before surgeons dared to operate. The big question glossed over by Mandy's doctors, her father, and her sister D'Ann was the state of her memory.

He'd seen pictures of her as she was transferred from the hospital in Los Angeles to the small airport. There she'd been secured in an air ambulance for the flight to Barrow Neurological Institute in Phoenix. The photos, taken by some jerk with a cell phone and rabbit pellets where his brain ought to be, showed her head swathed in bandages and her eyes glazed like the eyes on a porcelain doll.

He looked away from the SUV to see his crew lined up at the door of the bus. As the driver emerged, he spoke to the man at the head of the line. The firefighter pointed at Cam and the driver approached with a clipboard. A pen dangled on a string.

Cam met him halfway, looked over the list, and handed it back. "My number two is over there. He'll handle this."

"That's good, thanks. Hey, who's the big wig in the Lincoln?"

"Ford McCay."

"No kidding? Hey, is that blond girl that actress who got shot? That was a hell of a thing."

"Yeah, that's Mandy. The other girl is her sister." Cam hadn't seen D'Ann in person since she was a kid with skinned knees and braces, but he'd seen her half a dozen times on TV news. She'd left her nursing job in Oregon to stay beside Mandy through the surgery and painful therapy. Now, with the two of them standing side by side, their family resemblance was easy to see. D'Ann was about five feet eight, not quite as tall as Mandy. They both had long, thick hair and heart-shaped faces with a sprinkle of freckles. Mandy had the dimple.

"Pretty girls, both of 'em." The driver chuckled. "Their dad's some kind of peacock, though."

Cam nodded, his lips too tight with tension to smile.

"I've been eating his dust all the way up here," the driver went on. "I had to stop at every roadblock while he chewed a hole through the deputies. Says he's an F.O.G. 'Friend of Gill.'"

Cam recognized the acronym of Governor Gill Smyth's valued supporters. Cartoonists often made the S in *Smyth* and *Supporters* a dollar sign.

The driver spit in the dirt. "I think S.O.B. is more like it,"

"Money talks." Cam waited for the inevitable punchline.

The driver laughed. "Yeah, it talks to me. It always says, 'Goodbye.' Well, we ought to be out of here in a few minutes. It's two or three miles farther to the highway. I'll have you and your crew back to the staging area in an hour."

Cam shook hands and thanked him, but his attention was riveted on Mandy, downhill maybe twenty yards on his left. D'Ann had walked some thirty yards off the road to his right to look down to the highway. When Mandy started walking toward her, she wasn't completely steady on her feet. Against his better judgment, he chose that moment to walk back and retrieve his pack and helmet at the base of the tree. If their paths crossed, he'd blame geometry.

Her blond hair shimmered in the sunlight. He

closed the distance between them and she looked to her right, toward him. Her eyes were the color of ice deep within a crevasse.

For him, time didn't stand still. It rewound twelve years in two seconds flat.

For the cataclysmic love that used to be in those eyes, he'd played a starring role in the corniest show on earth. *The poor cowboy and the rich rancher's daughter.*

Suddenly, the toe of Mandy's right sneaker caught on a tree root and she started to fall. With lightning reflexes, he reached out.

"I've got you!" He clamped his big hands on her arms and kept her from landing on the ground.

"You okay?" he asked.

She regained her balance. When their gazes met and held, he searched her eyes but could find no hint of recognition. Instead he saw her look down at the arms of her white blouse, marred now by large black handprints.

"I'm sorry."

"That's all right," she said with a smile that could ignite wet wood. "I'd be dirtier if I hit the ground."

"Mandy!" D'Ann was approaching fast from Cam's right.

He apologized once more to Mandy and turned away to snag the strap of his pack and palm his helmet onto his head.

"I'm okay," Mandy assured her.

"I think we'd better wait in the car," D'Ann said. To Cam she added, "Thanks. I mean double thanks. For catching my sister before she landed face down in the dirt, and for working so hard to put out the fire."

He glanced toward them and nodded, not sure what to say. He wasn't sure what to think, either. How could he be standing six feet from Mandy? How

7

could their orbits cross? What were the odds? God must have a sense of humor.

As he headed for the bus, he watched D'Ann hold out her stiffened left arm to give Mandy something to hold onto.

Regret flared like a blowtorch in his chest, regret for the anger and pride that had driven them apart, the tangled web of lies and truth. He'd remembered—deliberately—her accusation, and blocked out so much more.

And yet, somehow, the taste of her last kiss was still on his lips.

****

"It feels...cammeled." Mandy pushed the power button to lower her car window. When they'd finally bounced off the old logging road onto the highway, she'd dozed off for a half hour or so. Now she got her first view of Bitter Falls Farm.

"Cammeled" was wrong but she couldn't think of the word she meant.

D'Ann had asked her how it felt to see the farm after being gone twelve years. She didn't add anything about why it had been so long, about choices Mandy had made, doors she'd slammed behind her.

"Try again," D'Ann said with her usual patience.

She'd been a rock these past months. Mandy took a deep breath. "Like eggs." She made the back and forth motion of beating eggs. "Crammeled."

"Oh, scrambled." D'Ann grinned. "You mean it's hard to get it all sorted out in your memory."

She nodded. She rarely mixed up words now, only when she was frightfully tired, as she was after this long trip home. Not even stepping out of the car for fresh air, back on that mountain pass, had helped her. Instead of feeling better, she'd nearly fallen. Her balance was more affected by fatigue than her vocabulary. She'd proudly graduated a

8

week ago to medium high heels, but it was apparent to that firefighter and anyone watching that she wasn't totally steady on her feet. That public pratfall knocked her pride down two pegs.

She looked at the handprints on her white shirt. The firefighter had a nice voice. His eyes, the color of dark brown sugar, reminded her of someone, but the impression was as fleeting as smoke.

D'Ann had talked her into wearing sensible sneakers for the trip. They hadn't announced their schedule, but someone at the airport might recognize her and snap her picture with a camera or a phone. CNN would love to get a shot of Mandy McCay falling down like a sobriety test flunky.

As far as she knew, no one had spotted her between Phoenix and Missoula. She and D'Ann wore jeans, sneakers and sunglasses, and all she had to do was keep her eyes on her sister and hurry down the concourse.

The drive home from the airport was an ordeal. They'd waited nearly two hours at three roadblocks before Ford McCay got permission to drive up the back way, skirting the burned area. D'Ann argued in favor of a motel, but Mandy insisted she could make it home. The last part of the detour they'd crawled up the hill in front of a U.S. Forest Service bus.

She was, however, on the ragged edge of exhaustion by the time they pulled into the circular drive. The island formed by the driveway was a riot of color thanks to coral, pink and purple dahlias. With a broad veranda and climbing vines beside the steps, the farmhouse was like the house in her dreams. But her subconscious hadn't manufactured this. The line between truth and fiction was blurry, but this house, these flowers, the view across a green valley—this scene was in her memory bank.

She held her arms out in front of her and slowly touched her little fingers to each other in one of the tests she'd mastered. She sighed. Yes, could shuffle cards and pour orange juice. She could give D'Ann and her doctors high-fives when she met a new goal.

What I can't do is remember chunks of my own life. The damage from the bullet was capricious.

Her memory of how to dance the rumba was gone, but she could recite the Gettysburg Address. She knew what she'd had for lunch the day she was shot, but she couldn't picture herself graduating from high school. And she couldn't recall why she left Montana at the end of that summer.

A petite woman in her late forties or early fifties, wearing a starched apron, stood at the top of the stairs. Strands of red hair escaped from a large hair clip and fell around her face. Her gray eyes were frank and confident.

"You must be Eleanor," Mandy said as she climbed the six stairs to the porch. D'Ann had supplied the name of the woman who'd worked for their father for two years, keeping up the house and cooking meals when he was there.

"Yes, Eleanor Mays. You look tired. All of you do. Come in. The house is nice and cool, and I made fresh lemonade. Or would you prefer tea?"

"Tea would be great," she said. "I think I could drink a quart without taking a breath."

"You go ahead upstairs," D'Ann said. "Eleanor and I will bring the tea and something to eat."

Her father carried their suitcases into the entry hall and excused himself to check on messages in his home office.

As she climbed the stairs to the second floor, she concentrated on the process. Lift the heavy right foot all the way to the next step, she told herself. Okay, now hold on to the polished banister.

Don't be discouraged. She smiled to realize that the voice in her head was her favorite therapist. *It's been a long day, Mandy. Cut yourself some slack.*

A little muscle weakness was not surprising; she'd be fine in the morning. Fine in the...

She grabbed the banister with both hands and held it tight. Her wayward right foot threatened to buckle at the ankle, then righted itself.

"Who am I trying to fool?" she muttered under her breath as she climbed the last three stairs. *I'll never be fine. Never.*

Her room looked exactly as she remembered it. Big four-poster bed with a white canopy, light oak dresser and chest of drawers. White louvered closet doors, a white phone.

But was she truly remembering it? Or was this one of the memories D'Ann and her friends in California tried to recreate by describing things and showing her pictures? After a while, she'd seen a picture of this room so many times that the dividing line between memory and its substitute was fuzzy.

She crossed to the window and looked at a cedar chest against the wall. It had been her great-grandmother's hope chest, brought to Montana from Wisconsin on a covered wagon. It hadn't been in the pictures D'Ann showed her, but twelve years ago it held crocheted doilies and an embroidered tablecloth and—oh, yes—a quilt made from scraps of flour sacks in a wedding ring pattern. As she lifted the lid, she had her own kind of hope.

Yes, it was all there. She'd recalled it on her own.

More would come. She leaned the hinged top of the chest against the wall and took out a doily to examine the delicate handwork.

Some things were better off forgotten, of course. She would probably never remember her stalker and the threats. Nor would she remember being taken hostage and dragged onto the highway overpass, nor the police blocking the roadway, nor the sound of the gunshot as the .22 caliber bullet burst through her skull.

No one showed her pictures of Ethan Koller dead on the pavement beside her, their blood pooled. She'd been told the helicopter landed on the cleared highway and that it was a miracle she got to the hospital in time to save her life.

Her memory was blank until weeks later, in Arizona. She'd awakened to a world of pain and confusion. Words had no meaning; objects had no context. All she did was cry.

No, she didn't want any of those memories to return. Shut the door, her counselor had said. Imagine a solid steel door and shut it. Your life is on this side of the door.

She'd done what the doctor suggested. She'd gone one step further, too. The shooting and all that pain was behind her, but so was her California lifestyle. She had no wish to revive it. No, it was better to come home to Montana. She'd been happy here, and secure. In sight of the mountains she loved, she could build on solid ground.

She folded the doily and set it back in the cedar chest; she lowered the top halfway then froze. Slowly, she opened it all the way and knelt as if at an altar. With her left hand, she held the lid open. Her right hand probed beneath the quilt and pressed the wood, seeking the latch on the secret compartment.

When she was a little girl, she'd spun elaborate stories about her great-grandmother and the love letters she'd hidden in the chest, letters from a man she'd been forbidden to marry. Mandy had never seen any letters. Probably it was nothing more than a story, more embroidered over time than the tablecloth.

Her thumb found the release and her fingers pressed the sides of the empty compartment. She sighed with profound disappointment, as if she herself had hidden something there and now it was gone.

The sound of D'Ann's voice in the hall brought her fully back to the present. She closed the top of the chest and rose to her feet. She heard a soft knock on her door and called, "Come in."

Eleanor walked in with a plate and a glass. D'Ann was right behind her with a fold-out tray.

"That looks delicious. Thank you, Eleanor."

She caught a fleeting look in D'Ann's eyes. She'd seen it in the eyes of other people, her publicist and her best friend—surprise that the "new" Mandy said thank you.

Had she been so selfish before the traumatic brain injury? Had she made her only sister dislike her? D'Ann ignored all questions like that, saying it was all water under the bridge, that she shouldn't waste her time looking for something that wasn't there. But Mandy couldn't help wondering. *Who was I?* If she couldn't answer that, how could she make sense of the other mysteries she had to solve?

Who am I now?

And...what about the rest of my life?

Chapter 2

On Tuesday morning, Cam trotted his sorrel gelding, Sunny, along the white fence back toward the ranch house and stable. His foreman waved from the round pen where he was working with a mustang he'd brought in from the BLM roundup in Nevada a week before. The young mare's eyes and nostrils flared at the sight of yet another stranger. Joey Dix calmed her down with his soothing voice and led her to the water trough.

Cam surveyed the pastures within sight of the house, proud of the eight brood mares and their healthy colts and fillies. Five of the mares had been covered by his champion stallion, Dar-Kanyon, soon after they foaled, and all were pregnant again. Most of Dar-Kanyon's colts and fillies were born elsewhere, but Cam kept close track of every one of them.

The other three had been covered by a red roan stallion, Jehosaphat, on a ranch two hundred miles away. They, too, would foal in the spring.

Last year, he recalled with pride, two colts by Dar-Kanyon and out of famed Arabian Perfection's Fire took champion and reserve champion prizes in the reining horse division at the Scottsdale Arabian and Half-Arabian Horse Show.

The three yearlings he still had on the ranch, plus the acclaim of colts like the two out of Perfection's Fire, would show prospective breeders what they could look forward to if they brought their best mares to Campbell West Ranch.

"The grass is good along the draw," he called to Joey. "Let's take Valley Girl out there tomorrow and Buckskin Molly next week." Their foals would be agitated for a while, calling for their mothers, but the weaning would go better with the mares out of sight and hearing. And the grass-only diet would help dry up the mares' milk.

He looped the reins around his saddle horn and slid to the ground. "They all look great. It's good to be home."

"You goin' into town?" Joey asked.

Cam nodded. "I saw your list on the kitchen counter. Do you think our order is in yet at Falls Feed?"

"Lester said they get their truck by noon, so it'll be there by the time you drive in." Joey kicked at the dirt with the boot on his prosthetic leg. His smooth-hair collie, Polo, squeezed under the bottom rung of the corral and showed up for muster.

As on all ranches, the dogs were part of the team. Cam's old Border collie, Marco, had been jealous of Joey's pup, but they'd learned to cooperate. Polo was bigger than Marco now, but she had no delusions of grandeur. Marco was the boss dog.

"Polo's getting fat," Cam said.

"Our girl ran off for a few days in June, while you were in Texas," Joey said with a laugh. "I lost track of her downtown at the festival. She came back preggers. I don't know what the little buggers will look like."

"Why that little tart!" Cam crossed his arms and studied Polo. "After all we've done for her!" Marco was in the clear. He'd been neutered long ago.

Joey shrugged. "Apparently the issue is what we *didn't* do for her. I didn't get her to Doctor Delgado in a timely fashion."

"I'll take her in today; make sure she's all right."

"I hope it was a love match," Joey said. "Not some tawdry back alley affair."

"Yeah, well, I hope the daddy wasn't a Great Dane."

Polo wagged her hindquarters, delighted to be the object of so much attention. Cam glowered at her. "We'd better keep our ears open for anyone wanting a puppy. Anyway, right now I've got to get to town."

"Money burning a hole in your pocket, cowboy?" Joey asked with a grin.

"Yeah, I'm going to belly up to the counter at the hardware store. Lay my money down for two pounds of nails and a new ax. Is that pretty redhead, Lana, still working there?"

"Hell, no!" Joey said with a snort. "Pretty girl comes to Bitter Falls, she gets snatched up and married faster than I can scrape the dirt out from under my fingernails, race into town, and display my wit and charm. It's slim pickin's, Cam. I was hoping you'd bring me home something special." He made the shape of a curvy woman in the air.

"Ha! Where I've been, the only way to tell the women from the men under the hard hats and grime is the women are the ones telling the dirtiest jokes."

"That works for me. Keep your eyes open in town."

Cam loaded Polo into the cab of his pickup and drove the back way down to Bitter Falls. Traffic moved better than the day before, but he still saw a lot of heavy equipment and fire management people.

He parked in the shade in back of the feed store and stepped out. Polo usually leaped down from the high seat but this time she looked down and whimpered.

"Oh, for pity's sake," he muttered and lifted her down. "Come on."

He strode in the back door of Falls Feed and

Tack and told the young man at the counter he'd be back for his order in an hour, possibly less. A custom saddle on display in the front window hooked his attention and delayed his departure.

The bell over the door rang. He glanced over and caught his breath.

D'Ann McCay walked in and spoke to someone behind her. Mandy stepped inside and pushed her sunglasses up onto her ash blond hair. She blinked in the muted light of the old wood interior. Looked at him and away. Not a scintilla of recognition.

He'd thought a thousand times what it would be like to see those glacier-blue eyes and big feathery lashes look into his own, but this was scenario one thousand and one. She didn't recognize him. He had to turn away to regain his composure.

He couldn't flatter himself that she was *acting* like she didn't recognize him. Beautiful, vivacious Mandy McCay had made a good starlet in Hollywood, but nobody ever claimed she could act her way out of a broom closet. She'd been a favorite celebrity in the fan magazines, pictured with movie and TV heartthrobs, often showing a lot of skin.

Cam knew this not because he'd followed her acting career, such as it was, but because the tragedy of the bullet in her brain had made Mandy so famous that he couldn't help but catch up on what she'd been doing for the past twelve years.

He turned back and watched the two women trying on leather riding gloves. To him, D'Ann was still a kid in braces. She'd been about twelve when he'd worked on her dad's ranch. Hell of a rider. She'd wanted to be a rodeo star and practiced barrel racing until both she and the horse were so tired he had to step in and rescue the horse.

He had to think a minute to recall why she'd quit racing. Oh, yeah. Her dad sent her to Virginia to live with an aunt and learn to ride like a lady.

D'Ann had joked about going to Virginia. "I'll be saying, 'Pip, pip and cheerio. Where did that cunning little fox go?'" But he'd seen her in the barn the night before she left. She had her arms around her mare, Blossom, sobbing into her withers.

That had been before Cam and Mandy fell in love. And, okay, in lust. Hard to tell which was which back then. Either way, D'Ann wouldn't have known about "them" unless Mandy had told her on the phone or in a letter, and he figured there was no chance of that. Her little sister would have spilled the beans to their father.

He picked up a hatband and went to the counter to pay.

"Cam?" D'Ann called. "Cam West?"

"Will that be all?" the clerk asked.

Cam turned his hat around in his hands and set the hatband to the side. "I don't think I'll get this after all, thanks." He turned to D'Ann and held out his hand. "Ms. McCay, you're looking well."

She was a striking young woman, light brown hair clutched in a leather strap at the nape of her neck. Her eyes were blue-green rather than aqua-blue like Mandy's.

"Thanks, Cam. And call me D'Ann. None of this Ms. McCay, stuff. You remember my sister, don't you? Mandy, this is Cam West. He taught me everything I know about riding a cutting horse. Then, of course, Dad paid good money to make me forget that and learn to prance around on an English saddle with my nose in the air like I had a burr up my butt."

Cam held out his hand and tried not to stare at Mandy's flawless complexion and eyes like...glaciers, topaz, Montana sky, bluebonnets, high mountain lakes. He sighed. Who knew he had such a poetic streak?

"Ms. McCay, I'm so glad to see you back in

Bitter Falls. Will you be staying long?"

Mandy's eyes went to D'Ann and Cam guessed she relied a lot on her sister to answer questions for her. Instead of answering, D'Ann turned to the clerk and asked about a special brand of gloves. The young man nodded and pulled a stack of narrow boxes to the counter and studied them, looking cross-eyed at what must be tiny print.

Mandy said nothing for a moment, then, "I don't have any plans to leave. I want to get, uh, re-uh...reacquainted with Montana."

D'Ann turned back. "Cam, did I hear that you're a firefighter for the Forest Service? Did you work on the fire that roared over Grail Mountain?"

"I did. I'm through for the season, though. In fact, I've retired from firefighting. I need to devote more of my back-breaking labor to my ranch."

D'Ann smiled and turned back to the clerk, who held up beige leather gloves. "I'm so glad you have them in stock. I'll take two pairs."

"If you ladies will excuse me," Cam said, "I need to take my dog to the vet. She's unexpectedly in a family way."

"Family way?" Mandy looked puzzled, then surprised. "Oh, you mean puppies?"

D'Ann and Cam burst out laughing and Mandy looked horror stricken at her inane question, but then joined them. Cam loved the sound of Mandy laughing. He always had.

"Yes, puppies," Cam said, "but we have no idea who the father is. I want the vet to make sure she can deliver them all right."

"What's her name?" Mandy asked.

"Polo. She belongs to my foreman, Joey Dix."

Mandy went down on one knee and let Polo lick her cheek. "I had a dog," she said softly. "A boy dog."

Her eyes looked off in the distance, then suddenly she grinned and her eyes had the old sparkle he remembered.

"Chester. We named him Chester because he had a limp." She stood and pointed a pink manicured finger toward D'Ann. "And you had a dog named Trouble."

Cam saw D'Ann beam with pleasure and even clap her hands. All this excitement for a dog's name? He wondered if more was going on here. Was she rebuilding her memory bank, one dog and pony at a time? Would she ever remember him?

And if she did, what then?

He put his hat back on his head and excused himself again. "Come on, Polo."

On the sidewalk, he couldn't tell if the hot flush over his body was due to the oven-like air temperature or to something else. He was pretty sure this August was on track to be the hottest on record for him.

****

Mandy watched the tall, broad-shouldered stranger stroll out of the store and repeated his name and his dog's name so she'd remember them. Recalling his face with that chiseled jaw and eyes the color of fireweed honey would be easy.

"How are you doing?" D'Ann asked. "Probably getting tired, huh? I know I am. This heat is awful. Ah, I have an idea. Let's go get an ice cream cone."

The taste shot into Mandy's mind and made her smile. "I want a root beer float."

"That's always been your favorite." D'Ann took her change and put the gloves and receipt in her large straw purse. "I heard that new owners took over the ice cream shop, but I'll bet they can figure out root beer and vanilla ice cream."

Mandy waited by the door while D'Ann thanked the clerk. Her little sister had been born sweet and never changed. Nursing was the perfect profession for her. *I was the one who rattled the cage all the*

20

time.

The August heat outside the store was brutal. As soon as they saw a break in the traffic, the two of them crossed the street on the diagonal. Tourism was apparently king in Bitter Falls, far more than she remembered. She looked at the businesses and recalled, in most cases, who had occupied those stores when she was a girl. Only a few were unchanged.

Since she'd returned to the house she'd grown up in, so much was coming back to her. Like her mom's death when she was twelve and D'Ann was seven. Mandy, D'Ann, and their dad had been the walking wounded, lost without Jane McCay.

Mandy recalled Aunt Sarah, her father's sister, coming from Virginia for a long stay. Then, saying Ford would have to handle things himself, Sarah returned to her own family and horse ranch.

After Sarah came a string of housekeepers. A couple of them were good; most were forgettable—even to someone with a good memory.

D'Ann stopped to admire shoes and purses in the front bay window of Mountain Made Apparel and Home Furnishings.

"What used to be here?" Mandy asked.

"The Keystone Café had about three-quarters of it and a used bookstore had the long skinny side next to Woolworth's. That was a long time ago."

"Yeah. I remember when Woolworth's closed and the art galleries started opening up."

"The new ice cream shop is another block down," D'Ann said.

"Do you want to go in here first? Those sandals would match your new sundress."

"Maybe tomorrow. In a town the size of Bitter Falls, you don't want to have all your fun the first day. Let's go get ice cream."

Memories tumbled into Mandy's mind as they

strolled down Main Street, pausing to admire a display of knit scarves and peer into a case of hand-dipped chocolates. The memories filled in a lot of gaps between what she'd been told about her life and what she truly remembered. It was the difference between a paint-by-numbers picture and a vivid, swirling, emotional work of art that filled a canvas and continued into another dimension.

Her dad had been gone more and more during the housekeeper years as his business got bigger and bigger. And when he was home he and Mandy had yelled at each other a lot. Perhaps that was normal; she couldn't remember what they'd yelled about. She did recall D'Ann crying her eyes out because Dad made her move to Virginia.

The girls behind the counter at the High Mountain Ice Cream Shop stared at Mandy; the unwanted attention made her nervous. She sat at a corner table while D'Ann ordered two root beer floats.

She had a sinking feeling that what she ordered and how she looked would end up in an internet gossip column.

She wished she could somehow outrun fame. She'd been pretty. Big deal. In Hollywood that was as common as having a credit card and red toenails.

Oh, she'd loved the attention at first. Mandy McCay and her cherry-red Thunderbird convertible; Mandy dating the hottest, youngest producer in Hollywood. Then she wasn't so new, so cute, so funny. To be noticed she had to keep dancing faster, had to spin more plates in the air. It wasn't enough to date; she needed to date "up the food chain." She remembered bragging to a girlfriend that she'd gone to five parties after the Academy Awards. Her sexy dress, the V in back plunging all the way to her butt crack, had gotten her onto *Entertainment Tonight* and pictured in *People Magazine*.

By the time she was twenty-two, she'd been engaged, jilted, engaged again. The second time *she'd* jilted *him*. She shopped and clubbed with all the right celebrities.

She was on a hit TV show; she was on a show that bombed. She hired a high-powered publicist. She went to Cannes and stayed a week on a yacht in the Mediterranean with a handsome producer, this time an older man. He was gay; she was his "cover." But she moved up the ladder.

And what had it gotten her? A stalker. A whacko who left a weird manifesto about how she was the Virgin Mary and he had to take her with him to paradise. He was nearly successful at sending her. The police sharpshooter sent him somewhere else.

She savored the fantastic flavor of the root beer float. She'd known she was recovering when she began to taste food again. And not only to taste it, but also to feel the texture, the temperature—and to smell the hundreds of aromas of fish and butter and chocolate. Fresh bread, marinara sauce, cold milk. To think she used to take apples for granted. In the past month or two, the juice of a crisp Fuji apple exploding in her mouth almost made her weep.

She'd never cooked in her life, but now she read cookbooks like a lot of people read mysteries. And to her it was a mystery. Did ordinary people make things like that? What must it feel like, to be able to do that? The only TV she watched was the Food Channel.

She drained the last drops from her float when motion caught her eye out on the street. "What is it?"

D'Ann went to the door and looked out. "It's a bus full of firefighters."

Mandy looked out the window. She'd seen faces like that yesterday, when her dad had argued his way past three roadblocks. Exhausted, sweaty men and women.

The firefighters came slowly down the steps of the bus. Someone approached them. The man with the dog.

Cam West and...Polo. He was laughing, pointing at the ice cream shop. Then he turned and came into the shop.

"I need forty ice cream cones, triple scoops. Surprise me on the flavors."

The two girls looked at each other, clearly panicked by the huge order. One of them squeaked, "Forty?"

"Could I help?" Mandy asked. The girls, Cam West and D'Ann all looked at her as if she'd grown a horn on her forehead.

"What a great idea, Mandy," D'Ann blurted. "We'll both help."

Mandy followed her behind the counter and the teenagers pointed out the hand washing sink and soap. In a minute, the four of them were leaning into the freezers and rolling up scoops of pastel wonders. Each time they had three ice cream balls seated firmly on a cone, they handed it to Cam and he passed it out the door.

When the rush was over, Cam paid the bill. Mandy washed her hands and followed D'Ann out onto the sidewalk. Forty people squeezed into the shade of the building, slurping the ice cream before it melted.

"Thanks, Chief!" several of them called as Cam came outside.

"I'm glad I didn't run into you guys in front of a steakhouse!" He laughed, then turned toward Mandy and lowered his voice. "Mandy, D'Ann, thanks for pitching in."

His smile and his brown eyes—hazel?—flecked with gold made her catch her breath.

Mandy wanted to know more about this man they called Chief, but couldn't think of a reason to stand there and gawk. Polo caught her eye. The reddish-brown dog had stretched out under a wooden bench and gone to sleep. With her belly on the ground between her front and back legs like a fat pancake, instead of hanging beneath her, she did look pregnant.

"How is Polo?" she asked.

"She's good. Doctor Delgado says it looks like five or six puppies and she thinks Polo can handle it—even though she's young to be a mother."

"When are they due?" D'Ann moved down the sidewalk to leave the entrance to the ice cream store unblocked. Mandy and Cam followed her.

"Joey Dix said she went missing when she was downtown with him for the Midsummer Festival. The doctor says based on that and the exam, she's probably going to whelp in about a week."

Mandy looked up at Cam West's warm, almost intimate, gaze and held it with her own. How long had he been staring at her? She was used to people staring, and it usually made her want to run the other way. But there was something in this rancher's eyes that had the opposite effect.

He broke off his stare and swallowed hard. Was it her imagination, or did his deeply tanned face just get a little redder? He wet his lips once, then again, and whistled to Polo.

"I hope you'll excuse me, ladies. I've got to pick up the feed and grab a peck of groceries. I've got hungry horses and four hungry workers waiting for me." With a tip of his hat, he stepped off the curb and into the street.

Mandy opened her mouth and blurted the first thing that came to her mind. "Would they like some cookies?"

Cam stopped in mid-stride and she covered her mouth with her hand to keep the laugh from coming out. He looked like a boy reacting to *Simon says freeze.* He turned slowly and stared at her, this time with wide, disbelieving eyes.

"Cookies?"

Her mouth—which had found it so easy to say anything that might turn Cam West around—was inexplicably dry now. There was something about his gaze and the sound of his voice that made her self-conscious.

He might be married, and here she was acting the fool on Main Street. Her stomach clenched. She tried to take a deep breath but had to settle for a string of mini-breaths. The doctors warned her that she might have a problem with acting impulsively, but she thought they were warning her not to go shopping with a fistful of credit cards. She would never have guessed she'd impulsively throw herself at a stranger, no matter how sexy he looked. No matter that his shoulders were so broad and the muscles in his arms showed to such advantage below the sleeves of his black T-shirt.

She couldn't make a sound. She shrugged and looked at D'Ann. From under her eyelashes she got a good look at Cam's left hand. No ring. But of course not all married men wore rings. Lord knows she'd found *that* out the hard way.

D'Ann looked from her to Cam and back and a slow smile spread across her expressive face.

"It's like this, Cam. Doctors told us that due to Mandy's injury she might display, well, that her personality might seem different. You've now glimpsed a facet of my strange new sister. Mandy is obsessed with cooking."

He grinned. "You like to cook?"

"I, uh," Mandy swallowed hard. "Not exactly. I like to imagine myself cooking." She felt a hot flush in her cheeks. "I haven't actually made anything yet."

"She pores over cookbooks, Cam. So far it's more

theory than action. Sort of like a spinster aunt reading romance novels."

Mandy groaned. She couldn't believe how badly this was going. She wished fervently that D'Ann hadn't mentioned romance novels. She instantly pictured Cam West clutching a lusty wench in torn clothing, one hand pressed to the side of her aching breast.

"Well, look at the time," she said brightly. "If we go straight home I'll be able to see *Emeril Live*." She took three long steps forward and thrust her hand out to Cam. As she gave him a hearty handshake she said, "A pleasure meeting you."

"I love cookies."

His voice was husky, and she couldn't help wondering what else he loved. As if he were reading her mind, he licked his lips.

She tried in vain to pull her hand free of his. Involuntarily, her tongue imitated his lick.

"You do?" She swallowed hard and cleared her throat, trying to get her voice out of lyric soprano range. "I suppose I could try a simple recipe."

D'Ann rolled her eyes. "I'll let you know when to expect us, Cam. This is something I don't want to miss."

"Is that a fact?" he murmured.

At last, he released her hand and once again touched the brim of his hat.

With a nod to her sister as he turned to go, he added, "You'll have to take a number and get in line, D'Ann. Behind me."

Chapter 3

Mandy paced in the kitchen like a father outside a delivery room. Even with the light on in the oven, she couldn't see well enough through the glass to be sure the cookies were done but not *too* done.

Eleanor had showed her where the mixing bowls and other supplies were and said she'd be in the basement. D'Ann disappeared, too. This project was Mandy's baby, so to speak.

Baby? She laughed, struck by the irony of the phrase "having a bun in the oven."

The timer buzzed and she jerked the oven door open. With a mitt, she lifted the first two batches out and examined them. They were pretty. No, they were exquisitely beautiful. Carefully, she took them off the pan with a pancake turner and set them on waxed paper. In five minutes, she had another forty lumps of cookie dough on the pans and the oven timer reset.

D'Ann came in and snatched one of the hot chocolate chip cookies, passing it from hand to hand to cool it. Mandy watched as she tasted it, ate the remainder, and licked her fingers, all the while making "Mmmm-mmmm" sounds. She picked up another one, held it aloft, and said, "As God is my witness, I'll never go hungry again!"

"Tell me the truth. Are they good?"

"Here comes Lefty. Ask him."

Mandy took off her apron and set the mixing bowl in the sink. "*You* ask him. Please?" To still her shaking hands, she grabbed a magazine and opened it at random.

"Good afternoon, ladies." Lefty Otway, the manager of Bitter Falls Farm since Mandy was a teenager, came in the back door and stood on the welcome mat. He took off his straw hat and held it in both hands. "Sure smells good in here. Do you know when Mr. McCay will be back from Spokane?"

Mandy looked up from *Horticulture Today* and said, "Sorry. I was asleep when he left."

"He called me from the road," D'Ann said. "He'll be back tomorrow night." She handed him a napkin with three cookies. "What do you think of these?"

Mandy looked back at an article about the economic impact on farmers of the developing biofuels industry. She tried not to watch Lefty's face, but she couldn't help herself. As he put the first cookie in his mouth, she could swear she tasted the chocolate herself.

He ate one and stared at the other two. "Delicious. Nothing better than homemade cookies right out of the oven. Thank Eleanor for me." He made quick work of the other two and said he'd be out in the old orchard if anybody needed him.

"I've got my cell phone." He eyed the tidy rows of cooling cookies. "Uh, do you think it'd be all right with Eleanor if I took a couple more of these?"

"I'm sure Eleanor would be flattered," Mandy said.

She watched Lefty close the back door behind him and burst out laughing at the same time D'Ann did.

"Well, Julia Child," D'Ann said, "how much proof do you need? These are wonderful." She ate another one.

"Stop eating them. I won't have enough for Cam West and his four *hungry* workers. And I'd rather be mistaken for Rachael Ray than Julia Child."

Forty minutes later, on a two-lane highway, D'Ann slowed the pickup. Mandy fluffed her hair off her neck, wishing she'd put it up in a ponytail.

"There's the turn-off to the state park," D'Ann said. "Cam said turn left at the second mailbox after the sign."

From the county road, Mandy couldn't tell anything about Cam's ranch, but when they came around a rise, about a half-mile onto his land, a wooden sign beside the pavement said *Campbell West Ranch*. Burned into the wood was a graceful silhouette of a horse rearing up, its mane flying. Shortly after the sign, she got her first view of the lush grass and expanse of white fencing.

"Look at the little baby horses! And that log house." She would have said "cabin" but the place was too big for that. Not huge, but spacious. She had butterflies, but at least she wasn't going to walk in and meet Mrs. Campbell West. She'd asked Eleanor and found out Cam West was a bachelor. In fact, he'd never been married.

D'Ann whistled. "I believe the one-hat cowboy I remember from my days in the corral has done right well for himself."

Mandy adjusted the big tin of cookies on her lap. "I can't believe I'm doing this. He'll probably laugh his head off downtown at the bar. Not to mention what the men who work for him will think."

"You worry too much."

Mandy rolled her eyes and did a mocking reprise of her question. "'Do you like cookies?' Good grief, you'd think I was twelve instead of thirty. Little Mandy Sue and her Easy Bake Oven."

"Hey, there are two things men never get enough of," D'Ann said with a chuckle. "And one of them comes off a cookie sheet."

"Stop right there! If I'm twelve, you're seven, so don't be telling me what the other thing men want is!"

"Okay, okay. I thought your memory might be squiggly on that point. Suit yourself." She arched her eyebrows. "Don't forget, though. I'm a medical professional. You can ask me anything."

"What I won't forget is that you're my little sister, and I'm not asking you about men." She pulled the visor down and checked her face in the mirror. She was so nervous she'd licked off all her lipstick. That's all right, she told herself. It was better that he didn't think she'd fussed over her appearance.

She snapped the mirror closed as they pulled into the front drive. "There's Polo. And there's Cam."

"Don't drool, Mandy. Campbell West puts his pants on one long, naked, muscular leg at a time."

She coughed. "Now that's a fine thought to put in my mind!"

Cam waved from the corral and started for the car. Right beside him was an equally tall, equally muscular man. Slung over the second man's shoulder like a backpack was a saddle most men couldn't have lifted. Both of them wore dusty Wranglers slung low on their hips. Three more men came out of the barn and shaded their eyes to see who the company was.

"Hell-o, Cowboy!" D'Ann said. "Five handsome men and only two of us. I might need to learn how to bake goodies, too."

"You sound like a buckle bunny," Mandy said with a hoot. "I thought you were a sophisticated big-city girl."

D'Ann answered with a sly grin. "Dad sent me off to Virginia to get me away from rodeos and cowboys. I've always wondered what I missed."

"You better watch out. I'll tell Daddy." She opened her door and stepped out, balancing the cookie tin.

"That's my line. I'm the little sister, as you pointed out. That means I'm the one to tattle on *you*."

Mandy took a moment to appreciate the irony. D'Ann wanted to know what she'd missed—while she wanted to know what she hadn't missed. Or did she? Perhaps some stones were better left unturned.

"Good afternoon, ladies," Cam said. "I'd like you to meet my foreman, Joey Dix. This is D'Ann McCay and her sister, Mandy McCay."

Joey set the saddle on the ground and wiped his hands on a handkerchief. "Ms. McCay, pleased to meet you."

He shook Mandy's hand, then D'Ann's, and they told him to use their first names.

"Let's get in out of the sun," Cam suggested. "I have iced tea in the refrigerator."

"I'll put the saddle in the trailer," Joey said. "Don't let him start on the cookies before I get there."

Cam steered them around to the front of the house. Up a wide set of redwood steps, they stood on the V-shaped deck and looked out across a vast acreage. To the west, an arched footbridge spanned a wide stream.

He told how he'd built the house in sections, adding on in the spring and summer with hired construction workers who carried on when he had to fight fires. He'd finished the inside, mostly by himself, by degrees in the winter.

"Come on in." He led them to a kitchen that could have been pictured in a magazine. Deep blue and yellow Mexican tiles flanked a gas range top with the brand sticker still glued to the surface. The sink was cobalt blue enamel; the wood was cherry, or at least some hardwood stained to cherry and burnished to a high luster.

Mandy felt like Dorothy waking up in Oz.

"Last winter I did the cabinetry in here." He opened a drawer and ran a finger along the edge. "In fact, I had the appliances delivered a week ago while I was working on the fire. I haven't even heated a can of beans yet. And beans with bacon is about the limit of my cooking talent." He looked at Mandy and cocked his head to the side.

She realized with a start that she must be standing there with her mouth hanging open. "It's gorgeous. Do you mind if I look around?"

"Feel free." He looked at the tin. "Are these the prototypes?"

Mandy opened it and he made a big show of savoring the aroma. She caught her breath as he licked his lips in anticipation.

"Excuse me," he said. "I'll go wash up. The tea is in the refrigerator."

She moved around the room, feeling the sealed granite countertop, admiring the cabinets, especially the built-in rotating shelves in the corners, and a walk-in pantry. A butcher block cooking island in the middle of the kitchen sat square beneath a skylight. It was a cook's dream kitchen, built inexplicably by a rancher who didn't cook.

She looked in the cabinet beside the Sub-Zero refrigerator to see what spices and herbs he had. His racks of wines in the pantry showed a lot more deliberate thought than his spices.

Salt, pepper and chili powder.

"The cowboy gourmet," she muttered. To D'Ann she added, "I've been out of the game for a long time. What wine goes best with chili?"

"I'll bet he's got something more appealing in the refrigerator." D'Ann swung the door open. "See? Cold beer, a head of lettuce and five pounds of onions. To a cowboy, that plus chili is all the food groups. If they need more vegetables they add jalapenos."

Mandy found the glasses and filled them with ice and tea. D'Ann found placemats and matching napkins in a sideboard and placed them on a round dining table. Mandy set out the glasses of tea and the cookies on a plate, then moved into the living room.

The front of the house was built like the prow of a ship, with big windows that came together at an angle. Between the windows and the three brick-red leather couches stood a freestanding fireplace and a massive metal chimney, also a dull red color. Standing by the window that began at ankle level, she could see out across the valley. A single contrail held a tight line against the sky.

Cam returned to see Mandy silhouetted against the window. He stopped to admire the image the way people stopped in museums, struck dumb by a portrait of a beautiful woman. Her hair had something like a halo. If he was dreaming, he hoped nobody said anything loud and woke him up. He was just getting to the good part.

"In the winter I scoot one couch forward," he said at last. "I put my feet on the hearth, and stare out at the snow. Here, let me show you."

He moved the sheepskin rug to the side and moved one end, then the other of the center couch. She said nothing, simply watched him. He sat and rested his boots on the river stone hearth that formed a circle under the chimney. He patted the couch next to him.

She smiled nervously and sat down.

"You need to put your feet up like this to get the right view."

She followed his example. "I see what you mean. It's sort of a theater effect."

"Of course, in winter I get the same feature over and over, but I change the musical accompaniment."

"For example?"

Her direct gaze was so magnetic that he had trouble thinking of an answer, any answer. Her blue eyes picked up the green in her frilly blouse. He wondered if D'Ann were to wear light blue if the two sisters might have matching eye colors. They were both beautiful. He was sure Joey would talk about this for weeks. Months.

"You were talking about music," she prompted.

"I was?" He forced himself to look at the fireplace, the bookcase, the CD player. Anywhere but into Mandy's eyes.

"Umm, yes, music." He cleared his throat. "I have a good music system. I like classical, like Rachmaninoff, and pop."

"Country and western? Somebody-done-somebody-wrong songs?"

"On occasion, sure." He turned back toward her and his laugh died in his throat.

Kenny Rogers' old song about, "know when to hold 'em," popped into his mind. The more his good sense told him to throw down his cards, hold his hands up, and step away from Mandy McCay, the more chips he shoved onto the table. Her eyes drew him the way the fragrance of a night-blooming cereus reels in the moth it depends on. He wanted to trace her lips—and so much more—with his tongue.

Luckily, she broke into his trance before he leaned over and made a fool of himself.

"What did you—?" she murmured. "Oh, yes, music. If you want me to get the full theatrical experience, you should put something on."

"Umm, sure." He stood, hating to move out of her potent force field. "I'll be right back."

He opened the drawer to his CD player and removed the one he had in. He'd been listening to Celine Dion the night before, a twelve-year-old CD he and Mandy had made love to. He dropped in the other one at hand, a collection of Chopin's work. He adjusted the volume and looked back at Mandy.

He saw D'Ann out on the deck, talking animatedly to someone, probably Joey. She moved down the steps and out of sight.

He took a deep breath and returned to the couch. He propped his boots back on the hearth.

"That's pretty," she said. "What is it?"

"Chopin. Polonaise."

"I wonder if I used to know that." She looked over at him and raised her hands, palms up. "Probably not. Evidence seems to indicate I was an airhead. I didn't go to college."

"You could go now, if you want to."

"I don't know what I want."

She sounded lost. He longed to put his arms around her, but kept his hands and hot thoughts to himself.

"D'Ann said you taught her to barrel race."

Clearly, she wished to change the subject.

"Yes, and it was a pleasure. She's an excellent rider, a true natural. I was sorry to see her go."

"I didn't go to Virginia."

She turned sideways and pulled her legs under her, studying him like she might examine a map with a magnifying glass.

"Did you teach me anything about riding?"

He coughed and his feet slipped off the hearth. His boots hit the floor with a loud thump. "Sorry, uh. Did I...? No, uh, you were busy with a lot of other things. And I had a lot of work to do. Lefty was a slave driver." He stood and held out his hand to her. "I can't wait to taste your cookies."

He hoped the cookies would get the image out of his mind of Mandy on a sleeping bag in the back of his old truck, and on the front seat of her dad's truck, and the riverbank. And in the motel room the one time they'd been on a bed. *Riding* was one verb that came to mind.

She placed her soft hand in his and rose gracefully. He waved out the window to Joey. At the table, he held out Mandy's chair then sat to her right.

"Was this in your family?" she asked. "It looks over a hundred years old. The sideboard, too."

"Good eye. They are antiques, but not from my family. I bought them at an estate auction in Whitefish."

D'Ann came in through the kitchen, followed closely by Joey and talking about horses. They sat at the round table and he saw D'Ann wink at Mandy.

"I want to ride Mustang Sally," D'Ann said, "but I was afraid Cam would eat all the cookies if we stayed out there."

"Good guess." He took four cookies and passed the plate to Mandy. She passed it to Joey. Cam could tell she was watching him out of the corner of her eye.

He was prepared to say the cookies were great no matter how they tasted, but he wasn't prepared for the melt-in-your-mouth wonder she had created.

"Okay, very funny," he said. "You had me believing you're a beginner. These are the best cookies I ever wrapped a lip around."

"Oh, stop!" She took one herself, broke it in half and took a bite. "Apparently cooking isn't as hard as I made it out to be."

"Or cooking is hard," Joey said, "and you're good at it. These are better than my mother used to bake."

Cam watched her face. She seemed to be struggling with something. D'Ann's attention was on her, too. "Is anything wrong?" he asked softly.

She shook her head, but he saw tears collect in her eyes and spill onto her cheeks.

"I'm sorry. Sometimes I feel, I mean, sometimes I think of something, uh, unexpected."

Cam handed her his napkin and she dabbed the tears off her cheeks.

In a transparent attempt to change the subject and draw attention away from Mandy's discomfort, D'Ann asked Joey something about the horses.

Cam tuned them out for the most part. Following D'Ann's lead, he said nothing more about Mandy's episode of sadness, but that didn't mean he wasn't thinking about it.

The Mandy he'd known and loved twelve years ago nudged her way into his mind. He'd only seen "his Mandy" cry twice, once in grief and once in anger.

"How long, Cam?" Joey asked.

"How long...? I'm sorry, what?"

"How long have you had Dar-Kanyon? Tell D'Ann about the roundup when you got him."

Cam rose and crossed to the wall behind Joey. With his arms wide, he lifted down the framed satellite photo of Steens Mountain, Oregon, and set it on the table, angled toward D'Ann and Mandy. Enhanced by technology, the photo showed the radical changes in elevation and even a hint of vegetation.

"This is in the southeast corner of Oregon," he explained, "southeast of Burns and Malheur Lake. Steens Mountain isn't a classic peak." He ran his thumb down the ridge running north and south. "It's a thirty-mile long shelf formed by a fault. The Kiger Gorge is this depression to the east, a gigantic U-shaped valley carved by glaciers."

He pointed out the Big Indian Gorge and the other canyons that cut through the mass of Steens Mountain. In his mind he saw it so clearly: the emerald grasslands carpeting the wide rocky culvert, willows along the river, juniper and sagebrush gripping the rocks and climbing the sides of the canyon, and a belt of aspens forming the timber line.

Beyond the gorge to the east lay the Alvord Desert, a vast plateau in the rain shadow of the lush, river-rich mountain complex.

"How do you get there?" D'Ann asked. "I mean, what's the closest you can get by truck?"

"There's a loop out from Frenchglen, along this river," he said. "That's as close as any road gets. The rest is tough, even for an experienced backcountry horse, but that's been good news for the Kigers. Keeps out the riff-raff, equine and human alike. The two herds in the gorge are the descendents of the horses brought by the Spanish conquistadors."

Mandy looked up from the map, as enthralled by the story as D'Ann was. Her eyes sparkled.

"What was it like to see them?"

She'd seemingly overcome whatever sadness had pulled her away. Sometimes she seemed so normal, so solidly "right here—right now," that he forgot she was still recovering from a traumatic injury.

"What was it like?" she repeated. "Was it love at first sight?" She cocked her head and smiled.

Was it love? That Mandy might slowly be remembering him, that the sparkle in her eyes might indicate more than interest in wild horses, came like a smack upside his head. What kind of crazy game was he playing?

For an instant Cam forgot the Kigers, forgot the first time he'd seen the herd—by moonlight—ten years ago. Hell, he forgot where he was now. The image that swam before his eyes was moonlight, all right. But the mane of hair tousled in the wind was Mandy's. And he'd wanted nothing more than to wind his hands in it.

He still wanted to.

"I'll be right back." He turned away and moved to the living room. As soon as his pulse returned to the normal range, he carried a framed photo into the dining room. Enlarged to two feet square, it showed a perfect Kiger stallion in the wild, the stallion that he'd named Dar-Kanyon.

"I took this a year after our first encounter," he said. "That first time, I was in the gorge was for a prescribed burn to get the sagebrush under control. Without a fire from time to time, the aspens get choked out by sage. When that happens, the horses, pronghorn, and big horn sheep have no cover."

He wiped dust off the glass with his handkerchief and pointed out the characteristics that set Kigers apart from other breeds.

"First there's the dun factor. Color ranges from buckskin brown to reddish brown to Dar-Kanyon's color, a shade of gray called *grulla*. You can't see it in this picture, but he has the breed's dorsal stripe down his back."

"I love the zebra stripes on the knees and hocks," D'Ann said. "And isn't there something unusual about their ears?"

He nodded. "They're hooked at the top with the outer edges lined in black and the inside a soft brown. Most Kigers have two colors in their manes and tails."

"He's magnificent," Mandy said.

Cam chuckled. "The first time I saw him, he was a juvenile delinquent. Young, male, and full of himself, a terror to his young siblings and cousins, a big aggravation to the mares. The dominant mare made it clear he'd shape up or be shut out, and for herd animals, that can be a death sentence. Cougars and black bears don't miss many opportunities to snatch game outside a herd's protection."

He laid the portrait of Dar-Kanyon to the side and replaced the satellite photo on the wall.

"I went back a year later when the BLM did a gathering. Instead of using helicopters, eight of us did it the old-fashioned way. Dar-Kanyon was full grown and ready to fight the roan stallion for his own mares, and I don't doubt he would have been the emperor of the gorge, but he'd gotten injured. The long trek to the pickup point was hard on him. When the BLM decided not to take him back to the wild, I got him."

"I wish I'd been here to see him," Joey added. "Cam says Dar-Kanyon took a saddle like he was born to it. Not to imply that he didn't have spirit. Goes to show what Cam knows about horses."

D'Ann furrowed her brow. "Spirit, hmmm. Wasn't the horse in the Disney movie a Kiger? Help me out here. I'm digging in the archives of my horse knowledge—with a rusty spoon."

Cam grinned. "Yeah. A Kiger stallion off a ranch in Oregon—not a wild horse—was the model for Spirit in the movie."

Joey stood and picked up the plate of cookies. "Anybody want to pry this last cookie out of my grasp? I didn't think so."

He bit it in half and rolled his eyes to show his pleasure.

"The rest," Joey said as he headed for the kitchen, "is history." He paused to wave an arm at the high ceiling. "This is the house that Dar-Kanyon built."

Cam invited them to go see the stallion. While they climbed on the fence of the corral, he put a bridle on Dar-Kanyon and led his horse outside.

Once Dar-Kanyon had committed to Cam as his leader, a mystical connection Cam couldn't fully understand, the gray stallion had been a precocious learner. He thrived on work and competition. No one who saw them at amateur rodeos could believe it was their first season.

Together they'd moved up in the professional rodeo world and into national rankings. Cam's part-time work as a firefighter paid the entry fees, and Dar-Kanyon's skill and fierce competitive nature paid for everything else. Cam's hope had been to make money in cutting horse competition, enough to buy more land and three or four mares with good bloodlines.

But Dar-Kanyon showed his brilliance in team roping as well as cutting. In six years of hard work, they made it to the National Finals Rodeo, and Dar-Kanyon's performance as a double champion was a legend. Once money started coming in, Cam had plowed it into more land, more horses, and better outbuildings. The first three years Dar-Kanyon stood at stud, Cam's horse barn and breeding barn were attractive enough to feature on a calendar, while his house was a dilapidated cabin.

Finally, three years ago, he'd been flush enough to start building his dream house. Seeing Mandy in his living room and kitchen, then at his table, and now perched on the corral fence, the dream was complete. Perfect, in fact.

Joey emerged from the house and leaned against the corral, right by D'Ann.

Cam gave the stallion the hand signal to stand up on his hind legs like a Hollywood horse. "That's good, fine. You have two new fans, my man."

He led the stallion over to Mandy and D'Ann and watched them pat his regal head and soft muzzle. Joey gave them each an apple and Dar-Kanyon took them delicately.

"We have three of Dar-Kanyon's yearlings out in the pasture and five colts born this spring," Cam said. "And I'm glad to say we've got a good waiting list for stud service with Dar-Kanyon and Colonel Jackson."

The big Arabian stallion he'd bought in Scottsdale, Arizona, would be arriving in a few days. The stable addition was ready for its high-spirited new tenant and his companion, a placid gelding who calmed the stallion down.

Joey explained how the ranch operations were expanding.

"The end of this week," Joey said, "we have the Japanese owners of a champion Arabian mare coming for a visit. The mare lives in northern California."

Worry nagged at Cam about the two events coming so close together. The mare's owners would be there to see Dar-Kanyon and his colts, but they'd expect to see Colonel Jackson, too. If he had a rough time settling into his new home, word of his temperament would spread. Bad news always traveled a lot faster than good news. One thousand jumbo jets landing safely went unmentioned in the face of one landing-gear malfunction.

A half hour later, he watched the McCay Enterprises truck disappear behind the hillock that sheltered the ranch house from the worst of winter's winds. Slightly more than twenty-four hours ago, he'd seen Mandy for the first time; now she'd been in his house and his corral.

What were the odds? Beyond his ability to calculate.

It was a miracle he could still walk a straight line, he was so drunk on the scent of her, a fragrance of something floral plus something like fresh grass in the early morning.

He chuckled. *All that, and a touch of vanilla.*

When Mandy had gone back in the house for her sunglasses, Cam turned to ask D'Ann about Mandy's progress, but a warning beeped in his head, like the alarm in certain cars that tells the driver there's a cyclist in his blind spot before it's too late. If he brought up his concern for Mandy's condition to her fiercely protective sister, he had a feeling D'Ann might pose a few questions of her own.

And he wasn't ready to answer any questions with "Mandy" in the subject line.

As soon as the pickup was out of sight, he got to work on the piles of paperwork that had accumulated while he was gone. Or at least that's what he tried to do. But it was like trying to read a contract while falling off a cliff. *The fine print might be important, but the distraction was infinitely more powerful.*

It had taken him twelve years to get where he was—longer counting the months he'd worked for Ford McCay and the year-plus before that when he'd contracted for ranch work alongside his grandfather. What a greenhorn he'd been. Thank God he was a fast learner.

Once he'd realized, deep in his bones, that he was born to raise horses, he'd never shirked from the hard work. When Mandy left, he'd grown even more determined to make his ranch and his horse breeding operation a financial and professional success. He'd made a solemn vow to himself to live life on his own terms. From that time on he looked ahead, always ahead.

Not back at the day he made that vow.

For the first few years, he had Mandy on his mind day and night, but it was like a spur to a cutting horse. The harder Cam worked and the more his muscles ached, the less he thought of Mandy and the pain she'd inflicted. After a while, she was less a memory than a ghost—no more substantial than a thin white curtain in a gentle breeze. A footnote.

There were plenty of other women in the world. As he worked, he kept telling himself that pretty soon—next year, then the year after that—he'd look for a nice woman to settle down with. Someone who'd make a good partner and a good mother. Someone satisfied with Montana, not on the run to something "better," something more exciting.

Such lectures to himself helped scab over the wound, the longing for Mandy. Then, about the time the deep pain stopped, Mandy was shot.

Eleven years and four months were nothing. His heart ached as if she'd left his bed and his life and Montana an hour before.

For more than a month, it had been all anyone in Bitter Falls talked about. Every TV network had an update on Mandy McCay on the hour and again on the half hour. He'd seen the footage, over and over, of the helicopter taking off with Mandy on board. Still on the pavement, covered by a sheet, lay the body of the man who'd stalked her, kidnapped her, and tried to kill her.

Cam had stared in disbelief at the surgeon pointing to an X-ray of Mandy's skull. There was the bullet lodged in her brain. Below the cold clinical X-ray was a logo of a gun and the words *Actress Clings to Life.*

The only good news Cam could see was the stalker had used a .22. If he'd known more about handguns, the TV coverage would be of her funeral.

Cam had left the TV on in his big empty house that night and driven around aimlessly. Christmas lights on the stores and houses in Bitter Falls seemed a mockery. *What* joy in *what* world?

At last, he'd stopped at Ford McCay's farm, about five miles as the crow flies from his land, and talked to the manager. Lefty Otway said Mandy's father had flown to Los Angeles the minute he heard about the shooting, and her sister had left her nursing job in Portland to stay right beside Mandy.

Cam asked Lefty if he needed help with the farm.

He said he appreciated the offer, but he had everything under control. Fall had been unseasonably warm and long, but now the snow had started and everything was under cover. Cam knew that Bitter Falls Farm was a small part of McCay's agribusiness empire with its gigantic fruit packing plants in Montana, Idaho, and Washington. He'd heard that about a third of McCay Enterprises' business was now with Japan.

Cam sat with Lefty for three hours, sharing a bottle of Jack Daniels, a crackling fire, and a whole lot of silence.

Cowboy therapy.

Lefty was one of damned few people who knew what a fool Cam had been. A fool for Mandy. He'd been Cam's boss then, back when Ford McCay kept some stock.

When his whiskey hangover eased, about noon the next day, Cam considered flying to Los Angeles. Fortunately, he came to his senses. The hospital was surrounded by satellite TV trucks; he couldn't possibly get in. And he had no business there. He had once known a girl named Mandy, but the high-living, big-spending, jet-set movie starlet was no one he knew. Life in the ultra-fast lane—that was her choice. *That* woman was clinging to life. The girl he called Mandy-by-moonlight, the girl with velvet skin and apple blossoms in her hair? She had ceased to exist eleven years and four months earlier when she'd sped south away from Montana. Away from him.

He was twenty-four then; she was eighteen. He'd done the honorable thing, and she'd hated him for it.

Hell, sometimes he hated himself for it. Honor was a cold bed partner on a long winter night. Honor didn't answer when a man called out, "Honey, I'm home."

Cam shook his head and turned back to the contract in his hand.

Chapter 4

Early Wednesday, before the heat got oppressive, Mandy tightened the laces on her expensive walking shoes. Walking on real ground would be a first for the shoes. She'd always had to work out in California to keep her figure; being thin was the gold standard. But she did her workouts in a gym. Treadmill and Stairmaster, followed by spinning class or, on alternate days, dance exercise. Then into the pool for laps.

You better, you better, you better fill out the sweater.

And you better not fill out anything else. Celery, anyone?

She stretched out her muscles, what little she had. She was thin, but far from the fit shape she'd been in all those long months ago. When it took all your mental capacity to train your knee to lift your foot and put it down six inches ahead of you, Pilates versus yoga wasn't something you talked about over lunch.

Lunch? Even that word was emotionally charged for her. She'd had to learn to use a spoon. The occupational therapists worked for hours, prodding her to squeeze a ball. She was so weak at first they could have used a live gerbil instead of a ball; she couldn't hurt it. So many times she'd stare at the ball in her hand, unable to make her fingers close.

D'Ann would make up silly stories about the ball, and the spoon, and the fork. She was the cheering section not only for Mandy but for everyone at the neurological institute.

Ford McCay had come to the facility in Arizona every weekend, no matter how far he had to travel. Her memories of his visits were jumbled in time, like a movie edited by someone in a drug-induced haze.

Of her weeks in the hospital in Los Angeles, she had no memory at all. D'Ann said their dad had been there all the time, as she had. The two of them had gotten a room in an adjoining building and left to shower and sleep in shifts while one of them was beside Mandy.

She finished her stretch and walked at a good clip past the small vegetable garden Eleanor kept up and out the back gate of the large yard. A man she hadn't met yet turned the far corner on a riding lawnmower and waved to her. She waved back.

A doe with twins so young they still had spots looked her over and dismissed her as no threat.

She looked back at the house, comforted that she knew this place. This was the bedrock of her memory bank. She knew how to get to the old orchard and where the footbridge crossed the creek and where she'd built a snow cave.

So many of the memories were entwined with her mom. It had been a powerful memory of her mom's cookies, sort of a time warp with chocolate, that nearly had her blubbering in Cam's dining room. D'Ann had said again, on the way home, that she should talk to a psychologist in Bitter Falls, but she resisted the suggestion. She'd been close to the clinical psychologist in Arizona. It was hard to shift her allegiance. Trust was hard to come by.

By the time she got to the orchard she was out of breath and glad she'd brought a bottle of water strapped to her belt.

It was too late for apple blossoms and too early for apples, but it was a perfect day. The old orchard with its gnarled branches was as close to heaven as she could be.

Why had she left?

D'Ann didn't know—or said she didn't—and her father changed the subject the four or five times she'd brought it up.

She remembered a lot about her years in California, and if she wanted to know more she could look in the boxes of magazines and ticket stubs and invitations she'd saved. Her girlfriends and her publicist, Kira Dawn, had arranged for all her clothes, makeup, books, and keepsakes to be packed and shipped to Montana. Correction—Kira, her *former* publicist.

Mandy's catastrophe had added the private phone numbers of a lot of TV producers and talk show hosts to Kira's cell phone. Once Mandy was well enough to say she would not be returning to California, Kira had moved on to greener pastures. D'Ann told her yesterday that one of Kira's new clients, an athlete, had been arrested three days ago at an airport with vials of body building chemicals, and another one, a movie star, had two women pregnant at the same time. So Kira was flying high. As she'd often told Mandy in their club hopping days, "There's no such thing as bad publicity. Not in Hollywood, anyway."

She walked slowly to the far end of the orchard. It had been her favorite place when she was a little girl. She'd made up elaborate stories—all starring Mandy McCay, of course. Most of them involved apple blossoms and a wedding gown. Raggedy old lace curtains did nicely for a gown.

When she finally had the sister she'd asked for, she expanded the cast to include a flower girl, then later promoted D'Ann to bridesmaid.

They had each other and Mom. They had their dad, too, but his business took off and he spent as much time in eastern Washington as he spent on the farm in Montana. The varieties of apples grafted by Ford McCay and his father, James McCay, from these old trees paid for land near Wenatchee, Washington. James had inherited the Montana farm and the original trees from his father, Otis, then had worked himself into the grave to build up the orchards.

Every penny James had earned went into more land, more trees. And Ford had worked even harder than James.

She sat on an ancient stump in the shade of a Tompkin's King tree. Hybridization, time, and machinery had improved apple production in giant orchards, but these heritage apples, some grown from seeds and others from grafts hand-carried across the country, had flavor her mom said you couldn't buy in any store.

Once her dad had bought and leased thousands of acres and built up the commercial orchards, he'd made the leap into packing plants and began shipping fruits. Across the region at first, then all over the United States. In less than five years, he was shipping tons of produce to Japan, China, and new markets in the Middle East. The McCay Enterprises logo was recognizable around the globe. In addition to spending time in the state of Washington, Ford McCay spent considerable time in Washington, D.C.

But his heart was on the land his grandfather homesteaded, Bitter Falls Farm. That's where Ford brought his bride, Jane, when he'd finally married. He'd been forty-one; she was twenty. All predictions by ladies in the area that "the girl" would outlive Ford McCay by twenty or thirty years were wrong. She'd died of cancer at thirty-three.

Their dad was a relative stranger to Mandy and D'Ann at that point, but he'd done his best, and the three of them were close. Mandy had bitterly resented it when he sent D'Ann, then twelve, off to Virginia. His reason—she could remember it quite plainly—was that he didn't want D'Ann to be as wild *and spoiled* as she was.

The sound of an engine caught her attention and she stood to see where it came from. Lefty and one of the other workers were coming across the pasture on two all-terrain vehicles. Lefty was towing a square trailer. As they got closer, she saw the tools in the trailer.

The two men got off the ATVs and Lefty greeted her.

"Good morning. This here is Springer. We're fixin' to work on the old irrigation line. See how dry this side of the orchard is getting? I got the parts in today. We'll have it back on line in a couple hours."

He lifted equipment out with Springer's help and added, "Say, if you'd like to ride back to the house, you can take Springer's vehicle. He can ride behind me."

"Thanks for the offer, Lefty, but I enjoy walking. And I'm not supposed to ride bikes or ATVs or horses for another month or so. The surgeons don't want their fine work ruined."

"Well, sure. I can understand that." He touched his fingers to the brim of his hat. "Enjoy your walk."

She turned away, then turned back. "I'm wondering about something, Lefty. How long did Campbell West work here?"

His expression changed. She would swear the question made him nervous. But why would it?

"Oh, I don't recall precisely." He examined the back of his hand. "Half a year, more or less. Your dad decided that fall that he didn't want to keep the horses. That was Cam's area of expertise."

She smiled. "My sister was plain crazy about horses. I didn't care so much for riding myself."

51

"That's right. I remember Cam teaching your sister about cutting horses. She won a lot of ribbons."

"Yes, she did. Thanks, Lefty. I'll see you later. Nice to meet you, Springer."

She walked at a faster pace back to the house; not for the exercise but to find her sister's scrapbooks. D'Ann had left for Virginia only a few months before Mandy moved to California.

If Cam West was working on the farm all that summer, the summer she turned eighteen, why didn't she remember him?

****

Cam rose early after a restless night and made a pot of strong coffee. Joey had left him a list of the jobs he and the other four men were working on. Contractors were working on three projects on other sections of his land, and the builder who'd nearly completed the new bunkhouse promised to come fix the problems Joey had discovered.

With a sigh, he looked at the desk in his office, satisfied that he'd made substantial headway by working straight through until two a.m. He put stamps on the envelopes he needed to mail and put them on the counter.

Two cups of coffee and a bowl of cereal later, he was ready to drive out to check on a water well being drilled on a section of land he'd bought last fall. Marco leaped into the truck and after a few minutes of riding shotgun on the wide front seat, he put his head on his master's thigh. The Border collie had learned long ago that Cam needed one hand to drive and he might as well put the other hand to good use smoothing fur and scratching ears.

Usually stroking a dog had a restful effect on Cam, but today it worked against him. He thought of Mandy instead, of a night close to twelve years ago. He'd driven her to town, to the movies, and they'd stopped up on Bitter Ridge to look at the stars. Yeah, like astronomy was so much on their minds. It was a cold night in early September; frost was predicted by morning.

Cam had driven one of her dad's trucks for their date. His old Chevy was in the shop. He'd managed to pay for four semi-new tires the month before, but now the transmission needed work. Paycheck to paycheck. At least he'd paid the back taxes on his land with his first two paychecks from Ford McCay. That meant he could see if not a rainbow, at least daylight in the distance.

Mandy's car was on order. A Thunderbird convertible, candy apple red. She'd expected to get it when she got out of high school, but Ford McCay was so pissed at a stunt she'd pulled on her senior trip in March that he canceled the order. She'd lived by Daddy's rules for the subsequent five months—at least her father thought she did—and the car would be delivered in two weeks.

Mandy had lain on the wide front seat of the F-250 and put her head on Cam's thigh. Her curly blond hair draped across his lap like a cloud; he looked down into her eyes. She unbuttoned her blouse and let it fall open to show her lacy blue bra. Then she'd licked her finger and raised it to his face, outlining his lips with fire.

"I don't see any stars," she said. "The windows are all steamed up."

"Well don't look at me. I quit breathing five minutes ago. It'll take a defibrillator to start my heart again." He'd smoothed the hair back from her face. "That, or a kiss."

"Oh, all right. If it's the only way to save your life."

They hadn't stopped with a kiss. Once they'd crossed the line, after her spectacular eighteenth birthday party in June, neither of them wanted to go back to teasing, tantalizing kisses. He could more easily put toothpaste back in a tube.

They were wild for each other. Her scent, the taste of her mouth, the feel of her lips, her tongue...He groaned as the unwanted memory made him hard.

Off to his left, three miles outside of Bitter Falls, he saw the manicured greens of the Falls Creek Country Club. His first thought, as always, was what a felonious waste of water.

His second thought was a lot more personal. Mandy's birthday party had been staged in the dining room and back lawn of the country club. Cam hadn't gone, of course. A hired man in a country club—not so good a fit. A bull in a you-know-what.

Well, the same way no bull ever enjoyed a china closet, the dance floor of Falls Creek Country Club held no appeal for him. No, he'd waited for her downtown. They'd driven over the pass to a motel.

He'd never told her he *could* fit in at a country club. In his former life, before Montana, he'd spent enough time wearing a tuxedo and dancing the foxtrot and rumba with debutants to earn his stripes in "society," but it didn't appeal to him. And he knew down in his bones that Campbell West in a dinner jacket, college graduate and sole son of Arabella Billings West, wouldn't have the same appeal to Mandy as *Cam West, dirt-poor cowboy.* She hated the stiff formality of the club, the rigid Harvard Business-Yale Law pedigrees of men deemed suitable for the elder daughter of Ford McCay. Mandy was a rebel, and Cam West was her bad boy of choice.

Nice work if you can get it.

Why ruin a good thing by dragging Mom and her money into his life? He had no intention of taking any of it, anyway. When he left Boston she'd threatened to disinherit him in favor of her new husband's son. It was her way or the highway; she never changed. He chose the highway. He'd seen enough of the damage done by inherited wealth. All he wanted was what he earned and the patch of Montana ranchland—with an overdue tax bill—that would someday come to him from his grandfather.

When he turned off the road and bounced cross-country, Marco lifted his head in alarm. The truck lurched to a stop close to the site of the new well.

"Come on, Marco. Let's do an honest day's work. The sooner we get this well working, the sooner you can have stock to herd."

Hard work was the only way he knew to get his mind off Mandy. He hoped it would work for him again.

Chapter 5

Three hours later, in clean clothes and driving his "new" Ford truck, only four years old, Cam cruised slowly down Main Street looking for a place to park. *There's one—no.* The man was getting out, not in. It was high season for tourists. All those out-of-state license plates meant money to the struggling businesses of Bitter Falls, so he didn't begrudge the space. He knew a better place anyway. Way out behind the courthouse was a dirt lot with shade from a cottonwood.

Marco rode beside him again. Polo was at home sulking that she didn't get to ride along. Joey told her to get used to staying home. In a few days, she'd have five or six hungry mouths to feed.

"And I'm not staying up all night with baby bottles!" he'd added. "This here is a ranch, not a doggie day care center."

Five other vehicles had claimed the shade before Cam got there, but he knew which way the shade would fall in an hour. As he parked his truck at the left end of the five, he saw that the car to his right was a silver Lincoln Navigator with a logo on the side. McCay Enterprises. Maybe Ford McCay was in town. Not likely. Or Lefty? No, he'd drive a pickup. That left D'Ann or Mandy—or both of them. The Sisters McCay.

He'd had a lot of time in the previous twenty-four hours to chew over their encounter on his ranch. And just in case he forgot about it for ten minutes,

Joey kept chiming in with a comment or a question.

"Joey," he'd said, exasperated, "have you ever heard that the ideal cowboy is the strong, silent type?"

"No, why's that?"

"That was supposed to be a rhetorical question." Cam had shoved a pitchfork into the bale of hay and tossed the hay into the feeding trough.

Joey picked up the farrier tools and fit them on loops in his work belt. "I think I might call D'Ann this evening and ask when she wants to go for a ride."

"She'll call you. Look, can we talk about something other than women?"

With a wide grin on his face, Joey tossed the hammer up in a circle and caught it in mid-air. "Sure thing, boss. We can talk about cookies."

"I give up. I'm going to town and get the new pump." He put the pitchfork against the barn, snatched up a shovel and held it out to Joey. "How about you and Douglas dig the trench so I can work the old pump out of the hole when I get back?"

His sour mood wasn't made any better by parking beside the McCay Enterprises vehicle. He needed to get Mandy *off* his mind.

If he didn't have so damn much work to do on the ranch, he'd stop in to the Aces High Saloon and see how Enid was doing. Joey had mentioned that the pretty waitress broke up with her boyfriend the trucker and was looking to get back into the dating game. She wasn't Cam's type, strictly speaking, but he liked her well enough.

Tomorrow night he'd stop in there. Or the night after. What he needed to lighten his mood was to get close enough to a pretty woman to smell her perfume and see her cleavage. Get his priorities straight. He'd been working too hard. He needed to loosen up, "press the flesh" as politicians say. But shaking

hands wasn't the kind of flesh he wanted—needed—
to press.

Cam held the door open while Marco jumped
down. He tried to think about Enid, or digging
trenches, or fence repair. In other words, *anything
but Mandy*. No such luck. Instead, he wondered
about hypothetical encounters. If he ran into her on
Main Street, what would he say? No, he should avoid
the shopping area altogether. He needed to go
straight to the plumbing supply store. TCB. Take
Care of *Business*.

His mind said Business, but his feet said
Adventure.

"Don't even ask what the rest of my body says,"
he muttered to Marco. As he headed across the
grassy expanse of the courthouse lawn toward a
flowerbed and a concrete bench, he steeled himself
for the adventure of Meeting Mandy. That
probability, and the image he'd stored of her
silhouette against his own section of the Big Sky,
made his pulse race more than sitting on Dar-
Kanyon right before the gate flew open.

Forget rodeo, he told himself. *Romance has more
heart-flipping thrills.*

Normal run-of-the-mill romance he could
handle. No problem. That was a language he
understood. Give and get. Mutual satisfaction
guaranteed. But this no-man's-land of Mandy's
faulty memory was laced with mines. He was a fool
to pretend he hardly knew her. What would she
think when—if—she remembered their past? She'd
probably hit him upside the head with a two by four
and ask him how *he* liked being the one with brain
damage.

His knees wobbled and he plopped down on a
handy bench.

Cam had handed the shovel to Joey, but he was
the one digging a hole.

Okay, things weren't too bad—yet. He hadn't actually *lied* to her. And what else could he do under these circumstances but say nothing? Should he chuckle and say, "I know you don't remember me, but I vividly recall how you used to shiver with delight when I trailed my tongue down your neck and flicked my tongue on your dark nipples and sucked gently on your breasts"?

And how you looked, naked in the moonlight. How you wrapped your long legs around me and made the sweetest sound I ever heard, a sound I still hear in my dreams. How I said you sound like a cat purring.

Maybe he should write her a short "Your Eyes Only" letter, state the facts in the least colorful way, and add, "I understand why you'd rather never see me again."

The least colorful way? What would that be?

"Dear Ms. McCay, It is incumbent upon me as a gentleman to inform you that you and I were once very well acquainted. That is, I knew you (in the biblical way) when you were 18.

"Yours truly, Campbell West, Village Idiot."

He patted the bench beside him and Marco jumped up and cocked his head as if to say, "You are a jerk, but I'm still your friend."

"Marco, I'm in a heap of trouble."

He gave the conundrum more deliberation and decided—to do nothing. To stay as far away from the lady as he could. If she remembered him, remembered what they'd been to each other, well, okay. If the spark plugs in her brain started firing, she would remember how she'd treated him. How it had ended.

His cheek still stung from her slap. And his heart still ached from what she did next.

Left town, headed south, without a backward glance.

Well, what did he expect? A postcard?

The best plan was to keep his distance. Be polite, that's all. *Neighborly.*

Say, "Thanks for the cookies, Ms. McCay." Tip his hat; smile. Say, "Call me if you need jumper cables for your car," or any other neighborly thing. Any neighborly thing...

Like lifting your hair off your neck and blowing softly on that spot that drives you crazy. And outlining your ear with my tongue.

Okay, never mind being neighborly. Simply be polite if he saw her in town and otherwise stay the hell away from her.

If she remembered her demand and his refusal, her accusation and his silence...if she brought it up, he'd be cool. *Oh, I forgot that a long time ago,* he might say. *The two of us had fun, then it was over.*

"Come on, Marco. I'm burning daylight." He headed for the plumbing supply store, but chose a route through the alley between Charms-a-Lot and The Happy Cooker.

Main Street was jam packed with cars and people. The ice cream shop had people lined up out the door. That, of course, made him think of Mandy yesterday, leaning way over to scoop ice cream out of the bottom of the cardboard barrels. Her v-necked top fell forward and he'd seen the perfect mounds of her vanilla breasts spill forward. The edge of her lacy pink bra, the color of strawberry sorbet, barely held her nipples inside.

He glanced at the windows of Charms-a-Lot. Whoa! Skimpy lingerie. Not what he needed to see right now. He turned quickly to the adjoining shop. The Happy Cooker. The last, uh, make that *next-to-last* store he would ever set foot in.

He glanced inside. And his heart downshifted as it rounded the last curve before the finish line. Yellow caution flags flashed by as he picked up speed.

There she was. Mandy McCay, fondling some kind of frying pan. Before his brain could send a text message to his feet, he opened the door. Marco looked for shade along the storefront and lay down.

Cam saw Mandy hold up a transparent pink apron as racy as the lingerie next door. He moved quickly out of the center aisle and tried to look interested in an assortment of jars on narrow shelves. Mustards. What? Ah—jellies and jams. That was more like it. He wondered what quince tasted like—and what it would taste like on Mandy's lips.

He took the jar from the shelf and held it up as if to study the label. A slight turn gave him the vantage point he sought. Over the lid, he had a clear view of Mandy. Now she was running her fingertips over a big oval pan. Now she was—oh my god—stroking...*massaging*...the hard length of a thick glass rod that narrowed to a point. He watched, transfixed, as she gently squeezed the ball on the other end. Once, twice. Cam hardened as a wave of heat moved through his body.

All his resolutions to keep his distance went up in smoke. He couldn't look away from her, couldn't stop erotic memories from churning through his mind. Couldn't stop new erotic possibilities from crashing through the roadblocks he'd set up twenty minutes ago...

Such as Mandy McCay wearing nothing but a filmy pink apron and whipped cream swirled on her nipples. For the first time, he understood the attraction of making love in a kitchen.

If Mandy looked over, if she saw his face, she'd know in a heartbeat what he wanted. For that matter, anyone who got a look at his jeans would know.

He managed to turn his back to her. Any shopper who saw him now—he hoped—would see a man who appeared to be held in thrall by shelves of jams and jellies.

Mandy glanced at the clock and sighed; she had an appointment a block away in twenty minutes. She gave the ball of the turkey baster another squeeze and handed it and the roaster pan to the clerk. She was assembling quite a lot of cooking equipment. She picked up the instructions for the Cuisinart blender and glanced through the recipe suggestions.

Hmmm. She would buy a bottle of Grand Marnier at the liquor store, in addition to the sherry, burgundy and Bailey's Irish Cream on her list. She thought of Cam West's wine rack and wondered what wine he would suggest to go with Chicken Marengo.

His wines surprised her. A quick look told her he had excellent taste. It didn't mesh with the single-minded hard-driving horseman and firefighter that he appeared to be. And it certainly conflicted with a man who would heat a can of beans on his top-of-the-line gas range.

She would like to get her hands on that range. She pictured a rack of copper-bottomed pans installed above it, easy to reach.

She was going to act on her desire to cook. She was. She wouldn't start with Beef Wellington, although that picture was so gorgeous it made her hands sweat. A simple *Boeuf Bourguignon* would be a good beginning. She hoped Eleanor wouldn't feel territorial about the kitchen.

She added an assortment of wire whisks to her order. She ought to say she was finished and have the clerk ring it up, but she couldn't resist a display of cookbooks. One subtitled "Romance Begins in the Kitchen" made her chuckle. She pictured the large island in the center of Cam's kitchen and had to cover her mouth to keep from laughing out loud.

A loaf of bread, a jug of wine, a can of beans, and thou.

She handed the cookbook to the clerk. "That's all, at least for today."

The clerk started lifting the booty onto the counter and reading the bar codes with the hand-held reader. Mandy was surprised to see how much she'd bought. And there were so many more items she had strongly considered.

A woman outside opened the door and called, "The bus is loading," and seven or eight women hurried out the front door. In the mostly empty space a tall man in a denim shirt stood out like a clown at a funeral.

Mandy sauntered over and looked at the shelves in front of him. "Hello, Cam."

"Oh, hi there. I saw you over the heads of the crowd. I came in to perk up my pathetic pantry. What could I do with sun-dried tomatoes?" He handed her the jar.

"These would be good with baby romaine, arugula, frissee and goat cheese. Can you find fresh goat cheese in the grocery store here?"

"That question was on the tip of my tongue." He sighed and turned to look at her.

She smiled, enjoying his sheepish look. *You are so busted.*

"I looked in your pantry yesterday, and I think pretty much anything on the shelf would improve it."

"Ah, that was cold. I'm a bachelor. Have mercy."

"Have mercy? I think that's probably the line you use when you're angling for a home-cooked meal." She fanned her face and spoke in an exaggerated southern accent. "Lord'a' mercy, Miz McCay, I'm a bachelor."

"If that line got me a home-cooked meal, I'd use it. I might be deeply ashamed, but I'd use it."

"I'm thinking about making *Boeuf Bourguignon.*

Now, I can't guarantee it will turn out, but if you're willing to be a guinea pig, you're welcome to come to dinner tomorrow night."

"I'd be honored. What can I bring?"

"Wine." She handed him the jar. "And sun-dried tomatoes."

"Ms. McCay," the clerk called, "I have it all rung up now."

She took her credit card from her straw purse and handed it to the clerk. She was dismayed at how many bags she'd managed to fill. "I'll go get my car and come back for these."

"I could help you," Cam said. He'd moved to the counter beside her.

"Thanks, Cam, but I'll pick them up in an hour. I have more things to do downtown."

"Is D'Ann with you?"

"No, this is my first time to drive. A whopping twelve miles each way, but it's a benchmark."

"Good for you. Well, I have to get over to the plumbing supply store. What time shall I come tomorrow?"

Mandy was aware that the clerk was hanging on every word of this conversation. By dinnertime tomorrow, there wouldn't be a bona fide resident of the county who didn't know Mandy McCay was cooking and Cam West was eating. At least he'd be a gentleman and not tell anyone if her *Boeuf Bourguignon* turned out to taste like canned stew. In fact, he probably liked canned stew.

"Let's say seven o'clock."

"Wild horses couldn't keep me away." He laughed. "And in my case, that's not a cliché."

She gave him a wave and turned back to the clerk to sign the credit card receipt. Her appointment, now five minutes ahead, wasn't somewhere she wanted to go.

When she'd gotten home from her hike to the

orchard, she'd surrendered to D'Ann's repeated reminders and called the office of the psychologist recommended by her doctor in Phoenix. Her thought was she'd set an appointment for the following week or—even better—the week after that. D'Ann would be satisfied, and Mandy could put it out of her mind for a while.

"Dr. Kahn has an opening today at three o'clock," said his perky receptionist.

"That's, well, so soon. Uh, next week would be better. Any day next week."

The receptionist chuckled. "Dr. Kahn will be leaving the end of next week on vacation. He's booked solid except for this one hour today, a cancellation. You must have good luck."

"I have some kind of luck all right."

****

Shortly before five o'clock, Mandy closed the back door of the SUV and climbed into the driver's seat. She had the bags the clerk had held for her at The Happy Cooker plus one more, a set of saucepans she decided she must have. She also had the bottles from the liquor store. She would have to drive into town in the morning to get the groceries.

She'd done enough for one day.

Dr. Kahn had turned out to be a nice enough man. Her first impression was that he was old enough to be her grandfather; then she did the math. Okay, old enough to be her father. But whatever his patina of "niceness," she dreaded opening up her feelings and especially her fears to him. She'd gone over the "What do you remember?" ground so many times already. It was like beating a dead horse.

She winced at the cliché. She'd better never use that one around Cam West.

Now she planned to take a long, leisurely bath and curl up with a good cookbook. When she pulled into the driveway alongside the kitchen, she was glad to see Lefty. He carried in all the bags while she made her way, slowly, up the stairs.

While hot water ran in the old claw-footed bathtub, she added lavender-scented bubble bath. She slipped off her linen pants, blouse, and underwear and dropped them in the hamper.

The hot fragrant water felt so good. It had been a tiring day, starting with her long walk to the orchard and back in the morning. D'Ann had brought her scrapbooks downstairs from her bedroom closet, then left to work at the free clinic for migrant farm workers.

Mandy had eaten lunch alone at the dining room table with D'Ann's scrapbooks and her own school yearbooks that she'd found in a bookcase open all around her.

She'd changed clothes and driven downtown; discovered The Happy Cooker—and had a deliciously close encounter with Campbell West, the wild horses man.

She'd impulsively invited him to dinner tomorrow—and he'd said yes. Guinea pig didn't begin to describe what he'd signed on for. In spite of the heat, her arms were covered with goose bumps.

She replayed their conversation in her mind. There was something in his manner that told her he wasn't totally sure he wanted to come. Something ambivalent in his eyes. What was that about? She knew he wasn't married, but he could have a serious girlfriend. Oh, wouldn't that be a shocker to little Bitter Falls. Page four below the fold: *Mandy McCay in a Stew with French Recipe.*

Oh, for pity's sake. She sighed and wound her damp hair on top of her head. *My instincts can't be that bad. The man wants to see more of me.*

She raised one leg out of the bubbles and reached for her shaver. She wondered what he'd think if he saw this much more of her. She surely would like to see him in this tub. There'd be a lot of man above the water line. She'd sponge his tired shoulders. Ummm.

No, siree. She didn't need her little sister to tell her the second thing men never got enough of.

She closed her eyes and sighed. Being physically tired was scarcely half of her exhaustion.

Instead of poking around at her memory as she expected, Dr. Kahn had asked her what gave her pleasure. She said the first thing to come into her mind. "The fragrance of spices."

In the process of finding the vanilla and baking powder to make the cookies, she'd taken down a dozen spices piled in no discernible order in the cabinet beside the stove. She'd sniffed the cinnamon, the ginger and the cloves, then sprinkled a dot of each on her fingers and savored them, imagining how they would taste in pies and cookies. There was a nutmeg tin, but it was empty.

She found it intriguing how spices, like tea, had changed the history of men and women all over the earth. People had risked their lives to sail to India for the treasures on the tips of her fingers.

Now she rested her neck on the back of the bathtub and summoned the pungent smell of curry to her mind. A world of scimitars, elephants and brass bracelets paraded by. There was so much more in cookbooks than most people knew. History, travel, comfort, romance. Even sex. Aphrodisiacs.

"Aphrodisiacs!" she said aloud and laughed. *What a splendid word.*

She lifted her other leg from the water and laughed again. She hadn't even *started* on the herbs. Seeing the variations on parsley, sage, rosemary and thyme at The Happy Cooker had given her a rush. So many taste buds, so little time.

Dr. Kahn hadn't laughed at her interest in

spices. Instead he talked about her scores on intelligence tests. Why had she never gone to college? Did no one encourage her to use her fine mind?

Without knowing it, Kahn had landed like a paratrooper in her zone of exclusion. The summer she made the monumental and apparently sudden decision to leave Bitter Falls—in fact, to leave Montana and go to Los Angeles, where she knew no one and had no plans—that summer was the biggest hole in her Swiss cheese memory. Neither she nor the doctors could say whether the memory was "taken out" by the bullet or if it was floating under the surface of the water like seven-eighths of an iceberg.

There were other gaps, to be sure. Everything to do with her stalker, for example. Seeing the documents she'd signed and the restraining order against Ethan Koller meant nothing.

And she didn't remember an escapade with another woman's husband on the set of the first *Pirates of the Caribbean* movie. The scandal had been widely reported, especially in England where it took Camilla Parker-Bowles off the front page for a day or two. Her friend Tally said she'd never denied it. Still, it didn't seem like something she would do. *Me, with a married man?* It sounded more like something Kira would cook up and feed to her flock of birdbrains.

Mandy's trip to Cannes and her stay on board a yacht—more than a week altogether—was reduced in her memory bank to one painful sunburn. Sure, that was her in the photos, topless and sun-roasted to medium well. Who knew a telephoto lens could be so crisp? But she didn't *remember* it. The psychologist in Phoenix had suggested that she didn't care enough about it to remember it.

How did he put it? She stepped out of the tub

and rubbed herself dry with the towel as she tried to recall his words.

He'd said something like, say you got a stain on a favorite dress, and the dry cleaner managed to remove it.

"Why would you care where the stain had been once it was gone?" he'd asked. "You wouldn't."

She considered his point. Perhaps she didn't care enough about Cannes or the so-called love triangle on a movie set to waste any brainpower remembering them.

But the summer she turned eighteen was different. Every time she tried to remember it, anxiety made her heart race and her hands get icy cold. Her father was deliberately evasive. He wouldn't talk about it except to say he'd been extremely disappointed when she took off for California. She'd had her choice of colleges and he thought she was going to attend the University of Virginia. Then, in September, she'd said she wasn't going. No reason. Or anyway, no reason that her dad would tell her about.

She had apparently dug in her heels and thrown her college admission in the wastebasket. *Why?*

She smoothed lotion on her legs and arms.

Her dad had been gone a lot that summer, shuttling between his new packing plants in Idaho and Washington and his distributors in Asia, plus trips to Washington, D.C. From the way his face looked now when he said she'd suddenly decided not to go to college, she guessed he felt guilty about leaving her on her own too much. He seemed to think that if he'd been a better father, she would have gone to college, and none of the California craziness would have happened. No starlet, no paparazzi, no stalker. No gunshot.

Clearly, she'd disappointed her father with her lifestyle. He didn't give a fig for any of her so-called friends in Hollywood and Beverly Hills. And that was saying something, because figs, hand-picked and hand-packed, were an extremely profitable crop.

If not California, she'd told him on the way home from the Missoula airport, she might have chosen another form of craziness. Her choices twelve years ago had been hers—good or bad—whether he was in Bitter Falls or Tokyo.

She wasn't surprised when he'd changed the subject.

Now she heard her dad's voice in the hall. She quickly dressed in shorts and a T-shirt that said *Life is short. Eat dessert first.* She padded barefoot down the hall to the room she labeled "Mom and Dad's" room, even though her mother had been gone for eighteen years. When Jane McCay died, Mandy had been a gawky twelve-year-old with scabs on her knees and a crush on a boy from the Blackfoot Reservation. His name popped into her mind, probably for the first time in seventeen years. Johnny Bowhunter.

Sometimes this memory thing was like being in a shooting gallery. Look away ever so slightly, and up pops a duck. Turn and fire. Bang.

Damn. That reminded her of another boyfriend. Sammy Sandoval won her a ratty-looking poodle toy at the state fair carnival, and then groped her out behind the horse trailers. At fourteen, she'd been taller than Sammy and probably could have decked him, but instead she wriggled away and ran for her dad and D'Ann in the horticulture judges area.

She combed through her hair with her fingers. She'd done enough tripping down memory lane. She knocked on her dad's door.

"It's me."

"Come on in." He was sitting on his bed, taking off his shoes. He looked older than she expected. In the picture she carried in her mind, her dad always looked like he did when she was twelve and her mom was alive.

That had been one of the hardest things to reconcile when she was in rehab. From the time she was twelve until she was eighteen, Mandy had seen her dad all the time. Well, as close to "all the time" as a working single parent could be seen. Then, when she was eighteen and he was sixty, she'd left home. She'd seen him at least twice a year in the twelve years she'd been gone. But in her altered state, coming out of a fog at the Phoenix facility, Ford McCay jumped from fifty-four to seventy-two with nothing in between.

She'd heard happily married old men say their wives still looked like the girls they'd married, and she'd thought, *Oh puh-leeze.* But her mental "bleep" of her father's aging process made her a believer.

What does the song say? Seeing through the eyes of love? Now she knew there was something to that.

"You look wiped out," she said, and crawled on his bed. Propping pillows up against the old maple headboard, the same way she and D'Ann had done a thousand times, she listened to his short summary of his trip. Tired or not, his love of his business was undeniable. It had always been that way, but now Mandy listened to him with different sensibility. When he talked about the variations between apples, the distinct taste difference between Cameos and Honeycrisps and Fujis, she thought of the curry powders from Madras, and Bombay and Ceylon. Like her dad and his apples, she knew it wasn't the devil in the details; it was angels.

"I walked out to the orchard today."

"That's a long way," he said. "The doctors said not to overdo exercise."

"I sat out there and rested by the Tompkin's King."

71

He smiled. "Your mom's favorite tree. She used to make a cobbler she called King Cobbler. She won first prize at the county fair."

"I can remember the taste."

He gave her a doubtful, *Yeah, right,* look.

"I'm serious, Dad. My taste buds are prodigious. It's like in a science fiction movie when the kid gets zapped by a space alien or something."

"Sounds scary."

"Not so much. I think you're the same way about flavors. It took a long time for me to be a chip off the old block, but I got here. Have you had supper?"

"No. Eleanor left a casserole in the oven. She called me a couple hours ago, said her daughter's baby is coming early and she has to go to Missoula. So after the casserole—the last supper—we'll have to eat out."

She smiled like the cat that swallowed the Copper River Salmon stuffed with Dungeness Crab nestled in a bed of whipped Yukon Gold potatoes.

"Not so fast, Mr. McCay. There's a new cook in town."

Chapter 6

"Any chance of you bringing home a doggie bag?"
Joey asked. He leaned the wheelbarrow against the
shed and gathered up the nails that had slipped out
of his carry-all.

"Not happening," Cam said emphatically. "I
intend to be on my best behavior. The lady likes to
cook and *Boeuf Bourguignon* only gets her halfway
through B in the cookbook."

"Well, I always say, the way to a man's heart—"

"—is through his stomach." He bit off the words.

"No, I was thinking of somewhere else. But the
stomach is a good alternate route." Joey grinned like
a politician who'd escaped indictment.

"I'd like to know the route to your mouth's on-off
switch," Cam groused. He led Dar-Kanyon to the
corral and tied his bridle rope to the top rung. He'd
hosed the stallion off and brushed him good. Now he
smelled more like wet horse than Dar-Kanyon did.
He hoped he could scrub himself hard enough and
long enough to smell like aftershave instead of
afterhorse. Joey had already said he'd feed the
horses and get the stallion settled for the night.

As if on cue, a mare inside the stable bellowed
and kicked at her stall.

Cam sighed. "You'd better move Regiment to the
new stable or none of us will get any rest."

A mare with excellent bloodlines, owned by a
good friend of Cam's, was in residence for six weeks
and was causing more trouble than a Hooters

waitress at a church quilting retreat. Hussar's Regimental Lady had been barren with two other stallions through two complete breeding seasons and was receiving hormone injections. Cam's friend brought her to the ranch in hopes Dar-Kanyon's "mojo" would help the artificial hormones work on her system. For the first four weeks it only succeeded in aggravating Cam's mares. But now, at the worst time, with the press of other ranch work, Regiment—or as the cowboys called her, "Hussy"— was showing clear signs of coming into season. Dar-Kanyon was getting antsy.

"I'm going into town," Joey said. "Probably go to Little Anita's and have a B for beer and a C for chimichanga. D for dessert, too." His face widened into a grin. "Speaking of D, D'Ann said she'd like to come over and ride with me on Sunday. I think we'll go up to the arch."

A shudder rippled through Cam. The arch. *Damn.* That was one of the places he and Mandy had gone that August twelve years ago. They'd lain side by side on a sleeping bag to watch the Perseid meteor shower. They ended up—no surprise— making skyrockets of their own.

He glared at Joey and strode toward the house before he said something he'd regret.

He stripped in the mudroom and walked naked up the stairs to his bedroom. His bathroom was totally masculine. Shower only. No girly tub for him. He showered the way he always did, turning off the water while he soaped and scrubbed. Anyone who ever depended on natural grass to feed his stock, and anyone who ever fought a forest fire, wouldn't waste water no matter how special the lady in question. He'd just scrub harder with the lava soap.

Waste not, want not.

That wasn't the way he was raised, back in Massachusetts, but it was the way he'd raise his children.

His children? Where the hell did that come from? Women who had trouble finding a husband could get something from a sperm bank and become mothers. But it didn't work the other way. And anyway, he didn't want it any "alternative" way. Man, woman, church bells. Pretty soon, it's cradle time.

All of which made him think of the old bumper sticker: *Save water. Shower with a friend.* Hmmm. His shower stall was big enough for two, and it had a convenient tile bench. If he ever had a guest, he'd use that fancy citrus soap and rub it gently into her breasts and down her thighs.

He groaned and turned the water on cold for his last rinse. Being around Mandy McCay was making him as antsy as Dar-Kanyon. This situation was not good. He'd made such good sense yesterday when he'd decided—firmly—that he would stay away from her.

And then? And then? *The spirit is willing, but the stomach is weak? Is that my excuse?*

He laughed out loud. No, his stomach wouldn't take the rap for this. It was another organ that was running the show right now, and he sure as hell didn't mean his brain. Parts of his body that he'd thought were on extended retreat in a monastery were back and clamoring for attention.

He toweled off and shaved for the second time that day. When had he ever done *that?* He'd shaved that morning just in case Mandy stopped by, or in the event he had to go downtown—where he *might* run into Mandy. Joey and the other guys laughed their butts off when he got to the corral at six a.m. for what promised to be a hard day of work.

Of course their humor was raunchy, about how the mares were sidling up to Cam and giving the cold shoulder to Dar-Kanyon.

"Whatever do you use on your face, boss?" Joey asked. "Your skin is so fresh, so supple."

"How'd you like to try a horse manure face masque?" he'd barked. "All organic."

Joey, a veteran of the Iraq war, and Douglas, an agriculture major at Montana State University, outdid each other telling "how you know a cowboy is horny" jokes. Turk, a thin but muscular guy who worked on the ranch half the year and the chairlifts at Whitefish Mountain the other half, chimed in about signs he saw posted on the big mirror at the Long Haul Bar out on the highway.

"Safe sex is in the palm of your hand." Turk grinned.

"Beer. Helping the ugly get laid since 1868." Joey's contribution.

"Wife and dog missing. Reward for the dog." Douglas again.

At least they knew better than to sit on their butts while they jawed. They probably figured—rightly—that Cam was mad enough to cashier the whole lot of them.

At last, half an hour early, he was dressed. Crisp white shirt with mother of pearl buttons and black piping on the yoke and down the front. Starched black jeans and a light tan western jacket with leather elbow patches. Bolo tie from New Mexico with a Zuni Pueblo sun face.

He'd set up the ironing board in his bedroom to make sure none of the men came in the house on an errand and caught sight of it. If they had, he knew that inside of eight hours every cowboy in the county would be calling him Suzy Homemaker.

He already had the flowers. He bought them while he was downtown on an errand and sneaked them in the front door and into the extra refrigerator in the garage, right beside the bottle of Kestrel Syrah, 2003, that should be perfect with *Boeuf*

Bourguignon.

He hadn't been this nervous before a date since he was about seventeen. On second thought, that was a cakewalk. This was more like a firing squad.

Bizarre as it was, he and Mandy had never had a "date." Since he'd been her secret lover—the bad boy, off-limits hired man—they'd made a game out of fooling people. Her sister was in Virginia, her father was out of town most of the time, and the McCays didn't have a housekeeper, only a lady that came in twice a week to clean. The only person who knew something was going on—a lot of "something"—was McCay's farm manager. Lefty was a man of few words, but he'd tried on two occasions to talk sense into him.

It hadn't worked, but Cam had at least *listened.*

Nobody on God's green earth could have talked sense into Mandy, not back then. She was dazzling, audacious, and sexy as hell. Cam had been blind to her faults because they were in love. And Mandy in love was better than sunrise on a glacier, moonlight on a high mountain lake, cherries right off the tree.

Mandy in love was better than oxygen.

And he was crazy as a howling monkey to walk into her house tonight with his heart on life support and a long, thin extension cord.

What the hell was he doing?

When Mandy remembered who he was and what had happened between them, she would reach around behind him and pull the plug.

He gave himself one quick look in the mirror and put the wine and flowers on the front seat of his truck. His *clean* truck—another source of hilarity for the boneheads who worked for him. Oh, how he wished a carload of pretty girls would break down in Bitter Falls. Give Joey and his sidekicks something else to yap about.

Actually, Lefty hadn't been the only one who

knew about Cam and Mandy. At the end, her father knew. Cam dreaded the day he'd have to meet Ford McCay again. Even if Mandy remembered everything, she wouldn't remember that. Only he and her father knew what had passed between them. And so it would stay.

On the drive to Bitter Falls Farm, he gave himself a strict rule. Dinner, once. Then he had to extricate himself from this quicksand. He'd waded in knowing full well what danger lurked.

He laughed out loud. It could be that there was more of his mother in him than he liked to admit.

He adjusted that admission. More of his mother when she was young and wildly adventurous. He'd never known her that way. By the time he was born, when she was forty-four years old, Arabella Billings West was a diamond-crusted snob. In her Boston mansion, she'd attempted to groom her only child to be a snob like herself.

Arabella had been an extraordinarily beautiful young woman, and exceptionally smart—smart enough to know beauty was a commodity with a shelf life. She'd moved from Montana to Massachusetts with single-minded determination to marry into a ton of money. Her husband—Cam's father—Edmund Astor West, had been much older than Arabella. After nearly twenty-five years of a childless marriage, Arabella had finally gotten pregnant. People told Cam that Edmund was delighted to have a son, but he'd died of a stroke when Cam was a toddler.

In the course of her long and extravagant life, Arabella West had accrued a bellyful of grudges at the people who had snubbed her. Once she had a son, she'd made up her mind that she was going to get even. Her son would be richer and more handsome and higher in society than any of them. She'd dangle Campbell Billings West as live bait in the wedding sweepstakes.

Not so fast, Ma.

Cam had turned his back on society and did the last thing Arabella could tolerate. He went to Montana and became his own man. His inheritance shrank from Arabella's millions to the land homesteaded by her grandfather and passed down to her father, an old man Cam had never met.

Although they were strangers, Cam and Michael Billings had grown close in that last year and a half of his grandfather's life. Mike was in his mid-eighties when Cam arrived, but all he had on his beloved land was a shack with no running water.

In an odd way, Mike and his daughter shared a flaw that ran through each of them like a vein of shining metal in hard rock. Arabella found her gold in a vault in the First Bank of Boston. Mike found his fortune twice, once in silver in Nevada and once in gold in Alaska. In the end, it had all been dust slipping through his fist.

No, not a fist. Mike always had an open hand to a friend in need.

"When I count my blessings," Mike had said as the two of them gazed at a sunset the color of a chestnut roan, "I don't do it in a checkbook."

The old man and Cam had gone on the road as latter day itinerant cowboys and construction workers. It served as an excellent apprenticeship for Cam. Every campfire and every grizzled old cowboy was a source of knowledge no book could contain. Every chance he got, he learned about horses. It didn't take him long to know his calling in life was to be a horse breeder.

When Mike's health failed completely, Cam took care of him. At the end, he buried his grandfather in a pine box on a hill overlooking the land Mike Billings and his father before him had struggled so hard to keep.

At age twenty-four, Cam had the land, a debt for back taxes, a lot of know-how, muscles like a mule, and nothing else.

No, that was wrong. He had something else. He'd inherited the respect Mike Billings had earned in his long, honest, and generous life. Word got around quickly that Mike's grandson needed a job.

He had hired out to Ford McCay's farm, taking care of stock and doing whatever labor was called for. It was another apprenticeship. Lefty had been a great teacher.

Cam had already gotten rid of his eastern accent and his tennis-player physique. He could have burned his diploma from Harvard for all the good it did him. In fact, it would be such a disadvantage in Montana that he told no one, not even Lefty.

Now he drove down the familiar lane. As he pulled up in front of the McCay's farmhouse, he loosened the bolo tie in hopes he could breathe better. It didn't help.

He'd heard around town that McCay had hired a big crew to paint the whole exterior of his house about a month earlier, once he'd been sure Mandy would recover. The fresh white paint reflected the late afternoon sun.

The last time he'd been here was the night he brought the whiskey. Right after Mandy was shot.

It seemed like yesterday.

Mandy stepped out on the porch and beamed a smile that she could rent out to light up the sky over a Hollywood premiere. He climbed the steps and held out the bouquet of lilies and baby's breath.

"Thanks, Cam. They're beautiful. Come on in. I'll go put them in a vase."

She had a smudge of flour on her chin and it was all he could do to keep from touching her, gently, brushing it aside. She turned and he admired the way her long, semi-transparent skirt swished around her legs. It was made of bright colors like a Mexican fiesta and she wore a sleeveless yellow blouse and a red sash. She'd been home two and a half days and already she had a glow to her skin.

He followed her through the living room to the dining room and offered to go in the kitchen to open the wine.

"No!" she said quickly. "No. I mean, I'll bring the corkscrew in here. You get comfortable."

"Oh, I nearly forgot." He took a jar out of his pocket. "Here's the sun-dried tomatoes."

She took the small jar and rewarded him with a smile.

"Thanks for remembering."

She returned from the kitchen with a corkscrew and the vase of flowers. While he opened the wine to let it breathe, she lit two candles in brass candlesticks. He watched her place the flowers on the table by three place settings. Why three? She'd told him D'Ann was flying to Portland for a couple days.

"My dad came home last night," she said brightly, "and he's excited about my first dinner party. I'm sure you two will find plenty to talk about."

Ford McCay entered the room in a navy blue blazer, tan slacks, and a blue silk tie. Cam didn't keep up with men's fashion, but he could tell quality when he saw it. McCay's hair was white but still thick. Their eyes met and Cam held out his hand. "Good evening, sir. It's good to see you again."

Mandy was probably right; the two of them would find plenty to talk about. But they wouldn't be talking about the last conversation they had. Cam wished he could forget it had ever occurred.

****

By the time she served the French vanilla ice cream in brandy snifters, drizzled with Grand

Marnier and topped with shaved dark chocolate, Mandy was so tired she was fighting tears. It was a good thing her dad was there to entertain Cam with talk of free trade and tariffs and trade deficits. At first she thought Cam was simply being polite, but he surprised her by knowing what her dad was talking about. Even more surprising, her dad was asking his opinion; something about supply chain economics. Her eyes glazed over.

The two of them were in complete agreement that China should float its currency. China. Float. Root beer float.

That's when she fell asleep and knocked over her water glass.

"Sweetheart!" Her dad's hands gripped her shoulders in time to keep her from sliding off her chair like gelatin in a warm room.

"Mandy! What's wrong?" Cam was on her other side. He put one arm beneath her knees and one around her back to lift her against him.

She started crying. "I'm so sorry. I'm sorry. Ruined the party." She put her face against Cam's chest and tried to stop her tears, but it turned into a gusher.

"She did too much. The doctors warned us not to let this happen. Now she's exhausted. It's my fault."

She didn't want him to tell Cam how hard she'd worked on the dinner. She'd been at it all day. She set the table in the morning, before she went to the grocery store, and when she realized she'd forgotten the balsamic vinegar and the ice cream her dad had driven into town for them. She'd barely had time to shower and dress.

"I'm sorry," she said again. "I'll be all right."

"Her right leg buckles when she gets this tired. It's a miracle she didn't fall carrying that heavy chafing dish in here."

"Why don't I carry her to her room?" Cam said.

"Follow me."

She protested, but not too vigorously. She didn't like to be discussed as if she were absent, but it certainly toasted her bread to be in Cam West's arms.

Fixing the dinner shouldn't have been that hard. But at every step she had to consult a cookbook, sometimes three of them. Once, in bewilderment at instructions to "add half a cup of chopped Sultana," she'd tried looking in the dictionary. Well, that was no help. According to Webster, that would be a half cup of the chopped "wife of a sultan." It had taken a call to the reference librarian to find out the recipe called for a particular brand of California dates.

"Orange zest" required two cookbooks. And she never did decipher *bouquet garnier.*

No wonder people bought Hamburger Helper.

Cam stopped in her room and she watched her dad pull down the covers. Cam set her on the bed and she released the hold she had on his neck. He took off her sandals. She smiled and closed her eyes.

"I'll come up and check on her in a while," her dad said.

Their footsteps retreated down the stairs.

****

Downstairs, Cam carried the dinner plates into the kitchen. Ford was behind him with wine glasses.

"Oh, my." Cam stopped dead in his tracks. He gave a low whistle and the two of them laughed. Now he knew why Mandy hadn't wanted him to go into the kitchen.

"If you can find room for the plates beside the refrigerator, I'll put the stemware back on the table until I make room for them," Ford said. "Why don't we have coffee? I can work on this later."

Cam found space for the plates and went back to the dining room. He took off his jacket and rolled up his sleeves. "Let's have coffee later. When we've earned it."

It took over an hour with both of them scrubbing, but the kitchen could pass inspection by the health department. McCay spooned coffee into the coffee maker; Cam said he liked his with cream.

"This is an excellent wine," McCay said, holding up the dark bottle. "Kestrel Vintners in the Yakima Valley. Are you acquainted with the owners?"

"No, just the wine. I admire a number of Washington wines."

McCay took the clean china plates and saucers out of the dishwasher. "These go in the hutch. This was the china my wife and I bought when we'd been married about five years. Mandy would have been four."

Cam put them away. Then he went out on the porch. A few minutes later McCay came out with two mugs of coffee.

They'd talked companionably while they worked, about farming, ranching, and politics, but now the personal strain between them was unavoidable. McCay sat in a wicker chair and crossed his ankles. Cam settled onto the porch swing.

"She doesn't remember you," McCay said.

Cam nodded. "I know. I guess I should tell her."

"I want to protect her, but this is damned awkward. She wanted to marry you. I was the one who stopped it. I should probably be the one to lead her on this trip down memory lane."

"You're the one that wanted to stop the marriage, but I'm the one who stopped it."

Cam knew what he wanted McCay to say, what he *ought* to say. Hell, he'd written the script for this moment fifty times in his head. Instead, his words went unanswered. Silence descended, as heavy as smoke in a deep ravine.

"Maybe she'll take it well," McCay said at last,

"and we'll all have a good laugh." His grim face belied his attempt at humor.

Cam wanted to bail, to abdicate. To let McCay break the news to Mandy any way he wanted, even to say that the man she was trying to impress—to the point of collapse—was the man who had refused to marry her. He didn't need any drama; his life was full enough without disinterring the past.

But he couldn't do that. His pride hadn't done him any favors twelve years ago, but somehow he clung to it now.

He tried to see her father's side. McCay knew little of what had gone on that summer. In fact, if he found out now how Cam West—the hired man, for God's sake—had been having sex with his daughter all over the county he'd probably break Cam's nose. Oh, the man wasn't naïve. He must have known Mandy and Cam had gone pretty far. But Cam had omitted a lot when he and Mandy's father had their one talk.

A gentleman didn't kiss and tell, that's what he told himself.

Not that kissing came anywhere close to describing what they'd been up to.

He finished his coffee, took the cup inside, and put his jacket over his arm. On the porch, he looked down at Ford McCay.

"I'd better be the one to tell her, sir. As soon as she feels better."

McCay seemed to be deep in thought. At last, he nodded.

"I have to fly to D.C. tomorrow, Cam. D'Ann will be back the next day, Saturday. I'd like to...I'd like to be here when you talk to Mandy. I mean here in town."

"When will you be back?"

"Sunday night late or sometime Monday." He stood and held out his hand.

Cam looked at it, paused, then shook it. Last time he stood face to face with the man, tension had blanketed the farmhouse like natural gas, needing a tiny spark to explode. The result was Mandy tearing out of Bitter Falls for California.

And Cam's life torn through top to bottom, like a sheet from a two-inch scissor cut.

McCay's request to wait was tough. Cam's instincts told him to get it over with. Rip off the bandage with one swift movement. But he'd shaken the man's hand, and he'd wait. Until Mandy knew the truth, he'd be her new acquaintance. A friendly neighbor. And he'd keep intensely busy looking anywhere but at Mandy McCay.

Because, God help him, every time he so much as looked at her he wanted desperately to take her in his arms and claim those lips.

Chapter 7

Mandy woke up Friday, astonished to see it was nearly ten o'clock. She had an eerie sense of déjà vu. When Cam carried her up the stairs, with her arm draped around his neck, she'd had the strangest feeling that she'd been in his arms before. It had to be a short circuit in her brain, but she couldn't shake it off.

Four or five months after the shooting she'd recovered enough to distinguish dreams from reality, but she still had difficulty when she first woke up to identify dreams about total fiction from dreams about memories.

It was like going to a movie in a theater, feeling her way to a seat in the dark, no posters or titles to say what was in progress. She knew the action wasn't taking place in front of her; the screen was not a window. But was it people she'd never known doing things she'd never seen, or was it a home movie replaying a scene from her life?

Tests of her hearing and vision were normal. She didn't think they differed in any way from the way she'd always heard and seen things. But her other senses were heightened. Her fingers and her tongue could easily read subtle differences in texture. At the same time, the conjoined senses of taste and smell were incredibly fine-tuned and overwhelming in their impact on her. She knew from her memory and California friends that she used to be indifferent to food. Things were salty, or sweet, or fishy or sour. Menus held no interest to her. Food was food.

It was pretty much the same with smells. She always thought it was a hoax on the gullible to label shampoos and lotions with extravagant names of the scent inside. The differences to her were insignificant. Who cared?

But now she was wildly in tune with every scent on the air. Flowers, grass, clover were a concert of aromas. And food? Something that "smelled good" to most people was exquisite to her. D'Ann joked that the X-rays and CT scans and MRIs had zapped her olfactory glands and taste buds with superpowers.

Well, D'Ann and her dad and the staff at the rehab facility could joke all they wanted about hiring her out as a bloodhound, but Mandy knew what she knew.

And she knew she'd smelled rancher Cam West's unique scent before. Up close and personal. And she was determined to find out how and when.

She grinned and slid out of bed. Her skirt, blouse and bra were on the floor where she'd left them around midnight. She'd slept in the first thing she found in the drawer without turning on a light. She saw now that it was a Looney Tunes T-shirt. Well, well. That fit her in more ways than one.

She winced when she saw herself in the mirror. Her mascara had run to form black war paint under her eyes and her hair stood out in all directions. Once she'd washed her face and brushed her teeth and hair she appeared less—what was that word? Aboriginal.

She put on a bra under the T-shirt and slipped on a pair of seersucker shorts. The house was quiet, but she heard a tractor outside. She pulled up the nightshade from the window and faced the blazing sun of another Montana day. The tractor sound died, then started up, died, started up and this time held steady. It chugged into sight beyond the new barn. Lefty was fixing potholes in their long driveway.

She went downstairs to make coffee and discovered an envelope propped against the coffee maker.

"Mandy," it said in her father's angular handwriting, "the dinner last night was fantastic! I'm so thrilled that you wanted to do that, and I'll have to say you sure looked like you were having fun. But too much is too much! You need to care more for your energy and your health. Yes, I *have* informed D'Ann and she's going to crack the whip while I'm gone. I'll be back Sunday night, if possible, but by Monday night at the latest. See you soon. I already miss you. Love, Dad."

Under that he added a P.S. "I enjoyed Cam's company and he was wild about the dinner, but I've warned him not to accept any more invitations to dinner until I'm sure you have your strength back."

She ground a quarter cup of Costa Rican coffee beans, spooned it into the coffee maker, and added water. She was relieved to see the kitchen clean, but feared her dad had been up all night scrubbing pans. She wondered if Cam had stayed to help. He seemed like the kind of man who never shirked from work. Some hostess she'd turned out to be.

As the coffee brewed, she couldn't tear herself away. The smell of coffee was incredible. She would never tire of it. And there were so many different coffee beans. She'd bought nine kinds at The Happy Cooker and was determined to learn to identify them blindfolded.

To the glorious smell of fresh coffee she added visual delight: sunshine on a hanging basket of flowers outside the kitchen window. Moving to the sink, she picked up a potted mint plant she'd bought at the grocery store and put in the window until she could plant it. The fragrance was delicious.

Something out of place caught her eye on the windowsill. A man's watch. It was the green-faced watch and custom tooled band she'd admired on Cam's wrist the night before.

He had been washing dishes last night. She laughed at the thought of the tall rancher up to his elbows in dishwater.

Hmmm. She ought to drive over there and return his watch. Her heart did a tap dance.

With her mug of steaming coffee and cream, she sat in the living room. The scrapbooks D'Ann had unearthed were on the coffee table. She'd thought after dinner the three of them might look at pictures of D'Ann winning her ribbons at local rodeos, but her embarrassing exhaustion put an end to that plan.

Poor Cam. Come for dinner and spend the whole evening talking politics and business, then work the night shift cleaning a kitchen that looked like a bomb had gone off in a flour canister.

She leafed through the scrapbooks again. D'Ann with her dog Trouble and her horse, Blossom. There were a few of Mandy with D'Ann and Dad. One of Lefty holding Blossom's bridle. None of Cam West.

She wondered, without much enthusiasm for searching, what had become of her own scrapbook. It might be in the attic.

The "Mom" book, the collection of all the pictures they could find of Jane Fuller McCay, was with a professional scrapbook artist downtown. Pictures were being carefully removed from the old paper, restored when necessary, and would be placed on acid-free paper. D'Ann said she'd found old report cards of Mom's and poems she'd written. She also found a shoebox with ribbons from county fairs Mom had entered.

Luanne Holt at Memories Mine would have it ready in another week or two. She'd said she would research old newspapers about county fairs when

Jane McCay was competing and see if she could write in details about the ribbons.

Mandy wanted to go through her mom's recipe tin now that she was fascinated with the process of cooking, but that, too, was at Memories Mine.

She finished her coffee and poured a second cup. For breakfast, she ate a ripe freestone peach from the fruit basket beside the microwave oven. The juice dripped down her chin and she laughed and ate over the sink. She relished the aroma of the peach, the soft fuzz, the red flesh at the center. It was like capturing summer in one perfect golden globe.

She liked to read about extravagant breakfast pastries and things like Eggs Benedict, but in August in Montana the best bed and breakfast would be a house with a good coffee maker, set smack in the middle of a cherry orchard. Guests could walk outside and browse off the trees like deer.

She picked up Cam's watch. Ooo-eee! As farmers liked to say, *Where has the forenoon gone?* But farmers were likely to say it around seven a.m., not at eleven-thirty.

She showered and dressed in pastel green Capri pants and a white blouse with a scoop neck and ribbons on the shoulders. Using a hair dryer would be superfluous when the humidity was probably six percent, so she brushed it back off her face and left it loose.

She had another appointment with Dr. Kahn at three. Apparently, when he discovered how interesting her case was, he'd opened up space in his appointment schedule. She'd stop over to Cam's ranch and then go into town for a late lunch at The Mineshaft.

She put her watch on one wrist and Cam's on the other—sliding it up her arm to keep it on—and picked up her car keys and purse. As she got in the SUV, something made her stop and look toward the grape arbor between the old barn and the new barn. Clearly, no one was there. Still, something about it made her pulse rate soar. Was it a memory trying to break through? She got in the car.

With the window down, she could immerse herself in the fragrance of the honeysuckle that grew like a weed all along the garage. She closed her eyes to savor the sensations: the sound of bees, the warmth on her skin, the fragrance of the flowers.

She wished she could think of a way to get close enough to Cam to smell his scent again. Something about it nagged at her. He was so handsome, funny, and yet a trifle bashful when he handed her the flowers. Okay, and sexy. Those muscles were made to be fondled. When she'd seen him in the black T-shirt, at his ranch, she'd wanted to trace the cut between his biceps with her fingers and tickle him by letting her fingers stray to his chest—preferably with his shirt off. And his lips. Yummm. They begged to be tasted, like raspberries hanging heavy on a vine.

As she'd looked at him across the table, with the candlelight on the wine and reflected in his eyes, warmth flowed through her. That tingle in her breasts and between her legs told her more of her body was healing than the therapists had worked on.

Campbell West was magnetically attractive. But at the same time there was something worrying at her, tugging on a loose memory thread the same way she could never leave a loose thread alone, even when she knew that tugging could ruin a sweater.

She drove down the driveway and waved at Lefty, but her mind was exclusively on Cam. At the mailbox she stopped. She saw his face to her right and turned. No. To her left. No. It was gone, out of sight. She'd caught a glimpse of his face, as if he were peering at her from the past. His face younger and every bit as handsome.

But angry, cold, bitter. *Why?* And was it a real memory, or a false one? In spite of the heat, she shivered.

****

Cam had ridden out before daybreak on Sunny. The black gelding he kept as a pack horse trudged along behind with heavy tools. His big chain saw, extra gas and chains for hauling. Cam was in a foul temper, and the fewer people he saw the better off they'd be. He'd left a note for Joey by the coffee pot and headed for the state park.

The ranger, Pat O'Runion, had volunteered on the fire line during the Grail Fire, and Cam promised to come help him with trail repair as soon as he got his feet under him back on the ranch. O'Runion told him that extreme winds in late winter had ruined a lot of trails and the park service didn't have the muscle power or the man power to affect much of a difference. The park hosts were a nice retired couple from Iowa. They could as soon move a mountain as a log four feet in diameter.

He stopped at the ranger's cabin to plan the work with O'Runion. The ranger spread out a topographical map to show him where the flood had taken out the road and four prime campsites.

"I've got an ATV and a chain saw," O'Runion said. "I'll swing around to the west and come down that side of the creek. Your best route in on a horse is this way." He dragged his finger up the map. "I'll meet you there."

Cam spent the morning and part of the afternoon slicing through the logs with the chain saw, then chaining them and using Sunny and Vector to haul each side away from the trail. The work was hard and dangerous if he lost his focus. He didn't have to make any conversation; he and the ranger communicated with hand gestures and arm waving. O'Runion left around one p.m. to call the state engineer and describe what he needed a work crew for.

Cam kept working. When he shut down the chainsaw for the last time and took off his ear protectors, he slumped bone weary onto a log.

And Mandy McCay washed into his mind like the tide. One wave was all it took to break down whatever sandcastle of detachment he'd been building.

His body ached from the hard labor, but it hadn't bought him anything. A Greek chorus was in his head, saying what Greek choruses always say. *We warned you! But would you listen? No!*

What would have happened last night if Ford McCay had been away on business? He leaned over and rested his head on his forearms. Good Lord, he smelled like a plow horse. Oh, he'd wanted to sweat, to sweat his craziness out of him. But he'd sweated out none of his pain and ambivalence.

He wanted her. God help him, but he did. If her father hadn't been there, he would have licked the wine off her tempting lips and caught her up against him so she'd feel how hard he was. He was certifiably the horniest man in Montana.

What kind of hell was this, that he knew every inch of her body—had *tasted* every inch of her body—and she didn't know him from the mailman? Her father had warned him to stay away from her, and the man was totally in the right. Mandy's body and mind had been dragged through a rat hole backwards, and she needed an environment with no stress.

The last thing she needed was him coming on to her with ulterior motives. He was playing with a loaded deck, five aces, and he knew where every one of them was. Like tracing his tongue around her nipple but not taking it until she was breathing hard.

All of Cam's relationships with women were, well, negotiated. Every little thing in the man-woman game was give and take. The art of mutual seduction. Win-win. Aretha Franklin said it best. R-E-S-P-E-C-T.

But this charade with Mandy was an explosive with a short fuse. One kiss would be all the spark he needed.

It was coming up on three o'clock when he got all the tools secured and started the ride home. At his ranch, Joey saw him coming and offered to take the horses.

"Thanks, Joey, I'm good. I might as well finish the job."

He was about to ask how the new pump was working when Joey interrupted him.

"Mandy was here, around noon. She brought your watch back."

Cam looked at his wrist and saw his watch, then recalled that he'd worn his dressy watch to dinner and taken it off by the sink. "Did she say anything?"

"She said her dad went to Washington D.C. and D'Ann will be back from Portland tomorrow. She was dressed up pretty, on her way into town."

Cam nodded and asked about the pump and the fence repairs. Two hours later the horses were cared for and the tools and other equipment were clean and back in place. His stomach was growling like a puma, but before he could fix anything to eat he had to shower. He caught his reflection in the window and laughed. He looked like a derelict who sold plasma next door to the bus station.

He peeled off his filthy clothes in the mudroom, thinking it would be a kindness to burn them instead of trying to wash them. He never threw any clothes away, thinking instead that his tattered jeans and shirts would be good to use for work clothes. Must be something he picked up from his granddad. Now he had a wardrobe that was ninety percent work clothes with "one more wearing" in them. It was time to cull the herd. He dropped the jeans and shirt in the trash bin right outside the kitchen door. Stopping long enough to grab a beer, he headed upstairs.

To shower. Not to shave. He had to stop "getting ready" to see Mandy. He had to stop forming sentences in his head that even had the word Mandy in them.

Sure, he could do that. About like he could breathe underwater. Nothing to it.

He came back downstairs in clean jeans and a tan T-shirt. The sun was nearly down; he turned off the air conditioner and opened windows instead. The ranch was blissfully quiet.

Joey and the men had gone into town to get hamburgers and see what was on at the theater. Luckily, Cam had stopped at the deli when he bought the flowers for his dinner date. Now he pulled Russian rye bread, ham and Swiss cheese out of the big refrigerator. He put a big slab of tomato on the meat and cheese and smeared stone ground mustard on the top slice of bread.

Mustard. Before he could even take a bite, he choked up.

She'd been so damn cute in that cooking store, poking fun at him. *Lord'a' mercy, Miz McCay, I'm a bachelor.*

Great. Now mustard could be added to the words that led him straight to a *Mandy moment.* Along with wine, candles, his good watch, his tan jacket. The sun coming up, the sun going down. It was a good thing he wasn't taking one of those psychological tests where they ask for association.

"Sandals?" Mandy's feet.

"Ribbons?" Mandy's hair.

"Heaven?" Mandy's scent, Mandy's skin,

Mandy's moan of pleasure when she comes.

"It's only mustard, damn it!" he said aloud.

He opened another beer and sat to watch the Mariners on TV. After a while, the sandwich wasn't on the plate and he wasn't hungry, so he guessed he'd eaten it. Food was merely food without Mandy.

"Damn it!" He turned off the TV and put on his boots. He'd told Joey he'd check on Polo. Out in the barn he called to her softly and heard her whimper. He crouched down beside the blanket Joey had spread out for her on fresh straw. Marco sniffed her and she growled and snapped.

"Better stay back, Marco. Polo's going to be pretty ferocious once those puppies come. She probably won't even let me touch them." He reached out and petted her head.

"You're a good girl, Polo. I know, it's rough. But the doctor said you'll be fine." He checked her as best he could without moving her too much. She kept her big eyes on his face and he didn't miss the low growl and the show of teeth when he looked under her tail.

"Well, girl, I know a thing or two about whelping, and you're going to have a few mewling little bundles by morning."

Chapter 8

Cam heard a car come into the yard. It didn't sound like Joey's truck. He stood and worked the kinks out of his knees and headed outside in the afterglow of what had been a spectacular sunset. It was nine-thirty, but at this latitude there would be light until ten.

"Cam!" Mandy jumped back. "Oh, you surprised me."

She wore tight denim shorts and a red off-the-shoulder blouse. And no bra. Cam got hard and couldn't find his voice.

"I brought you an apple coffee cake. I thought I could invite myself for the coffee I missed last night. In fact, I brought coffee. It's decaf. From Kenya." She blushed. "I should have called."

"If you had, I would have said to come over." He wondered if Joey had casually mentioned that he and the other men would be gone tonight. Half of him cursed Joey and the other half—the bottom half, of course—blessed him.

"I meant to ask you yesterday," she said, "how's Polo?"

"I was in the barn now checking on her. I think we'll have puppies by morning."

"I hope she'll let me see them when they're tiny. Nothing is cuter than puppies."

"Well, I'm kind of partial to foals, but all babies are cute. Here let me carry that. You can come see Polo. I think she'll be more comfortable with a 'sister'

98

right now. Marco came close to losing an ear and she showed her teeth to me."

Inside the barn, Mandy made cooing noises like women always did around baby anythings. Usually it sounded goofy, but she could read the phone book and he'd think it was better than Shakespeare. She didn't try to touch Polo; instead she held out her hand with the back of it toward Polo's face and told her how beautiful her puppies would be and what a fine mother she'd make. Polo wagged her tail and licked her hand.

Cam laughed. "That proves it. Sisterhood is powerful, even across species."

In the kitchen, he made the coffee while Mandy cut two squares of the coffee cake. He gestured with his chin. "The plates are to the right of the sink."

While they waited for the coffee to brew he told her about the damage in the state park and what had been accomplished in a day of work by two men, one ATV, two excellent horses, and a couple of powerful chain saws.

He got down mugs and added the coffee and cream. "Let's take this outside. The air is cooling off now."

He carried the mugs and she carried the two plates out to a picnic table under a willow tree. She took a deep breath—which, of course, made her breasts move. Cam had to swallow hard to keep from swearing.

"Dinner last night was wonderful. Thank you."

"You're welcome. You and Dad found a lot to talk about."

"He's a fascinating man. I was lucky to keep up my end of the conversation. I spend most of my time with men who consider the swimsuit editions of sports magazines to be fine literature."

"You didn't seem to have any trouble keeping up. Are you a secret reader of the *Wall Street*

Journal?"

"Shhh! Someone might hear you. I'm already getting a barrel of grief over washing my truck."

She studied his face. "How long did you work for my dad?"

He hoped he was wrong, but it sounded like a loaded question. He even wondered if she was starting to remember something from that time.

"Oh, about six months, give or take."

"So we knew each other?"

"Uh, sure." Don't lie, he told himself. You don't have to spout like a geyser, but do not tell a lie.

She said nothing for a long while. "I don't remember you."

He fervently wished he could say the same, but he was still conjuring an icy shower in his mind, trying to get his jeans to fit better.

She went on, sparing him the task of thinking of a response.

"I went to see the psychologist again today. Dr. Kahn. He thinks it's odd that I can't remember leaving Montana. My dad sort of clouds over like a storm coming in when I ask him about it. Then he quickly changes the subject. D'Ann wasn't here. She's no help."

"So what do you think happened?"

"Well, I know I bailed on college. I was accepted at University of Virginia. Here's what I think. I think I had a humongous fight with my dad— probably over nothing—and I hauled ass out of town. Not to my credit, I hauled ass in a convertible he'd given me!"

"You didn't come back." An anvil settled on his chest. The days after she left were the most painful days he'd ever lived through.

"I must have been as stubborn as that awful mule we used to have. Remember Oscar?" Her blue eyes widened.

He laughed. "Oscar would have made good shoe leather. He sure wasn't good for anything else. Lefty got rid of him about a month after I started working on the farm."

"I like to think every animal has a redeeming quality that makes them useful, if only to clean up carrion off the highway. But Oscar was the exception."

She laughed and he couldn't help but see her breasts bounce.

Even with her breasts dancing around like two bunnies in a tight pillowcase, the sound of her laughter was the most erotic thing about her. He grinned. That was like saying, *Sure, K-2 is a big mountain, but get a load of Everest.*

"Cam, would you come over here?" She patted the bench on her side of the redwood table.

"Over there?" He moved slowly, but his mind was racing down the track, somewhere near the quarter mile mark. *Keep it light,* he told himself. He sat on her side of the table, leaving a good two feet between her thigh and his.

"What's up?" He took a mouthful of coffee.

She scooted close to him and smiled. "Ask me no questions, I'll tell you no lies."

He choked, spraying coffee like Inspector Clouseau. She'd inadvertently said *his* line, the one that went around in his head like a pinwheel in a trade wind.

"Is something wrong?" She handed him a napkin and he tried to cover up his embarrassment.

"I'm fine. Sorry. It's uh, I swallowed wrong."

"Bear with me. I want to satisfy my curiosity." She leaned closer, closer. They were touching from thighs to shoulders and still she pressed closer. In his ear she whispered, "I won't bite."

Instead she nuzzled his neck with her nose. He had to grab the table with both hands to stay on the seat. *Have mercy, Miz McCay.*

Mandy breathed in the scent of Cam West. Nothing but a man and his soap. No aftershave; he had a day's growth of beard. She wanted to let her fingers explore, but she'd acted crazy enough as it was. She moved away and looked at him.

And laughed. "Cam, don't take this the wrong way, but you look like a wild horse must look when he feels his first saddle. Your eyes are the size of half dollars, and I could swear I saw your nostrils flare!"

"Now, how could I take that the *wrong way?*" He sighed. "I look like a horse. Well, do I pass muster in whatever scratch and sniff survey you're taking?"

She grinned. "Ask me no questions..."

"All right, all right."

She moved to the other side of the table. It was nice to be close to Cam, but it was awfully nice to look at him, too. And if truth be told, she was afraid she might lean so close she'd end up in a kiss he might not return with the enthusiasm she was feeling.

"What was I saying before I went on that brazen olfactory safari?"

"That you stayed in California so long because you and Oscar the mule have a gene in common."

She nodded. "Oh, yes. I used to be stubborn. But I'm thinking you already know that. Any questions?"

She stared into his eyes, expecting a teasing remark, but what she saw took her breath away. If eyes could eat, his would devour her. She blushed and dropped her gaze to her lap.

In little more than the time it took to swallow, he stood and slid around to her side of the table and took her in his arms.

"This is not a question," he said in a deep voice.

Before she had time to think about it, his lips were on hers. It wasn't any butterfly kiss, either. More like Clark Gable saying, "Kiss me, Scarlett."

She turned her head to the side and opened her mouth a fraction to his tongue, then happily surrendered to a delicious sensation.

She wriggled her arms free from her sides and put them around his shoulders. She heard him groan and wound her fingers in his hair. When they broke for air, her heart was racing.

"All right, Mr. West," she said between shallow breaths that had the unfortunate side effect of rubbing her sensitive nipples against his chest, "if you feel so strongly about it, you may ask me a few questions."

"I don't have any questions, only answers."

He claimed her mouth again. This time he slid one hand from her back forward along her side. Forward, half an inch at a time. Then he stopped. He was driving her crazy! Her breasts were aching to be held, the nipples swollen. She pulled back and without moving his hand, he had her breast. She rocked side to side slightly, trying to ease the wanting.

He froze short of touching her nipple and moved his hand to her back, but he deepened the kiss. This time it was her turn to moan. She knew two things now. He wanted her, was aching as much as she was. But he didn't want to act on it.

She knew a third thing, too. She wanted him with a sexual need she didn't know she had in her. When she felt his tongue again she pulled her chest away until she could clasp his hand with hers. This time she guided it to her breast.

And this time he cupped it gently and kneaded her nipple through the material. He lowered his mouth to her neck and she lifted her chin, lost in the overwhelming sensation. The V between her legs was wet and throbbed with her racing pulse.

Cam took a shallow breath—all he had time for—and kissed her chest, butterfly kisses this time, and moved lower. With his right hand he tugged the elastic top of her cotton blouse down. Two inches, three, down until her nipples popped free and he could taste the skin in the cleavage between her breasts.

"Mandy, Mandy," he moaned, moving his tongue like a paintbrush over the landscape, to one side and the other.

She heard a truck and jumped back as if startled from a deep sleep.

"Cam."

He swore but straightened up.

Cam took one look at Mandy's flushed face and the way her lips were swollen—and knew they were fifteen seconds from an embarrassing situation. It was bad enough that he'd be razzed to the state line and back, but he didn't want Joey and the others to see Mandy like this. She tugged her blouse up over her breasts.

"Quick, into the house!" he said.

He helped her up from the bench and they ran up the lawn and in the back door. They stumbled through the mudroom, laughing, and into the living room. She caught a glimpse of herself in the mirror over the hat rack.

"Oh, my. Can I use your comb?"

Her hair wasn't the sole evidence of their close contact. Her chest was scratched red from his beard. He started to direct her to his bathroom, upstairs, off his bedroom, but his good sense kicked in—finally.

"There's a comb in the cabinet in the downstairs bathroom."

He hated to admit it, but Joey's bad timing was a blessing in disguise. He'd been leaning off the cliff, dizzy with the scent and smell and feel of her, ready to leap into the river and go over the falls. Thank goodness his head was clearing now.

What was I thinking? It looked like the only way

he could keep from taking Mandy to bed was to board a plane to the South Pole. All his careful planning about working until he dropped, not going to her house, taking cold showers, keeping his word to her father—and she had to drop by with coffee cake.

Apple coffee cake.

His own Eve. But she was twice as tempting because she didn't know what the hell was going on. There was an innocence to her that was...well, virginal. She must have had lovers after him in twelve years of pretty wild living—if one-tenth of what the tabloids said about Hollywood starlets was true.

She'd been engaged twice.

But there was something so fresh about her, so open and honest. It sounded crazy, but it was as if she were eighteen again. And Mandy at eighteen was—well, there weren't words for it. Mandy at eighteen was why men wrote hit songs that a hundred million other people made love to.

And from what he could tell in their brief but intense tussle in the back yard, Mandy at thirty would leave that girl at the starting gate.

He had to get her out of here. *Something has come up. Business. I have to go to Missoula.* No, she might offer to come along. Seattle? Hong Kong?

The phone rang as she came out of the bathroom. She was back to looking like she had when she arrived. Of course, that had been enough to make him hard. He picked up the phone.

"Cam West."

There was silence, then a throat clearing. He looked at the caller I.D. Blocked. *Figures.* "This is Campbell West."

"Campbell, this is your mother. I'd like to talk to you."

They spoke by phone about four days a year, and

this wasn't one of them. "Why don't I call you back in half an hour?"

"I'm in Bitter Falls."

"You're *what?* Where?"

Mandy said she'd been stubborn to stay away from Montana for twelve years. Compare that to—he did the math quickly—compare it to sixty-one years of stubbornness. Oscar the mule was a pussycat compared to Arabella Billings West.

"I'd like to see you, Campbell. I know it's late tonight, and I'm tired from the trip."

"Where are you staying?" he winced, hoping she wouldn't make a scathing remark about what Bitter Falls called *lodging*.

"I'm at the Victorian Inn. It's quite pleasant."

He waited, expecting her to follow that with a snide remark like, "Pleasant if you call bottled wine spritzers and pretzels a cocktail hour." Or, "Pleasant if you enjoy the conversation of tourists from Iowa." She could make Iowa sound less appealing than the Black Hole of Calcutta.

He waited. She didn't add anything. She'd said it was pleasant and left it at that.

"Good, I'm glad you're comfortable. I'll pick you up in the morning. Would you like to see my place?"

Part of him wanted her to say no. He'd come to enjoy his "high ground" in their impasse. She was unreasonable; he was reasonable. She was cold, snobbish and materialistic; he was the soul of solid middle class values and a paragon of generosity.

Hmmm. Perhaps he should think about this a smidgeon more.

"I would like that, Campbell. I'll see you at, say, ten o'clock? Goodnight."

"Ten o'clock is good. Goodnight."

Having his mother in Montana, coming to his ranch, was more unlikely than him jumping on a plane to Hong Kong.

Mandy was cleaning out the coffee pot. "Sounds like you're expecting company."

"Unexpected company. My mother is here from Boston."

"Boston? Did you live there? Or did she move there?"

"Both. She's lived there most of her life, ever since she was nineteen and left Montana. I lived in Boston a long time, until I grew up and moved to Montana."

She wiped her hands on a towel and smiled. "That's an interesting reversal. Well, I'd better go. Dad will call and if I'm not home he'll worry."

He put his hands in his pockets. "I hope I get to keep the cake."

"Of course. I have conquered apple coffee cake and moved on to greater challenges. The cookbook is open to Strawberry Rhubarb Pie."

She crossed and gave him a kiss on the lips. He kept his hands in his pockets. The fact that it was dark outside and they were inside a well-lit showroom—and that four cowboys were probably strolling by to see what Mandy looked like tonight—helped his self control.

"Good night," he said. "Thanks for coming over."

She looked into his eyes with an intensity that made him edgy—and hornier than ever. The fragrance of her perfume, the one he recalled so well, was about to drive him to his knees. And if he went to his knees, he knew the next thing he wanted to do. What if he backed to the wall and turned off the light switch...?

"Cam, did...? Did you ever, I mean, did you ever hear me argue with my dad?"

"Argue? No, why?"

"I want to know what made me leave Bitter Falls in such an all-fired rush. Dr. Kahn says if my dad and I had an argument, it's not worth

107

remembering, that all teenagers rebel."

"Dr. Kahn is right."

"But that's not enough for me. I want to know why. When Dad gets home, I'm going to insist on knowing the whole story."

"I hope whatever you learn helps you heal. That's all everyone who loves you wants."

She leaned forward again, this time to the side of his face. As she had before, she nuzzled his neck and sniffed.

"Tonight was not the first time I've kissed you, is it?"

He said nothing. He didn't want to open that door. And even if he did want to, he'd promised Ford McCay he wouldn't.

"No, it's not the first time." He licked his lips. The next thing he said could lose his balance on this high wire. It had to be true, but not too true. "I'll tell you what, Mandy. You said, 'Ask me no questions, I'll tell you no lies.' I'll go one better. You *can* ask me questions—not tonight, but soon—and I'll tell you no lies."

Showroom be damned, he took her in his arms for one heart-pounding, unforgettable kiss.

"Goodnight, Cam," she said when they stopped to breathe. "Enjoy your visit with your mom."

"Enjoy? We're not close. I think the dictionary describes it as estranged."

She put her hands on her hips. "Hey, I wish *my* mom could come see *me.*"

Chagrined by her tone as well as her words, he smiled. "You're right. I need to be more…accepting."

"Call me," she said.

He watched the gentle bounce of her breasts as she walked out toward her car. He turned off lights in the kitchen and living room and stood at the front window, watching the taillights of her SUV disappear up the long driveway.

Did he dare hope? Yes, he had to. But he dreaded the full return of her memory.

Chapter 9

Mandy turned off her headlights and her engine. In the silence, she stared at the dark windows of the farmhouse where she'd grown up. In the time it had taken her to drive there from Cam West's ranch, darkness had cloaked everything. The only light anywhere was in a window of Lefty's cabin, a half-mile away. She toyed with the notion of calling him from her cell phone and asking him to stop up to the house.

She turned on her phone, relieved when she saw there were no messages. She should have taken it inside at Cam's house. Her dad would call their home phone, then her cell, and then probably the sheriff. She took the phone off the car charger and dropped it in her purse. Should she call Lefty?

No. I am an adult. I don't need anyone to walk into the house and turn on lights for me. Still, she sat in the car.

She'd locked the doors of the big house before she drove to Cam's place. She wished she'd thought to leave a light on. In the silence and the darkness, fear rattled at her like a snake in a crevasse, unseen and ready to strike. Fear...

She had no memory of being grabbed as she started to get in her car in Pasadena, and no memory of the horror that followed. She knew the parking lot surveillance photos had been on TV a thousand times. Frame by frame of her stalker appearing out of nowhere, knocking her out and driving her away in her car. So, too, the lurid footage of her being airlifted from the bloody mess on the highway was said to be everywhere. Replayed on TV, spread across the world on the internet.

Mandy had not seen the pictures; she'd been shielded by D'Ann, and her dad, and the staff at the rehabilitation facility. Now she could see anything she wanted, but if she never saw those images it would be fine with her.

As she'd told Dr. Kahn with a laugh, "That's probably why I watch the Food Channel with such single-minded devotion."

But still, somewhere deep inside her was a lump of fear that festered, as if her body were saying, "You say you don't remember? Your brain doesn't remember, but I do!"

Damn! Out here in the country it got so freaking dark. No moon tonight. She looked up beyond the trees and saw two shooting stars at the same time. Another one, and another.

She bolstered her resolve to go into the dark house alone by saying aloud, "I am perfectly safe here."

She stepped out of the car and closed the door to kill the dome light. In a few seconds, her eyes were used to the dark again. Instead of going inside, she walked to the back of the house. A picnic table like Cam's sat square in the freshly mowed yard. She sat on the bench and craned her neck up to see the night sky. A minute of that was enough to give her a crick in her neck. She climbed onto the table and lay on her back so the sky was above and seemed to surround her.

Too many shooting stars passed overhead for her to make a wish on each. She counted up to twenty, then gave up and enjoyed the show. She'd done this before. August, meteor shower...she tried to remember what it was called.

Oh, yes. The Perseid Meteor Shower. She'd watched it from high in the hills, a clearing somewhere. She couldn't think who had gone with her, but she was sure she hadn't been alone.

She roused herself from her star-struck lethargy and unlocked the back door. In a couple minutes, she had the place ablaze with lights and the curtains drawn closed. Still, she couldn't shake the anxiety. She made a cup of herbal tea and tried to comprehend why she felt so uneasy.

"Well, duh." She laughed. Not only was this the first time she would spend a night alone since the shooting, it was probably the first time she'd been this alone so far from other people—and this much in the dark—in twelve years.

The phone rang and she jumped. "Hello?"

That call from her dad was followed in short order by a call from D'Ann. She told them both she was fine and was on her way to bed. She sidestepped her dad's question about what she'd done earlier in the evening. She said she'd baked a coffee cake; she didn't say anything about using it as an excuse to see Cam. Her conversation with D'Ann did not go as smoothly.

"I'll be home around four o'clock," D'Ann said. "Let's go to dinner at The Mineshaft."

"Dad put you up to that, didn't he? Trying to get me out of the kitchen."

"In fact, no, he didn't. My motives, while ulterior, are all my own."

"And those motives would be what?"

"There's a dance floor at The Mineshaft and a live band on Saturday night. I want to go boot scootin'."

"You? You? My little sister with her nursing degrees from University of Virginia and experience at Johns Hopkins and Doernbecher's? What alien spaceship replaced my sister with a girl in tight jeans and Tony Lama boots?"

"Surely you're not saying people who like country western music are dumb! Do you think Cam West is mentally deficient?"

He'd talked about international trade, protective tariffs and currency variants with her dad. No question he was smart and well-read.

"Okay, your point is made. But you're dancing without me. I can't remember how to dance."

D'Ann laughed. "Your *body* remembers. Give it a chance. It's like that other thing. The thing men like more than cookies."

"I can't believe my sister called me to talk dirty."

"And I can't believe my sister is such a prude. Loosen up, girl. You're thirty, not eighty."

She wondered if Cam might show up at The Mineshaft. That reminded her about the phone call he'd received.

"Hey, did you know Cam is from Boston?"

"Boston? Get out of town!"

"He told me so. His mother is in town from Boston for an unexpected visit."

"And he told you this when?"

"When I was over..." She stopped. *Busted!*

"Over where? At Cam's ranch? Come on, 'fess up. Were you over there? What was your excuse?"

"I'm not admitting anything."

"You're not denying it either. What did you do, bake something and happen to show up on his doorstep?"

"Wow, look at the time. I need to get to sleep. See you tomorrow." She hung up before D'Ann wheedled any details of her trip to Cam's ranch.

That didn't stop her from thinking of the pounding throughout her body when he took her breast in his hand, and how he'd pulled the elastic top of her blouse down until her nipples were free of the material. And what he'd done with his tongue.

D'Ann was so wrong about her being a prude.

She made sure the doors were locked, and left a floor lamp on downstairs. In her room, she crawled into bed. She lay there, tossing restlessly, when she recalled where her scrapbook and mementoes were. Oh, yeah. She'd stashed them in an old broken-down bureau in the attic before she left for California.

Climbing those dark stairs was too much to ask when she was already nervous about being alone. She'd retrieve them in the morning.

Sleep wasn't any closer twenty minutes later. She turned on the bedside light and opened a book, "Cooking in Tuscany," and was soon engrossed in a recipe for Chicken Tetrazzini; a dish, she learned, that was named for Italian coloratura Luisa Tetrazzini.

Maybe she'd invent a dish, something ultra spicy, and call it Chicken West. Named for a rancher who—if her instincts could be trusted—was trying hard not to let friendly friction through two layers of denim ignite something he couldn't stop.

****

Cam was ready to go up to bed when he remembered their mugs and plates still on the picnic table. When he went outside to get them, the shooting stars caught his eye. He counted a few with his neck craned up, then sat on the end of the table and leaned back on the cool wood to watch the show.

He was doomed for all eternity to think of Mandy when he saw meteors. The two of them had driven up an old logging road that August night...

They parked and hiked; he carried a sleeping bag. He could even remember what they talked about. Mandy had gone shopping in Missoula and "visited" the car she would get in September. She also showed him a letter from D'Ann, who missed Blossom and begged Mandy to stop their dad from selling her. By the time they got within sight of the natural stone arch, Cam had been light-headed with anticipation of their lovemaking. Hell, the memory of it *now* made him light-headed.

Remembering Mandy by starlight, the scent of honeysuckle in her hair and the feel of her skin against his own...No, let it go. He gathered the mugs and plates and headed for the kitchen. He'd stepped inside when the phone rang.

He picked up the old wall phone in the mudroom, the one without caller I.D. "Hello."

"Hi."

Mandy's voice was soft, intimate. He suffered a moment of embarrassment, as if she could see him. He was still hard as a lead pipe after his trip down memory lane.

"Hi, there." He cleared his throat. "Hold on a second. I need to change phones." He let the handset dangle while he went in to get a portable, then hung up the wall phone. He welcomed the interruption as a chance to cool off. He got a beer out of the refrigerator, opened it, and took a good swallow. What he wanted to do was put his head under the faucet in the sink.

"I was outside looking at the meteor shower," he said.

"I saw it, too. It's the Perseid, isn't it? I don't know why I remember that, or what it means."

"Yes, the Perseid. Meteors that radiate from a point in the constellation Perseus. Are you, uh, are you remembering a lot more now that you're home?"

"I am. Not about my big black hole, about why I left Montana like an outlaw on the lam. Do you suppose I have a dark criminal past?"

"I'm pretty sure you're clean. Besides, it's not like you were hiding out. The sheriff could have tracked you if he needed to." He chuckled. "You were definitely *not* hiding."

"Thanks for the reminder. I shudder to think

what my father said when he saw that dress I wore to the Academy Awards."

Cam whistled. "Pretty much everyone in town had something to say about that."

She groaned. "I was young."

He closed his eyes. *I know. Young and beautiful and very much in love with a man you can't remember.*

"Weak defense, huh?" she went on. "Anyway, to answer your question, yes, I'm remembering things. It's an odd feeling when something clicks into place. It's as if the wheels on a slot machine are spinning and I see a flash of cherries and big red sevens, but they keep spinning to tease me. Then ka-ching."

"For example?" He took a swallow of beer.

"My eighteenth birthday."

Cam froze. His heart might jump out of his chest and roll across the floor. "Your, uh? Oh. Your birthday."

"My dad threw a big party for me at the country club. I don't remember much about it, but tomorrow I'll go up in the attic and get my scrapbook. When I see the pictures I'll remember more." She yawned.

"You should be asleep."

"I know. I went to bed, but I couldn't fall asleep. Something about the shooting stars, I mean meteors, made me kind of squirrelly."

"Starstruck."

"That's it! Yes. Well, I'd better say goodnight. I hope your visit with your mother is pleasant."

"That makes two of us. Good night, Mandy."

He set the handset back in the charger and turned off the lights downstairs. The couch he'd scooted forward to show Mandy his winter theatrical was still in its place. He sat, propped his bare feet on the fireplace, and stared without focus at the sky.

Mandy's eighteenth birthday. How much would she remember? Ford McCay might not have this play out the way he wanted—that he could be home when Mandy found out.

Cam swallowed more beer.

He would keep his word if he could. But he wouldn't lie to her. If she remembered enough to ask the right question, he wouldn't lie to protect her, or her father, or himself.

Memories of her birthday washed over him like a gentle lawn sprinkler on thick green grass. Summer solstice, the longest day of the year. Their shared midsummer night's dream.

It had been the longest day of his life. He stayed busy, trying to get the long hours to pass. From the corral he saw Mandy come out on the porch of the farmhouse with a camera. She wore a long, slim dress, a shimmery vision in silver and white slit up about five inches above one knee. Her friend came out, too, in a shiny red gown.

Ford McCay had already left for the country club in his tuxedo, so Mandy had called out to Cam.

"Can you spare a minute? I want to get a picture of us before we wilt in this heat."

He'd walked over from the corral and taken the small camera from her. Of course she'd winked and licked her lips to remind him of their plan to meet later.

The two girls had posed like beauty queens on a TV show and Cam had snapped a picture. She'd wanted him to shoot more pictures, but the film ran out.

"Oh, rats. Dad has the film with him. Well, you got one, anyway." Mandy slid into her friend's Miata convertible and they drove away.

That dress has to be a bitch to dance in, he remembered thinking. Jealousy had flared within him to know a roomful of "suitable" men would be dancing with her. But she wanted to be with him; she'd told him that. They'd been kissing and going pretty far in the few weeks they'd known each other, but tonight would be the night. He had a motel room reserved. It was crazy, but he was a nervous wreck about it. He knew making love with Mandy would be wonderful, but he wanted it to be nothing less than spectacular for her. She'd told him she wasn't a virgin, but he had a sixth sense about it. There was something off about her claim. It might be her first time, or not. But he was damn sure it would be her best, something to remember always.

Yeah, he'd been thinking about making their first time memorable for her, but look how it turned out. *She* didn't remember it at all and *he* couldn't get it out of his mind no matter what he did—or who he did it with. It was all Mandy, all the time with him.

"Pretty sad!" he said aloud.

He toyed with the possibility of putting Celine Dion back on the stereo, but he was already miserable enough. He put his empty bottle in the kitchen and headed upstairs to bed. Instead of thinking about Mandy in the hour it took him to go to sleep, he wondered about his mother. What collision in the cosmos, what conjunction of planets had gotten her back into the state of Montana sixty years after she left? And what effect would this unexpected visit have on his life?

Chapter 10

The delicious smell of strawberry-rhubarb pie cooling on the kitchen counter permeated the old house. Even in the attic where Mandy stood, staring with trepidation at an old wreck of a bedroom bureau, the scent of cinnamon was in the air.

Was she afraid of old dead photos? No. Live spiders? Hell yes. She took off her shoe and held it at the ready as she tried, unsuccessfully, to get the bottom drawer open.

She sighed and put the shoe on top of the scratched furniture to use both hands. Pull, shove. Harder—pull, shove. The third pull put her on her butt on the floor and the drawer completely out of the bureau. She skittered backward in fear of spiders—and heaven knows what other pests. She hated spiders even more than snakes—and she was terrified of snakes.

Aunt Sarah said Jane had been thrown from a horse while pregnant with Mandy. Cause of the accident: a rattlesnake striking the horse. No wonder Mandy feared snakes. She wouldn't even go inside a herpetarium at a zoo.

With the toe of her sandal, she lifted the long box that said Bitter Falls Florist and dropped it back hard. She did the same with the corner of the thick scrapbook. Nothing ran out, but that didn't mean they weren't full of black widows. How much did she want to see these old pictures? Maybe she'd wait until D'Ann was home and get her to bring them

119

downstairs. The two of them could go upstairs, armed with a can of bug spray.

No! I am an adult. She went through the same litany she'd recited the night before when she was afraid to go into the dark house. She weighed the pros and cons of touching the things in the drawer and went downstairs for a large garbage bag and thick gloves. Back in the attic, she lifted all her keepsakes into the garbage bag, folded over the top, and carried it downstairs like a butler carrying a breakfast tray.

She went straight out the back door and laid the bag on the picnic table. Still wearing gloves, she slid the bag free and tossed it on the ground; then she removed the lid from the florist's box and opened the ratty, disintegrating scrapbook to its midsection. Should she spray the whole thing with insecticide? No, that seemed like overkill.

She gave everything another shake.

At last, she removed the gloves and sat beside the table, ready to be a forensic investigator. She'd played a part in one episode of *CSI,* the one set in Las Vegas, but she'd died in the opening credits and her "acting" was on a slab in the morgue. This time it was *CSI: Montana* and she was the star.

Most of the objects in the box provoked the same question in her. Why on earth did I save *that?* One tangled glob the size of a head of lettuce was all corsages. She didn't remember going to that many dances. A playbill from the Broadway show *Forty-Second Street* made more sense. Her dad had taken her and D'Ann to New York for a week when she was fourteen. A rubber band held a batch of tour guide brochures together. When she touched the bundle the rubber band crumbled.

She opened the brochures and smiled in delight to remember all the fun they'd had. Radio City Music Hall to see the "Christmas Show." The Tavern on the Green for dinner. Wall Street; the New York Public Library; the Statue of Liberty. They'd done the town.

There were so many souvenirs of trips. Chopsticks and a menu from Chinatown, San Francisco. Postcards that folded out accordion style from Seattle. Pens and pencils from hotels; a four-inch bear wearing a Marriott T-shirt. Cardboard 3-D glasses. The script of a school play written by Gerri Melman's mother. She and Gerri had been friends, and occasionally rivals, all through school.

She opened the script and laughed. Gerri had been sure she'd get the lead role of her mother's play. When Mandy won it at auditions Gerri had a total meltdown.

So much to remember. She didn't think anything so far was a "lost" memory that she was yanking into the "recovered" pile. They were simply things she hadn't thought about in so long they were sort of forgotten. That kind of thing must happen to everyone.

She turned to the scrapbook. Each picture she found with her mother in it she removed carefully. She'd take them to Memories Mine and ask Luanne to put them in the scrapbook.

There were pictures of her and D'Ann at every gawky stage of their lives. Then things improved; she got her braces off and started wearing a bra. She went to formal dances. Each of those photos showed a corsage. Several showed her dates. Apparently she liked to go out with skinny boys with long bangs and bad posture. To be fair, she didn't look so hot herself.

Other pictures. The color guard at the county rodeo, Gerri with the U.S. flag and her with the state flag. They'd patched up their feud after the school play.

She grinned. There they were in suits and hats, both with banners from right shoulder to left hip that read "Homecoming Princess." Between them was the Homecoming Queen. Selena Robertson. The three of them had worn sophisticated stiletto heels that had sunk into the mud on the field. With every step there'd been a sucking noise as they tried to keep their shoes attached to their feet.

She ran her hand through her hair, trying to remember something. Oh, yes. Selena dropped out of school after Christmas to go live with her aunt and have a baby.

She laughed aloud and brushed her hands together to get the dust off. No wonder she had so much trouble remembering important things. Her head was filled with useless confetti. Like how Selena won the election for queen by one vote because she and Gerri split the votes of their mutual friends.

A photo of herself in a cap and gown. She'd changed a lot in the months since that homecoming court picture.

Then she turned to the back part of the scrapbook. Had she saved the best for last? Yes, there she was with Gerri, on the porch of her house. She wondered if Gerri still lived in Bitter Falls. No, probably not. She married somebody in Texas. No, wait. Didn't she get a divorce? She could ask her dad about the Melman family; he knew everyone in the area.

In the snapshot, she and Gerri were dressed fit to kill—Gerri in a red satin gown and herself in a silver and white sheath. She'd posed like a beauty pageant contestant; her ultra high heels making her seem not just tall but statuesque. Her hair was long and tousled.

Cam West was working on the farm then. Had he watched them preen and pose and show off? What had he thought of Miss Mandy McCay? Had the boss's daughter been a dreadful tease to the handsome hired man, bestowing a kiss like an imperial gift? That would account for the awkwardness between them.

Or did she have it backwards? Could the reticence she detected be regret on his part? Had *he* come on to *her*? Had he cornered her in the grape arbor and kissed her? And had she acted like a haughty princess, too good for a poor cowboy? That would certainly result in embarrassment.

What she wished was that she had no past with Cam, that the two of them could meet with a clean slate, nothing to make either of them gun-shy. Or in this case, kiss-shy. If she reassured him that she didn't remember him at all, perhaps they could start the game over. Nobody has a hotel on Park Place; nobody owns the railroads. Boy meets girl; boy kisses girl. Boy takes girl to state of ecstasy. She wasn't looking for happily ever after. Happily *now* worked for her.

She turned the last page and saw a full-length photo of herself in that same dress. It was a professional photo. She tapped her finger on it, trying to remember. Then she shivered.

"Yes!" It had been taken at her extravagant birthday party. All the guests were photographed with lights against a pale blue backdrop with topiary trees on both sides. She recalled the set looked cheesy in person, but the effect in photos was elegant. Careful backlighting made her hair look like a golden halo.

Dad had called it—what? She rubbed her forehead. He'd called it—her Miss America picture.

She stared into her own eyes and remembered... nothing. It was as if a pod person had taken her place at her party and none of the memories transferred to her. Why? Why was it so hard to remember? Not only that night, but the summer. What had she done from the time she graduated until she stuffed her scrapbook in a drawer and threw her clothes in the trunk of her car—and drove off toward the edge of the earth? Or, more precisely, the edge of the continent.

Again she massaged her forehead with her fingertips, but the headache that had begun in the attic was worse. She was trying too hard, forcing her brain to work. She had to back off. Let things come when they were ready to come. Or accept that she had a deep, wide pothole in Memory Lane and move on.

Not everything...Wait, try again. *Not everything that we remember is worth remembering. And not everything that we forget is a loss.*

Somebody said that. Who? She groaned. Her headache was worse now. She gathered up the flotsam and jetsam of her early life and took it inside. Still not believing the spiders were gone, she left it all on the bench in the mudroom.

She took one painkiller and drank a tall glass of milk. Rather than climb the stairs, she lay down on the couch. The cool air from the air conditioner seemed to brush her skin, caressing her like a lover. Like...a rancher with a teasing tongue, pulling her blouse down one tantalizing millimeter at a time.

Gradually her dream changed. Instead of a red cotton blouse, she wore a long silver and white dress. Cam walked toward her; she held her breath. He looked down at her and his eyes darkened. Without a word, he unzipped the side of the dress. Now he lifted her hair and blew softly on the back of her neck. He outlined her ear with his tongue. How did he know that drove her wild?

****

On his way to the Victorian Inn, Cam counted his blessings. Not the big ones. Right now he was thinking of little ones. His truck was clean; and he'd ironed a second shirt the day he'd smuggled the ironing board up to his bedroom like contraband.

Two less things to do. As it was, he'd hit the ground running to get about half of his morning work done. He had calls to return from owners of mares and from buyers for colts and fillies; a brochure to proof and send by overnight mail. He had to arrange to breed Regiment if her examination by the veterinarian went as he expected it to.

"It's love, I tell you," Joey had said as they mucked out the stalls before seven o'clock. "That mare is a fool for Dar-Kanyon. If we let her, she'd wear lipstick." He stopped and leaned on his pitchfork. "I swear, I don't know what gets into some females. Raging hormones, I guess."

Cam said nothing, intent on his work.

"There's no accounting for the taste of particular females in, uh, particular males." Joey again.

"What are you jawing about? Of course the mare is turned on by Dar-Kanyon."

"I was thinking of another female. Initials M.M. You ought to think about putting up curtains, boss."

"That does it. I'm going to wire your mouth shut. With baling wire." Cam hung his pitchfork back on the wall rack and headed for the house.

Now, showered and shaved, he tried to concentrate on his mother's visit. What was she doing here?

His mind kept running along an alternate track, however. *What's Mandy doing? Is she thinking about being in my arms?*

"Work," he said aloud. "Think about work."

He should make his reservations soon for a trip to Fort Worth to talk with investors who wanted to retire a champion cutting horse and stand him to stud. Was Cam interested in managing that transition? Would his ranch be big enough, they'd inquired, to handle the champion in Montana all next winter and on into the early spring breeding season? The answers were yes and yes.

Cam hated to quit the firefighting profession, but he'd turned a corner and had to concentrate on the ranch. The firefighting had begun as a way to make good money, but year by year it had become a calling. He already missed his crew.

In moments of utter honesty, he'd admit a second reason for fighting fires. It had helped him forget Mandy. When his life and the lives of other firefighters plus God knows how much property was on the line, losing the girl he loved didn't seem so damned important.

He pulled up in front of the old mansion, newly renovated into a B&B. He delayed going inside, using time to wipe the dashboard with a paper towel and make sure the dog hair was off the front seat.

He'd seen his mother once a year for the past nine or ten years, always in Boston, New York, or her winter home on the Gulf Coast of Florida. The first two years after his departure for Montana she'd refused to take his calls, so there had been no contact. He'd notified her of her father's death through her attorney.

He credited the attorney, Hugo Andrews, with the thaw in their relations. Left to her own devices, Arabella would never forgive what she called "Campbell's insolence." And she'd sure as hell never admit she was wrong to be so controlling. So they arranged brief visits with no mention of the two years she wouldn't speak to him. In much the same way a million other families dealt with whatever elephant danced on its hind legs in their living rooms, Cam and his mother never spoke of his move out of Boston and out of her sphere of influence.

He'd seen glimpses that she was proud of him. Of course, as she saw it, Cam's success proved he was the son of Arabella Billings West.

He figured his stubbornness did more to prove

that bloodline.

Why was she in Montana after all these years of avoiding not only Montana but three-quarters of the country? She seemed to him to be living in the America of Thomas Jefferson before the Louisiana Purchase.

The happiest day of her life was not her wedding, nor was it his birth. It was the day she was admitted to the D.A.R., the Daughters of the American Revolution. It cost a fortune, but she'd managed at last to trace an ancestor of her maternal grandfather to the correct side of the Revolutionary War.

She'd been bitterly disappointed when she discovered that her husband, Edmund Astor West, was as wealthy as he claimed, but of no lineage at all when it came to Boston society. Edmund had inherited an empire of textile mills all over the east coast from his father, Mortimer. Old Mort had turned a modest fortune into huge sums during World War I.

But Edmund Astor West might as well have made his money in the lottery for all the respect it bought in Boston's Back Bay. How the name Astor got in there was a state secret and apparently no source of pride. Cam's guess was that somebody had failed to get to the church on time.

These intrigues held zero interest for him. He wished, however, that he'd known his father. From what he'd been able to discover about the textile mills, his old man was something of a pioneer of fair labor practices.

He stuffed the dusty paper towel beneath his seat, stepped out of the truck, and put his Stetson on his head. On his way up the winding paved walk through a formal garden setting, he saw movement at the curtains. She was watching him. He waved.

He came up the steps to the veranda and

admired the front door flanked by beveled glass windows. Not certain of the protocol at a B&B, he gave a light tap on the door and removed his hat. A tall, plump woman with platinum blond hair opened the door and gave him a big smile.

"Come in, Campbell." She put out her hand. "I'm Gerri Woolery. I'm an old friend of Mandy's."

She said it with an odd emphasis on Mandy's name, sort of a nudge-nudge-wink tone. He went on the alert immediately. She was too friendly. Why did she bring up Mandy's name to him? Gerri—what did she say? Woolery. Did he know her?

"I'm glad to meet you." He shook her hand, but she held on to his longer than he expected. He turned away and crossed to his mother in the living room. She wore a lavender suit made of a super-soft wool, probably cashmere, and a white blouse with a ruffed collar. Amethyst earrings matched the suit. Her hair was dark brown and full, in a French twist held against her head by a mother of pearl comb. She looked closer to seventy than her real age, eighty on her next birthday.

"Campbell," she said, putting out her cheek for his kiss. "I was about to have a third cup of coffee. Would you care for a cup?" She waved her hand at the antique sideboard.

A china coffee pot and matching teapot flanked a small crystal sugar and cream set. A silver tray of muffins and croissants lay on one side and a large bowl of fresh fruit on the other. He wondered what Mandy would think of the muffins.

There I go again. He sighed. *Another Mandy moment.*

"Coffee would be good, thank you."

His mother poured coffee into two delicate cups. He always feared he'd crush such cups in his big paw. He had mugs in his kitchen. Tough pottery mugs that held enough coffee that a man knew he'd had coffee. What did this one hold? Four fluid ounces? He added about a half teaspoon of cream.

Out of the corner of his eye, he saw that Gerri Woolery was hovering. Well, she wasn't going to hear anything but the weather report from him. If his mother started to say anything personal, he'd hustle her out to the truck and off to the ranch.

The notion of hustling away reminded him of Mandy in front of the ice cream shop. *Well, look at the time,* she'd said. *If we go straight home I'll be able to see "Emeril Live."*

"Did you have a good trip, Mother?" He tried to sound as if she did this frequently, instead of at sixty-one year intervals.

"Yes, thank you. The airport in Missoula has good connections. Oh, before I forget, Hugo Andrews asked to be remembered to you. He's retiring soon. Well, he should, he's nearly my age."

Cam nodded. Andrews was a true gentleman and had always tried to repair the relationship between his client and her son. It was from Hugo that he'd learned of the death of Arabella's second husband eight years ago. Cam had sent flowers immediately and asked Hugo to feel her out on the idea of his coming to "help her out." The words "comfort her" seemed a bit of a stretch.

She'd never taken the name of David Pascal. When Cam had visited her in Boston a year before David's death, she didn't even mention him or his son.

It was Hugo who told Cam, without his asking, that Arabella's stepson was serving a long sentence for securities fraud. Hugo had detected Junior's criminal bent early on and made sure he never got a dime from Arabella.

Of course, she never spoke of that. She knew that Hugo told him, and he knew that Hugo reported back to Arabella. Once, as a tongue-in-cheek gesture, he'd sent Hugo a bouquet of flowers on Father's Day.

Gerri Woolery waited about thirty seconds after they sat in two loveseats before bringing the china coffee server over.

"Would you care for more coffee, Mrs. West?"

"No, thank you."

"Cam? More for you?"

He didn't miss the message in Gerri's question. She wanted him to think they were on a nickname basis.

"No, thank you, Ms. Woolery. We'll be going out shortly."

"I should have introduced myself by my maiden name. Melman. Mandy and I went to high school together. I'd say we were *best friends*. Well, excuse me. I'll be in the office if you need anything."

He didn't miss the implication this time. Gerri Melman Woolery knew a lot about Mandy when they were teenagers. Did that mean she knew about Mandy and him?

Oh, crap. Suddenly the picture flashed in front of his eyes. Gerri was the friend with the Miata convertible. She'd driven Mandy to the birthday party at the country club—after he'd snapped their picture on the porch of Bitter Falls Farm. She'd weighed about fifty pounds less and her hair was brown.

"She's a nosy one," his mother observed as they watched Gerri cross the dining room and the wide hardwood entryway. "She told me something of her history in the mistaken notion that I would then drop a hint of my business." She leaned forward and smiled. "You can guess how that turned out."

Something like inviting a piranha to a swimming party. He grinned. "She's an amateur in the presence of a true professional. What did you discover of interest in her history? Horse thieves?"

"None yet, but you should lock your barn doors.

The former Miss Melman has been divorced twice and is looking to commit matrimony again before her cellulite gets any worse. She's here because her father left her the Inn, not because she has any aptitude for hospitality."

"You're a force of nature, Mother."

"I do try to keep my hand in. It's not so interesting in Boston anymore. Most of the qualified players are dead. So many in the new generation are so...egalitarian. All money is created equal. New, old, and imaginary. I refer, of course, to dot-coms and hedge funds. It makes me nostalgic for bank robbers who tied a scarf over their noses and said, 'Put your hands up.' Robbers now sit at computers and do the same thing with a few keystrokes. It's all so impersonal, isn't it?"

Was she thinking about her stepson? Cam had never met David Pascal, Junior. He'd met Pascal, Senior, once, before Arabella married him. Senior declared himself to be an expert on Pre-Colombian art, but Cam doubted that from the get-go. There was something off about him. His credentials seemed to be deliberately obscure, a lot of work in "private collections" in Europe that "didn't want publicity."

The same would be true if Pascal were a charlatan and had deluded people with private collections. No one who had been duped with stolen or fake art and artifacts would announce their embarrassment. He'd said that once to his mother, who'd bristled like a porcupine. Shortly after that he left for Montana, so he didn't watch Act II.

He finished his coffee and set the cup and saucer on the table between them. Arabella did the same. A grandfather clock chimed the half hour.

"Would you like to see my ranch?" He tried to sound relaxed about it, but his mind was racing with things undone. Flower beds not even set apart from the driveway with dividers, much less planted.

"Hugo printed out a picture of your house and mailed it to me," she said. "It's striking. I'd like to see the view."

"You didn't see the photos I emailed to you?"

"My computer needs work. It probably needs to be replaced. I know the pictures are in there somewhere."

"Well, the house has changed a lot since then, anyway." He stood and she did the same. The two of them went to the front door and he took his hat off the rack.

"Wait a moment, Campbell. I need to get my handbag."

She walked down the narrow hallway that began beside the stairway. He feared Gerri would use the moment's delay in their departure to make another strafing run at him. Sure enough, she came out of the registration desk area carrying a manila folder like a stage prop. Her lipstick was the wet-looking kind. She kept tucking her hair behind one ear, a habit he always found annoying.

"I hope you have a nice visit," she said. "I believe Mrs. West said she hasn't been here in several years."

"That's right."

"I haven't seen Mandy since she came home. I might drive out there this afternoon. Is her sister here?"

"I don't know. I saw the two of them downtown a few days ago." He saw his mother coming and opened the door. "Would you excuse me, please?"

Arabella said nothing to Ms. Woolery, breezed past her as she would past hired help and put out her hand to take Cam's arm. He put his hat on and closed the door behind them.

He could appear to ignore Gerri Melman Woolery, but her insinuations were eating like acid in his stomach.

This was like...He tried to think of an analogy.

This was like rehearsing a play with three players and three acts, a low-key domestic drama, memorizing all your lines and cues—but on opening night a fourth player walks in from stage left. With a trumpet. Wearing a G-string and pasties.

Chapter 11

The visit from his mother turned out as a pleasant surprise. Lord knows they'd had more than their share of arguments leading up to his sudden departure for Montana.

Their rupture was more dramatic because it was unexpected. At least from her point of view. He'd been unhappy with the life she planned for him, but he hadn't articulated it clearly. Of course, she wasn't known for listening, so who knew if talking would have made a big difference.

He'd gone to the best prep schools money could buy, then Harvard for a bachelor's degree. Next on Arabella's agenda was a year at Oxford to polish his rough edges, then Harvard Business School for his MBA. She would use that time to explore his career and marriage options.

She'd never counted on him being as strong-willed as she was. He'd said, "No, hell no!" to Oxford and packed his bag to head the opposite direction.

Packing hadn't taken long. Wool worsted three-piece suits, tweed jackets, tuxedos, white dinner jackets, silk neckties and ascots, tennis whites—good riddance. He left three full closets and expensive leather luggage. He took underwear and shirts, blue jeans, and a lined canvas jacket, packed in an ugly suitcase he found in the attic, probably discarded by a servant.

His move toward independence had begun quietly five years before when he'd insisted on getting a job at a summer camp in the Berkshires. He'd saved his money and used it as a nest egg for Wall Street investments all through college. By the time he got on the train to Montana, he had enough to live on for a couple years if he lived a simple life. And that was his intention. Find his grandfather, make up for lost time, and learn a whole new way of life.

He had access to a trust fund set up by his father—not under Arabella's control—after he reached twenty-one, but he left it fully invested and untouched. A trust lawyer took care of paying the taxes and sent him essential paperwork once a year. It was a matter of pride to leave it untouched.

He stood in his living room now and watched his mother examine his small collection of pottery and stop to hold a photo of her father as an old, old man.

He'd never dealt with his mother on his own turf. He'd visited her in Boston, New York, and Florida, and she'd adjusted to his independence. Nothing he'd done had been precisely what she wanted, but she revised history to better match the results.

As well as the visit was going, however, Cam still didn't know why she was there. He'd driven her around the ranch, showed her the mares and their colts and fillies, and driven up the hill on the southwest corner of the land to show her the unadorned granite cross on her father's grave.

She didn't want to go in the barn, and he knew better than to take her to the breeding shed. Even if he'd convinced her that the Queen of England was not above keeping a close watch on the breeding of horses, Arabella wanted nothing to do with it.

She'd toured the house, and admired the view. She offered lavish praise for his kitchen, but he doubted she knew one brand of refrigerator or type of counter surface from another. He'd enjoyed a lot of fine food as he grew up, including excellent homemade cookies, but it wasn't his mom who'd mixed the batter.

Was it his imagination, or did the kitchen still smell like apple coffee cake? Mandy seemed to feel right at home in his kitchen. She hadn't seen the rooms upstairs yet. Well, she'd only been in his house twice.

He wondered what she'd think of his bedroom.

He made coffee while his mother looked at his bookshelves in the living room. While it brewed, he leaned on the oak kitchen island and answered questions about what he was reading.

"Jack London's *Call of the Wild*. It's as good the fourth or fifth time I've read it. And *Grapes of Wrath*. It gets deeper as I get older. I re-read *The Good Earth* by Pearl Buck last winter but I don't like it any better than I used to."

"Interesting observation and, by coincidence, a segue to why I'm here."

He brought a tray with two mugs of coffee and a pottery sugar and creamer set into the living room, which he'd straightened and even dusted before dawn. He placed the tray on the table he'd made out of black walnut. Once they had their coffee, they sat on the middle couch. The coffee was a stage prop; neither of them wanted more than they'd already consumed.

"You were saying *The Good Earth* segues to something?"

"The farmer's sons turn out to be materialistic nabobs who sell off the land the farmer and his wife slaved all their lives to own and cultivate. The sons lie to him on his deathbed and say they'll keep the land when all they want to do is sell it and live like reprobates off the money."

"And that brings you to Montana?"

She picked up her mug, looked at the coffee, and

set it down again. Her gaze fixed on something in the distance, beyond the white fences.

"I have amassed a lot of money and Hugo has convinced me—in spite of all my objections to his adamancy—that I can't take it with me." She sighed. "I need no reminding that my son is not a wastrel but is, in fact, a better steward of his great-grandfather's land than I ever dreamed of being. I watched my father work like a slave to make something of what his father left him, and I wanted nothing to do with sweat equity. I wanted blue chip stocks and the good life. What an odd turnabout that my son would forswear his fine Italian wingtips and revert to cowboy boots."

"And yet, that's precisely what happened."

She sighed. "Do you recall the line from *Hello, Dolly* about manure?"

"Musical theater was never one of my pleasures." He picked up his mug to have something in his hands.

"I surmised as much. You were more a fan of Shakespeare. But I digress. Dolly Levi says her late husband always told her, 'Money is like manure. It's not worth a thing unless it's spread around, encouraging young things to grow.'"

"An excellent philosophy."

"I thought you'd see it that way, particularly as you are so well acquainted with manure. So, Hugo flattered me about my wisdom and generosity until I finally gave in and agreed with him. I'm forming a charitable trust. I want you to manage it, Campbell. I'll offer my suggestions for worthy causes, but it will be your decision."

He set his mug down, almost missing the edge of the table.

"This is an amazing surprise, Mother. What kind of charitable work do you have in mind?"

"It's more a matter of what I don't have in mind.

I'm sick to death of appeals to fund art galleries and chamber orchestras and historic preservation in Boston. Oh, and I wish to God you'd never set foot on the Harvard campus. They have no shame when it comes to asking for donations to the endowment. I'm growing hoarse with saying no. I want the whole issue of putting money to good use to be in a trust. People can write to you. Of course, you can appoint a manager and you can have a board if you wish to do so. I know you have a full life without managing a twenty million dollar trust."

"Is that all it is?"

"It's not so much, I know, but invested well it could be worth more."

"I was being facetious, Mother. You've been in Boston too long if you think twenty million dollars is a small trust."

"I thought we'd call it the Billings-West Charitable Trust. I considered using my grandfather's name, or my father's, and I thought of using Edmund's name—after all, he left everything to me. But I should use *his* father's name, too, Mortimer. Too many names. Billings-West is enough."

Cam said nothing, stunned by the change in his mother.

"I brought paperwork from Hugo. Is this a good time to look at it? It's a preliminary outline. Hugo wants to get the trust formed before he retires." She pulled a thick sheaf of papers out of her pale blue leather handbag.

Ideas flooded his mind, ideas for schools, hospitals, farmland preservation, water conservation, and the performing arts center that had been designed for Bitter Falls but scrapped for lack of money.

"If I do this, Mother, the bulk of the projects will be in Montana."

"And you think that surprises me?"

Her hazel eyes, identical to his, sparkled with humor.

He reached for his mug but stopped. No, he didn't need any more caffeine; his mother's news was the equivalent of a quadruple espresso.

"Let's move to the dining room table so we can look this over," he said.

****

At three o'clock, Mandy sat across from Dr. Kahn's leather armchair. He'd ushered her in and excused himself for a moment to take a phone call at the receptionist's desk. Bristling with nervous energy, she stood again and examined the state license to practice clinical psychology granted to Ilia S. Kahn.

"I apologize for the delay," he said as he returned.

"I apologize for imposing on your weekend." She returned to her chair and crossed her legs one way and then the other.

"Don't feel sorry for me, Mandy. I'll be on the beach in Hawaii in a week, getting all the relaxation I can stand." He moved books and folders from the table beside her to his desk and settled comfortably into the high-backed chair. "How are you?"

"Okay. Mostly okay. I'm just so...edgy. Anxious. I don't know why. When I got home to Bitter Falls I was quite calm and...placid, I guess. Passive. But each day this anxiety increases."

"What has changed? You said your dad and your sister both left on trips and you've been alone. Is that bothering you?"

"No. Well, that might be part of it. I was afraid to go in the house alone last night. But I went in and turned the lights on and I got over it. I don't think that's it."

"What has changed since you arrived at home? I

have to admit, you seem different since our first meeting on Wednesday." He looked at her hands. "You're clearly agitated."

She looked down and saw that she'd ripped a handful of facial tissues to shreds. She stuffed them in her purse.

"Maybe I need medication."

He shook his head. "Maybe you need to get answers to your questions."

She nodded. One of the first questions Dr. Kahn had asked her Wednesday was why she hadn't gone to college. Her intelligence test scores were high. Had no one encouraged her to use what he called her fine mind? She'd explained that her father expected her to go to college. She'd applied and been accepted; she'd planned to go.

But something happened late that summer that changed her mind. *What?*

She'd tried to find out from her father on Thursday what he remembered from that time. He'd put her off because she was so busy—overwhelmed, in fact—with preparing her first dinner party. But she could see through his evasion. He didn't want to talk about it. She'd sensed that he was as agitated by the question as she was now.

She'd seen Dr. Kahn again yesterday and they kept circling back to that void in her memory.

"Before I went to sleep last night I remembered where I'd stashed my old scrapbook. So this morning I went up to the attic and got it."

"Did that help you fill in the blanks?"

She shook her head. "It reminded me of things, like being homecoming princess when I wanted to be the queen." She laughed nervously and pressed a hand over her mouth. The painkillers she'd taken for her headache were roiling in her stomach.

Slowly she lowered her hand, but held rigidly still, as if movement would trigger an eruption.

"The scrapbook reminded you of things?"

"Yes, insignificant things. But my anxiety kept building. More and more I have the feeling that something happened, something involving Cam West. It's like I'm waiting for the other shoe to drop. I hate clichés, but that's the only way I can describe this."

"Have you asked Cam?"

She took a deep breath and let it out slowly. "I went to see him last night." She smiled. "You've undoubtedly figured out I find him very attractive. But he's just as evasive as my father. I told you he worked for my dad, but I don't remember him."

She laughed and added, "Now that's a sign of serious mental illness! Cam West is not a man any red-blooded young woman would forget."

Dr. Kahn put his fingertips together and smiled.

"I asked him last night if he'd ever kissed me. Well, let me rephrase that. We kissed and *then* I said, 'That's not the first time you've kissed me, is it?'"

"And he said?"

"He admitted that he'd kissed me before. But he wouldn't tell me anything about it. I never thought the saying 'Gentlemen don't kiss and tell' could apply to the woman who was the 'kissee.' He said— wait, I'm trying to remember how he put it. It was odd. Oh yes, I'd said, 'Ask me no questions, I'll tell you no lies.' And he said, 'I'll go one better. You can ask me questions—not tonight, but soon—and I'll tell you no lies.'"

"It sounds like you might have answers pretty soon."

"That's why I'm so jumpy, Dr. Kahn. I'm afraid of what he'll say. And don't expect me to make any sense with this. I go all around it in my mind, one way and the other, that I was a flirt and teased the hired man. That's an ugly thought. Or he was fresh and stepped out of line."

"Or could it be that the two of you were kissing because you liked each other? As you so clearly do now. Maybe you're looking for skeletons and the closet is empty."

"That's what I want to believe! But there's something wrong, I know it. Something that makes him not *want* to kiss me. I mean in his mind. The rest of him was interested."

A half hour later, she thanked Dr. Kahn for seeing her on a Saturday afternoon and made an appointment for Wednesday. Nothing had changed by going to see him. The big questions, the Swiss cheese holes in her memory were still there, but it helped to talk about it. Didn't it? At least a little?

Okay, no. It didn't. She was coming around to thinking something she didn't want to think, that her lost memory of that summer and a handsome hired man had nothing to do with brain damage and everything to do with suppression. Why, why, why did she not let herself remember?

When she got home, D'Ann pulled into the farm driveway right behind her. Over iced tea and pie, they caught up on the past three days. Mandy had already told her most of the grand culinary adventure of Thursday night, the elegant party that had ended with her being carried to bed by her guest, and then her guest and her father having to clean the kitchen.

"I want to hear more about the apple cake caper," D'Ann said with a wink. "You went to Cam's ranch last night. Come on, spill the good stuff."

"Nothing happened."

D'Ann hooted. "If I believed that, I'd say there's something wrong with Cam West. He didn't even kiss you?"

A blush heated her cheeks. "Okay, a kiss. A fantastic, mind-exploding kiss. But that's all. Joey and the gang came in like the cavalry and my virtue was saved."

"Did you *want* it saved? And by the way, saved for what? You're not getting any younger." She waved her hand in the air.

"My virtue is not up for discussion. Or dissection. And I do have a few good years left in me, thank you."

D'Ann smiled indulgently. "Suit yourself. Me, I'm going to take a power nap."

It was a knack Mandy envied, the ability to lie down and go right to sleep—and wake up refreshed in an hour. D'Ann had honed the skill in nursing school. If Mandy slept an hour she'd wake up as groggy as a drunken sailor, but D'Ann would be ready to work another shift as charge nurse.

"Wake me up at six, please." D'Ann yawned. "I want to take a leisurely bath before dinner. The reservation I made at The Mineshaft is for eight o'clock."

Mandy put their cups and plates in the dishwasher and climbed the stairs. In her room, she sorted through clothes, trying to decide what to wear to the restaurant. At the back of her closet, a plastic bag caught her eye. She pulled it out and lifted the plastic. A chill rippled down her back and her throat barely let air pass.

Beneath the brittle plastic hung the silver and white sheath from the photo, the one she'd worn to her eighteenth birthday party at the country club.

The silky dress she'd dreamed Cam was unzipping.

She took off the gray slacks and blue knit shirt she'd worn to Dr. Kahn's office. With her heart hammering, she slipped the dress on over her lacy bra and panties. The zipper was on the side. The lining had a cool, slippery, sensuous feeling. She closed the door to her room and looked in the full length mirror on the back of the door.

To her surprise, the dress fit except in the length. It wasn't as tight in the bust as it looked in the pictures; she'd dropped a size there with her weight loss.

She looked in the bottom of her closet and found an old pair of stiletto heels. She wasn't steady enough to wear them for long—and she didn't care if she never wore such painful shoes again, anyway— but they lifted her enough to make the dress the right length.

She closed her eyes, imagining herself at the country club. Yes, she was dancing, and laughing. The photographer was asking her to come back for another shot, then one with her father. He looked fantastic in his tux.

She started to unzip the dress when another memory nearly knocked her off her wobbly feet. Cam West's hands. Unzipping her dress, reaching in and taking her breasts in his hands. Their lips together, hard, almost violent. Then softer, parting, welcoming. His tongue claiming her. His hands like velvet against her nipples.

He pulled her dress up, over her head. He said, "You're so beautiful." He lifted her off her feet and carried her to a bed.

She looked in the mirror.

That wasn't a dream. It had happened. He'd made love to her. Gently, tenderly. Reverently, as if their love was a miracle. It had been incredible.

She kicked off the shoes and lifted the dress over her head. While she ran water in the tub, she folded the dress and placed it gently into a shopping bag. She smiled and stretched lazily.

It occurred to her that rancher Campbell West could use a jolt to *his* memory.

Chapter 12

Mandy walked into the crowded entry lobby of The Mineshaft, self-conscious about her extremely showy western boots. Sure enough, people stared. The irony did not escape her. For about eleven years, everything she put on—and that included footwear—was selected to attract stares. The girls in *Sex and the City* had nothing on Mandy McCay when it came to shopping and strutting their stuff.

But these hand-tooled boots that cost her dad about a thousand dollars meant more to her than money or the admiration of others. He'd placed the ostrich boots on the dresser of her room at the rehabilitation center with a hand-lettered sign she could see from her bed: These boots were made for walking.

Looking around at the crowd waiting to get in, she should have worn jeans, but it was too hot for pants. She'd worn a full skirt instead. She told D'Ann on the phone the night before that she wouldn't be dancing, but her resolve crumbled like a sugar cookie under a flamenco dancer.

After her bath, she'd gone through the clothes Eleanor had unpacked and hung up before she got home, all the items from the huge boxes shipped to Bitter Falls from Los Angeles. At last, she found what she was looking for—the circular midnight blue skirt with a matching cotton vest. Once she tried it on, with a filmy white shirt under the vest, the idea of twirling around was irresistible.

145

Of course, that wasn't the only reason she was hugging herself and twirling around her bedroom. Ever since Cam had kissed her, in his back yard, she'd climbed about ten rungs on a ladder out of whatever hole she'd been stuck in. And now that she'd tried on the silver sheath and practically melted with the hot memory of his hands and mouth—and more—she wanted another opportunity to taste his kisses. Of course, it wouldn't happen for as long as his mother stayed in town. He'd be busy with her.

She sighed. *Think about something else.*

She and D'Ann moved up to the hostess's station and waited for the petite young woman to return from seating the party of eight that preceded them.

Mandy glanced around the rough wood walls at the rusty pick axes fastened to the planks. Authentic historical photos drew her attention, pictures taken at the silver mine out in the hills above Bitter Falls. Grizzled, bearded men, who were probably half the age they appeared to be, stared at the camera and—through the lens—into the future.

She'd done the same thing, sometimes into forty or fifty lenses at once, but the cocky self-assurance she'd shown from eighteen through her early twenties was a universe away from the miners. To them the future probably meant, "Where will my next meal come from?"

While it was good to remember past events as she did by looking through her keepsakes and scrapbook, plus an old stationery box of snapshots from high school that she'd found in the top of her closet, pictures were two dimensional and engaged only her sight. It was all removed from true *sensation.* Would she rather see a color photo of the best strawberry she'd ever eaten, or bite into one tonight?

D'Ann was correct in saying, "You're thirty, not

eighty." But in some ways she was thirteen, not thirty. When a person has been as deep in pain and despair as she'd been after the shooting, any new day free of pain and terror was better than Christmas. Mandy had clawed her way back from an abyss—back from clinical death, in fact—when her heart stopped and the paramedics performed a miracle to bring her back. Why should she not dance?

Yesterday she had her first kiss in her "second life." Tonight, she might attempt her first dance. How she wished it could be with that rascal, Cam West.

Her spirit had soared like an injured wild bird restored to flight when Cam, at his picnic table, had gently caressed her breast. Their breath had commingled, and her heart and his had pounded like timpani in the deepening twilight.

She shivered at the vivid memory. Maybe she had another "first" to explore.

Correction—not *maybe*. She was definitely interested in exploring that incredible sensation. She knew it would just be a fling. A bachelor Cam's age who looked as sexy as he did probably had a girl in every port. Or whatever the equivalent was for ranchers. A girl at every stock show?

Then why did he seem reluctant to fondle her last night? He was definitely holding back. She'd been the one to take his hand and place it on her breast.

Again, she ordered herself to *think about something else.*

The hostess returned and said, "Who's next?"

"We are," D'Ann said. Under her breath she added, "You look fantastic. Now move forward or I'll run over you."

"Has anybody ever called you Nurse Ratched?" Mandy hissed.

"Yes, but nobody lived to say it twice. Any other questions?"

The hostess stopped by an ugly little table for two against the back wall. D'Ann shook her head and asked for a table for four near the dance floor. When Mandy whispered that there were only two of them, D'Ann shushed her.

"Follow me. Pretty soon we'll have our pick of men. Mark my words."

Mandy knew who she'd pick if she had a choice. Too bad he wouldn't be there.

Whoa! She'd no sooner named the man than he materialized right in front of her, seated with an elegantly dressed woman, probably his mother. He had a black credit card holder open and a pen in his hand. He laughed at something his mother said.

This man has seen me naked!

Her face burned and her heart thumped like the sound effect in a horror movie when the heroine should turn and flee for her life. She considered turning on her heels before he could see her. She might make it out to the car before D'Ann realized she was heading alone to a table for four. The doctors had warned D'Ann that she might act impulsively; this was a good time to make that prediction come true.

But then Cam turned his face toward her, and she knew how sunflowers felt when the sun came out from behind a thick cloud. Damn, but that man could smile!

"Mandy!"

He sprang to his feet beside his table and held out his hand, not to shake hers but to touch her arm gently. A jolt of warmth surged into her from his touch.

"Cam." She cleared her throat and took a deep breath. "How nice to see you."

D'Ann turned and came back.

148

"Mother, I'd like you to meet Mandy McCay and D'Ann McCay. This is my mother, Arabella West."

"How do you do, Mrs. West?" Mandy shook her hand and D'Ann repeated the handshake and greeting.

"I hope you're enjoying your visit to Bitter Falls," Mandy said.

"Yes and no," Arabella replied. Her eyes were red, puffy and watery. "Excuse me, please." She broke off speaking to cough into a handkerchief.

"I'll be right back, Mother." He put his hand on Mandy's arm. "I'll walk you to your table."

The hostess stood beside the table with menus. "Did you say four?"

"Yes, four." D'Ann responded. "This will be fine."

Mandy stepped aside so the hostess could pass and looked up at Cam. "Is your mother ill?"

"I'm afraid so. The combination of the altitude and the residual smoke in the air from the forest fires is making it hard for her to breathe. I'm taking her to Bitter Field to catch a plane in half an hour."

"Won't a plane make it worse?" D'Ann asked. "Or did you get something pressurized?"

"Yes, a Lear Jet. It's on its way from Missoula now."

"Are you going with her?" Mandy wanted to put out her hand and grip his arm, stroke his shoulder, anything to feel more connected to him, but the most popular restaurant in Bitter Falls—on a Saturday night—was not the same as his backyard by starlight.

"No. I'll see her off. She's going to rest in the Bahamas. We've made plans to meet in Boston in two weeks."

"Well, please give her our best," D'Ann said.

"I will." He took a step away, then turned back and looked at Mandy and down at the menus. "It looks like you're expecting company. Did your father

149

get back earlier than he expected?"

D'Ann laughed. "No, Dad is still gone. We don't have dates or anyone to dance with, but we're, uh, casting about."

"Does Joey Dix know about this?"

D'Ann grinned. "I may have mentioned it in passing."

Cam smiled at D'Ann but when he turned his face toward Mandy he went from forty watts to a whole chandelier of candlepower. Leaning close he murmured so only she could hear.

"Save me a dance."

He held her chair out until she was seated. "Excuse me, please. Mandy, D'Ann."

Her face burned like coals in a sudden draft of pure oxygen. She studied the menu with the intensity of a biblical scholar examining the Dead Sea Scrolls.

"You have it upside down," D'Ann said.

"What?" She looked up, confused.

"The menu. You have it upside down."

Mandy gasped and she closed the menu, looked at the cover, then opened it again. Glaring at D'Ann, she snapped, "It's right side up!"

"Oh, I guess you're right. But you had to look, didn't you?" She glanced over Mandy's shoulder and waved.

Mandy turned in time to see Cam holding his mother's chair and securing her hand in the crook of his arm while she got to her feet. She could also see how many other women were looking at Cam as he escorted his mother out. He looked over to their table and Mandy, too, gave him a wave. Her pulse pounded at the thought of being in his arms soon, on the dance floor. And later? Would they be alone together?

"Did he look even half that good when I was twelve?" D'Ann mused. "I must have been paying way too much attention to horses."

Mandy had wondered the same thing until about two hours ago when she'd had that gushing geyser of memory. Yes, Cam had seen her naked, but—oh my goodness—that went two ways.

Yes, she wanted to tell D'Ann, *yes, he was every bit as handsome then as he is now.* Cam West fully aroused was amazing. And now she recalled, he'd made the sexiest sound in his throat when she'd stroked him...

She forced her wildly erotic ramblings to vamoose the heck out of her head. Finally, she focused on the menu. After back and forth discussion with D'Ann, Mandy settled on a fiesta salad. D'Ann ordered the petite filet mignon with baked potato; she also ordered a bottle of cabernet sauvignon and asked for a pitcher of water and a plate of sliced lemons.

For a change, the two of them had time to talk about D'Ann's career plans.

"It's not that I meant to put you off," D'Ann said as she tasted the wine and nodded for the waiter to pour. "I had too many options and none of them clearly defined."

She talked about what she liked best and least about her job in Portland. Mandy asked for explanations of terms she didn't understand.

The waiter brought the steak, medium rare, and the salad in a big tortilla shell. She wondered if she could even put a dent in the great mound of food. Especially when her throat was the size of a soda straw thanks to nerves.

Cam is coming back. Cam is going to dance with me.

"A piece of strawberry-rhubarb pie around five p.m. sort of takes the edge off the appetite, doesn't it?" D'Ann laughed. "But it was so great I have no regrets."

"Thanks. I have a recipe for Black Forest Cookies I'm going to bake tomorrow." The image of a large bowl tucked against her and the rhythm of beating batter gave her a rush of anticipation. The ridiculing voices in her head were there, but less loud, less caustic.

Dr. Kahn had told her most people lived with those voices. Writers heard, "What moron told you that you could write a novel?" Singers and instrumentalists and actors heard, "Everyone is better than you are. People are only clapping because they're so glad it's over and they can go home!" Mandy hoped that Dr. Kahn was correct, that the less she listened, the less the voices would snipe at her.

"This steak is perfect!" D'Ann ate American style, slicing with the knife in the right hand then transferring the fork to the right hand, tines up.

"I'm glad Aunt Sarah failed to indoctrinate you in eating in what she called proper table style."

D'Ann rolled her eyes and switched the fork to her left hand, delicately packed tidbits of meat onto the back of the fork and placed the fork in her mouth, tines down.

"I went along with a lot of what she wanted, but not this. It's un-American."

"I found your Utensil Manifesto in the back of your horse scrapbook yesterday. Laughed my butt off."

"No kidding? I'd forgotten about that."

The essay, a witty, ironic look at manners and how they brand people, had taken first place in a writing contest. Aunt Sarah must have ground her molars.

Mandy sipped her wine. "In contrast with your fork chauvinism, I went over to the dark side. When I moved to California, I wanted to look sophisticated. Going to Cannes made me more insufferable."

When the time came for occupational therapists to teach her how to feed herself, D'Ann had insisted they teach her to eat as people did in Montana. Mandy had no idea of the issue at the time, of course. She was simply hoping to get food from the plate into the hole in her face with a minimum of spill.

She returned to the subject of D'Ann's plans. "Don't you like living in Portland?"

"I love Portland, but it's not my home. My home is right here, as yours is." D'Ann put down her fork and rested her chin on her hands. "I know it's too soon for even a preliminary thought to your future, but Montana offers so much. Dad wants you here and so do I. If you start to think, 'Well, it's nice, but it doesn't have blah-blah-blah,' then let's see if that blah-blah is something Montana truly does need and see if we can get it here."

"You're making my head swim." Mandy put down her fork. She wasn't prepared to plan her life over her entrée.

"Let me think of a couple examples. There are things Bitter Falls doesn't have and their absence is good news because nobody wants them. Traffic for example. Gang violence, Lamborghinis. You following me so far?"

Mandy grinned. "Traffic and violence, you have my vote. But I think I like Lamborghinis."

"Okay, scratch that. My point, however, is that there are things that would improve Montana, and we should try to get those things."

"Such as?"

D'Ann nodded and held her hands palm up. "Better emergency facilities at the Bitter Falls Hospital. Better facilities at the only large animal veterinary hospital in the region. A new indoor municipal swimming pool."

Mandy studied her wine in the candlelight. "So

you're saying rather than leaving in search of something, I should look for it here. Possibly even try to move it here, or create it, if it isn't here already."

"Exactly. So what is it you want? What would make Bitter Falls more attractive to you?"

"I don't know." She rubbed her forehead. "A college?"

"We have a satellite campus of Montana State University. It's a new building down on the flats near Bitter Field; it opened a year ago. Go on."

Mandy rested her chin on her folded hands and stared at her half-eaten salad.

D'Ann put out her hand and grasped Mandy's elbow. "I'm getting way too involved in your thinking process. I'm sorry. Whatever you want to do and wherever you want to do it, Dad and I will be behind you one hundred percent."

"Even if it's far away from here?" Mandy sighed.

"Even if it's in Katmandu, or Patagonia, or Nome. All I'm saying is, don't rule out Montana because staying seems like the easy thing to do."

The easy thing to do? Staying or going, nothing seemed easy. She was holding onto a ledge with her fingers bloody, trying not to lose her grip and fall in love. What was easy about that?

The waiter took their plates and asked if they'd care for dessert. They both laughed. "No thanks," Mandy said. "We ate dessert before we came." She handed him her credit card but told him to leave the tab open for drinks.

"Would you like another bottle of wine?" he asked.

D'Ann answered. "No, but I think we'll be ordering beer pretty soon." She waved her hand to catch someone's eye.

Mandy turned around and saw Joey Dix saunter in. D'Ann had told her Joey had a prosthetic leg below his right knee, a result of a roadside bomb in Iraq, but she'd never guess it. His very slight limp was common to a lot of Montana cowboys.

The way Joey's eyes laser-spotted D'Ann, everyone else in the restaurant could be plastic mannequins. The man might as well have S-E-X spelled out in electric lights on his giant belt buckle.

She leaned closer to D'Ann and murmured, "If I tossed water on that man he'd sizzle like a red hot skillet. I hope you know what you're getting in for."

"Don't worry about me," D'Ann whispered.

"May I join you ladies?" Joey asked.

The waiter took the last dinner items from the table and asked if Joey wanted to see a dinner menu or a wine list.

"No, thanks. I'll have a Moose Drool on tap."

"I'll have the same. Mandy? Anything for you?"

"No thanks. I'll stick with my wine." She was on her second glass and knew she wouldn't even finish that.

Joey and D'Ann talked about her trip and what he'd been doing while she was gone, and where they were going to ride the next day.

Mandy listened, glad to see D'Ann having such a good time. One of the great regrets of her life was that she hadn't known D'Ann the way she should after age twelve. The two of them had been together daily for the past eight months, but her healing was all anyone talked about. She wanted to truly understand and appreciate her sister.

How interesting that she planned to come home to Montana. And that she hoped Mandy would, too.

"Say, Mandy," Joey said, "I'm an uncle! Polo had her puppies around six this morning. Four males, two females. They're all fine."

"Oh, I'll bet they're adorable. When can I come see them?"

"You can stop by tomorrow, but Polo is pretty

fierce about anybody touching them. You can look at them. Their eyes are closed."

"Do they look like anybody?" D'Ann asked.

"You mean do we have enough evidence to bring a paternity suit? No, they look like puppies. They're all the same color as Polo, reddish brown. I hope the father was a working breed and not a dumb lap dog. I've been watching downtown, and I see a male red heeler running loose sometimes."

D'Ann laughed, held up a peppermill like a microphone and sang, "I met him at the candy store—"

Mandy grinned. "Karaoke time, big finish."

Together the two of them sang, "And that's when I fell for, *the leader of the pack!*"

The waiter arrived with the beers and Mandy signed the credit receipt for dinner and the drinks. Joey objected and tossed an extra tip on the tray.

"It makes a better story this way, anyhow," he said with a wink. "I walked into the bar—all the good stories start out that way, a cowboy walked into a bar. So, I walked in, and two beautiful women invited me to sit with them. That's already a stretch that my buddies will howl at. And then I'll say the women plied me with liquor. Hell, it's the best Saturday night I can remember, and it's barely getting started. I have a feeling I can live off this story, with proper embellishment, through a long, cold winter."

"Would the two of you excuse me?" Mandy asked. She scooted her chair out and Joey stood.

In the ladies' room, she applied lipstick and brushed her hair. How long had Cam been gone? Nearly an hour, and he was putting his mom on a private jet. He could return anytime now.

Back at the table, she watched the band set up and test their microphones. D'Ann and Joey tried to draw her into a conversation about rodeos, but her mind kept wandering. Now that she remembered making love with Cam, she couldn't think about anything else.

She looked around the room, wondering if she'd see a man more attractive than Cam. Hmmm. Not over there, not over there. Nope. A waste of time.

Sooner than she expected, the band started their first number. "All My Exes Live in Texas."

"I'm just in time!" A deep voice. Behind her.

A shiver ran up her arms and a flush climbed into her cheeks. In an instant, a wave of warmth— no, a geyser of steam—flooded her body. She stalled before turning her face. If he looked in her eyes now, her desire would embarrass her.

She dropped her napkin and bent to retrieve it.

One deep breath. Another. *Clear my throat. Look surprised.*

"Cam." *Smile; don't scare the man away.* "Please, join us."

Chapter 13

Cam shrugged out of his sport coat and hung it on the fourth chair. He tipped his Stetson to D'Ann and Joey who were already half way out of their chairs.

"Mandy? Let's dance."

She ordered the voices in her head to shut up. She might be clumsy to start; she might have to count out loud to get the rhythm. So what? The handsomest, ruggedest, sexiest man in Montana was standing there with his hand out to her, looking at her like a wolf looks at a lamb chop, so why not take a chance? She put her hand in his and he pulled her chair back a foot.

He complimented her on her outfit, especially her boots, and answering his questions kept her mind off her dancing ability. Pretty soon she'd picked up his rhythm and settled in. They moved with the flow of men and women around the room. Nearly all the men and a few of the women were wearing cowboy hats as Cam was. She saw waiters moving tables back a few feet to give the dancers more room.

Cam swung her out and wrapped her back against him. He was easy to follow. She liked the part where she was close to him. When she faced him, the top of her head was shy of his chin.

"You smell good," she said. "Like leather and rainwater."

"The leather is probably indelibly worn into my

body from reins and saddles. The rainwater, however, is totally artificial. I used the fancy soap and matching aftershave my mom sent me for Christmas two years ago. Don't tell her I didn't open it until today."

Two dances later, the couples separated and lined up in a big grid. She stayed right beside Cam, trying to keep up with the intricate steps of the line dance. She'd just get it right and the band would speed it up, again and again. She'd be slapping leather behind her and the other dancers were doing step to the right, step, hop, shuffle, scuff, back step. Who knew what they were doing? It was a blur. Pretty soon she was laughing so hard she settled for turning around when everybody else did and trying not to fall.

The next dance was slow, thank goodness, because it was followed by two fast ones. Pretty soon she lost count of how many dances they'd done. Every once in a while, D'Ann would fly past with Joey.

A fast two-step stopped and Mandy leaned on Cam.

"You're getting tired," he said, kissing her forehead.

"I have enough energy for one more—unless it's like that last one." She continued to lean, not because she needed to, but because she flat out wanted to.

"We're gonna slow it down now," the lead guitarist said into the microphone, "with a song for all you lovers and dreamers. Miss Lee Ann Womack won the Grammy for Best Country Song of 2001 with this number. So put your arm around someone you love while Miss Elsie Jay sings, 'I Hope You Dance.'"

Tears filled Mandy's eyes as Cam tugged her close against him. She knew every word to this song, and suddenly—like every truly great song—it seemed written for her alone. She pressed her wet face against his strong shoulder and moved with the music, an easy thing to do thanks to his solid lead.

Cam knew the lyrics, too. He murmured into her ear about not taking life for granted.

He kissed her temple, and her private, quiet tears threatened to overwhelm her. She clutched tighter to his shoulder as the singer moved into the refrain.

He pulled a soft handkerchief from his pocket and she pulled it in to her face. When the song ended, they stood there a moment.

"And now," he said, "it's time to get you home."

"My home or yours?" she asked in a faint voice.

"Ma'am, a gentleman always lets a lady answer that question. Let's go find my truck."

He picked up his jacket off the chair at their table and tossed down a tip for the beer he'd hardly touched. D'Ann and Joey danced past them and Cam waved.

"We're calling it a night," he said. "We'll see you when we see you."

She smiled at D'Ann, who was clearly having a blast, and pointed toward the exit. D'Ann waved over Joey's shoulder.

Cam leaned close so she could hear him over the loud music.

"Joey talked so much about D'Ann and the ride they've got planned for tomorrow that the other hands threw him out of the bunkhouse last night. He had to sleep in the barn."

Cam watched Mandy try to get a solid foothold so she could boost herself up to the passenger seat of his Ford truck. Her foot slipped off the step twice, so he put his hands around her waist and lifted her up.

The shape of her hips, the feel of that curve, and the opportunity—however brief—to stare at her butt, was ecstasy. And agony.

On his side of the truck, he stalled before he opened his door. Anyone looking at him would think he was having trouble finding his key. The truth was that he was having trouble deciding which way to go once he turned on the ignition. He'd told her in a joking tone that a gentleman left it up to a lady, but the lady in this equation was not qualified to answer the question. He still held five aces. What was the term? *Informed consent?*

Finally, he got in. Put the key in the ignition but didn't turn it.

"I hope your mother is better by now," she said. "It's a shame she was here such a short time."

"She assured me that her general health is good. She had a problem with the smoke and the altitude due to asthma." He looked over at her and took a deep breath, then another.

"I'm going to take you home. Your father made me promise not to accept any dinner invitations from you and I know full well he meant 'or anything else that wears her out.' I'm pretty sure he'd be getting out his shotgun if he saw me waltzing you all over the floor until you were ready to collapse."

"Ah, don't blame the waltz. The waltzes weren't the problem. The two-step and the polka and the line dancing, I'll admit, that was too much. But I loved every minute of it."

He turned the key. "Seatbelt, ma'am."

"In a minute."

She stretched toward him and touched her lips softly to his. "Come to my house and I'll give you a real treat. Strawberry-rhubarb pie. One of the best things I've ever baked. Okay, one of the best out of the three things I've ever baked."

"Irresistible."

"But let's drive around first."

He grinned. "Okay. Any place in particular?"

She paused and pursed her lips. "The country club."

It seemed an odd choice, but he was glad to go anywhere with her. He turned the ignition and Celine Dion's voice filled the cab immediately. *Oops.* He reached out to turn it off, then decided that would look odd. The cab filled with the beautiful sound of the CD he'd played on his way to the Mineshaft.

Mandy hummed along and joined in on the refrain.

Smooth, West. Very smooth. Promise her dad you won't tell her about the two of you until he gets back, and then booby trap your truck with her favorite song. How many times had they lain side by side and hummed along to Celine? If this didn't remind her what they'd been to each other, he'd bet his truck that her memory was and would remain blank.

"You dance as well as you used to," he said. "No memory problem there."

She looked at him with her eyebrows knitted together. "You sound like you're familiar with my dancing ability as it was twelve years ago. How's that?"

"Well, I never danced with you, but I saw you out a couple times." He waited for lightning to strike him dead.

Using the strictest possible definition of dancing, what he said was true. He hadn't danced with her. No dance floor, no band, no pretty dress and corsage. But visions of how they'd stood, naked, pressed against one another from ankles to his chest, how they'd swayed to the music while doing the tongue tango, well, even a half-assed debater could make a case that Cam West, a cowboy with a lone dollar in his pocket, had in fact *danced* with the lady.

He pulled into the sweeping driveway of the

162

Falls Creek Country Club. "Do you want to go in and have a drink?" He parked in an open spot a good hundred yards from the entrance. The place was crowded tonight.

"No, I have a wild hare to walk around and look at it. To help me remember something. It's probably a waste of time."

He disagreed. Being anywhere with Mandy was no waste of time. He stepped out and strolled around the truck to help her down. He put his hands on her waist and she leaned into him, kissing him.

"I've been wanting to do that all evening," she said softly.

His good intentions melted in the heat of her mouth and hands. Her father was unreasonable to ask him to lie to her. And to pretend he didn't want Mandy in his arms was a lie the size of Alaska.

The truth was coming out for better or worse, and a lot sooner than later.

He set her on the ground and took her hand. Without speaking, they strolled down the sidewalk and in the front door. The large lobby had color portraits of the men and women who'd built the club. He knew most of them, or their kids and grandkids.

"Are you a member here?" she asked.

"No. I don't play golf, and I'm a homebody." He didn't add that he equated "country club" with idle socializing. Doing time at debutante events had made him an inverse snob. "Fighting fires, constructing my house and building up my horse breeding business have been all-consuming."

They looked in the trophy cases and at more photos on the wall. Suddenly Mandy stopped. There on the wall, framed, was a portrait of her. She was wearing the silver and white dress. It was the same picture she'd seen in her scrapbook, but that had been eight-by-ten. This was a poster.

Cam put his hand on her waist. "You're more

beautiful now."

She put her face against his chest and her shoulders shook. Was she crying? He rubbed her back and she pressed herself against him. Of course, the closer she leaned to him, the harder he got.

She pulled away and looked up with a strange—cocky?—grin on her face. Clearly, his erection wasn't a secret.

He shrugged. "You weren't the only one looking forward to tonight."

A high-pitched laugh off to his left made him shoot a glance in that direction. He folded his arm around her shoulder and walked her beside him toward a door to the outside.

"Where are we going?" she asked.

"I need fresh air. Let's go look at the pool."

Instead of walking over by the well-lit pool, he stopped in the dark alcove. "It's a beautiful night."

"Why did you hustle me out here?" she asked. "Are you avoiding someone? I think I saw this on 'I Love Lucy.'"

"I guess I got some *'splainin* to do, huh? Okay, here's my confession. I didn't want to run into Gerri Melman, now Gerri Woolery. I saw her this morning when I picked up my mother. She inherited the Victorian Inn from her father and she's—in theory, at least—in the hospitality business."

"You don't sound convinced."

"She was too interested in my mother's business and too eager to discuss her own. And she kept telling me what close friends she was with you. She brought up your name to me about three times in as many sentences."

Mandy tilted her head to the side. "That's interesting. Today I looked through my scrapbook and I happened to see pictures of us together. In fact, I was thinking I should call her if she's still in town."

"Oh, umm. I see." This conversation was like walking in the dark across a pasture. The next step might be into an ankle-breaking hole. "Let's stroll around that way and out to the truck."

"You seriously don't want to run into Gerri, do you?"

"I don't want to share you." That was true. If a line judge were watching him from the tennis court, he would get credit for telling the truth. Fifteen-love.

"If she sees you she'll never shut up," he continued, "and you'll get completely exhausted and your dad will shoot me, and the worst part of all this is I won't get any pie. Strawberry pie with rhubarb is my favorite kind. The only thing I like better is strawberry-rhubarb pie with ice cream."

"I still have that French vanilla in the freezer."

"Then what are we waiting for? Let's book it."

He took her by the hand and they crept out of the alcove, behind a stack of chaise lounges, and out the side gate of the pool area. They entered the parking lot and reached the tailgate of his truck when she lost her footing. He caught her and swung her into his arms; placed her in her seat and fastened her seat belt.

And stared at her full, tantalizing lips, inches from his own. Not kissing her when he was so close was not possible.

One quick kiss wasn't possible, either. As soon as their lips touched, she draped her arms around his neck and pulled him close. He wanted to stay that way and proceed to more contact, but the dome light was a reminder to him that they needed to get out of there. Any minute, they could hear that annoying laugh and face a game of Twenty Questions with someone who probably knew twenty-one answers.

He didn't know a lot about teenage girls, but he figured they talked a lot to their "best friends." And they probably talked about sex. And they might talk about the cowboy one of them was meeting at midnight after the big party.

Gerri Woolery was a loose cannon with a lit fuse.

He knew now that he had to move up the curtain time on Show and Tell, whether Ford McCay liked it or not.

Chapter 14

Mandy's mind was made up. She and Cam West were going to break through some barriers tonight.

"Cam, I know I promised you pie, but let's pick it up at my house and take it to your place." She watched his Adam's apple as he gulped.

"Sure," he said. "That sounds good."

She'd wished as recently as this morning when she looked through her scrapbook that she and Cam had no past, no reason to avoid one another. Since she'd found the dress, she'd begun to recall—with vivid detail—that they not only had a past, they had a *past*. All caps, no quotation marks. That kind of past.

No wonder he was hesitant to touch her breasts last night. He wouldn't take advantage of her. What a dear man. But now her memory of that night after her birthday party was filtering through the fog, and every new detail was more provocative than the one before.

She looked over at him and smiled—and wet her lips with her tongue. Like D'Ann said when they drove up to Cam's ranch with her first batch of cookies, *Hell-o, Cowboy*.

When they got to her place she invited him in. "I want to get these boots off and put on flats. I think I've worn a couple of blisters." She waited for him to help her down from the cab and hobbled to the back door. Under the porch light, she used her key to get in. She'd left lights on in the kitchen and living room.

Cam followed her inside. "Come sit on this stool," he said. She sat on the stool by the high section of the counter and winced as he gently pulled the boots off her feet.

"They're a gift from my dad," she said when he held them up to admire the tooling in the leather. "They looked so right for the Mineshaft, but I never broke them in." She stood and limped toward the stairs. "I'll be right back."

In her room, she put bandages on the blisters and found a pair of sandals that didn't rub the sore spots. She changed into Capri pants and a camisole top with no bra but decided it was too brazen. Too brazen? Yeah, like the pull-down blouse she'd worn the night before—with no bra—was prim and proper?

Still, she didn't want to shock him. That is, she didn't want to shock him *yet*. She put the bra back on and wore a cropped shirt. She tossed a light sweater into the shopping bag on top of the silver and white sheath and went back downstairs.

"I'll get the pie and ice cream." She packed them in a paper sack and held it out to Cam. As she expected, he didn't ask about the other bag.

"Is your dad likely to call and worry that you're not home?" he asked.

"D'Ann called him right before we went to dinner and he was leaving for a long, boring convention program. He still thinks he'll be home by tomorrow night, so she cleverly said to call us from the airport. I think her exact words were, 'So you don't wake us up.'"

"So what you're saying is that you and D'Ann don't have anyone checking on your whereabouts. Your sister is devious. I like that in a woman."

She held her arms out to the side and bowed at the waist. "I like to think she learned something from me."

In the truck, they talked about a major fire in Oregon that was on the news, and he explained how much training hotshots had to have. When she prodded him for stories, he told a few of his scarier firefighting experiences.

The way her mind was racing on to her plan to get him naked, he could have said, "Then I leaped on a dragon and flew through the air," and she wouldn't have batted an eye.

"Go on." She watched his profile as he talked, imagining the taste of his lips. She'd never made any headway as an actress in Hollywood, but right now she had one man fooled. She told herself her appearance of rapt attention was all for a good cause.

At his house, she hurried to serve the pie and ice cream like a waitress with one more customer at five minutes until closing time.

"Aren't you having any?" he asked. "This is great."

"I'm so glad you like it. I had mine before we went to dinner. You know the saying. Life is short, eat dessert first."

He ate the last bite and took his dish to the sink. "Cam?"

"Yes?"

"I was thinking. This is the third time I've been here, but I've never seen your second floor."

Again, his Adam's apple made the gulp. She wanted to kiss him all down his neck and start on his chest. He had exceedingly sexy chest hair. It formed a line that disappeared into his jeans. And she knew what else was in his jeans.

"Umm, sure. I hope I didn't leave a towel on the floor."

"I'll take my chances." Her chances were getting better by the minute. She turned on the small light over the stove and turned off the overhead. As they headed for the stairs, she snagged the paper handle of the shopping bag.

"Did you do all this woodwork on the stairs and railing? It's a beautiful job."

"Thanks. I'll show you the second bedroom first. It's for guests, or..."

"Or what?" She gave him her best wide-eyed innocent look.

What could he need a second bedroom for? For that matter, why did he design that fantastic kitchen? *Have mercy, Miz McCay.*

She smiled. Campbell West, bachelor, was building a nest—and he didn't even know it. Her smile widened into a grin.

"If I ever, uh..." He cleared his throat. "It's for guests." He flipped on the light.

She walked around the room and glanced into the bathroom.

"This is roomy. And is that a skylight?"

"Yeah. In the winter all my skylights cheer the place up. I have one in my room, too."

Perfect room for a nursery.

She followed him out, turning off the light as she did.

"You certainly like to conserve energy," he commented.

"At times." *Like now, when dim light is more romantic.*

She stepped ahead of him into the master bedroom. "Wow!"

The king-sized bed had a headboard made of hand-hewn wood. The duvet and shams were chocolate brown, and a light brown throw draped across the foot of the bed. He turned on a lamp beside an armchair and she turned off the overhead. She'd like to turn off the lamp, too, and light six or eight candles.

The room was masculine, but warm and inviting. Like a man with hard muscles and a soft touch.

The armchair was beside a blue enamel woodstove; on the other side of the chair sat a small pine table, six books stacked neatly on top.

She walked to the far side of the room to see it from a different angle. She stopped by the armchair and glanced at the book on top of the stack. *The Grapes of Wrath* by John Steinbeck.

"I thought you said the upstairs might be messy. This looks ready for a spread in a home decorating magazine. Titled 'Living Large in Big Sky Country.'"

He laughed. "I didn't say it was messy. I said I might have left a towel on the floor of the bathroom. Remember, my mother was here for the first time today. Of course I had everything slicked up. Come see the balcony."

He slid the glass door open and she walked outside. The balcony looked out over the ranch.The smell of hay and freshly mown grass combined with night-blooming flowers—and the scent of his aftershave.

"This is beautiful, Cam." She felt him close behind her and turned. Her arms seemed to fit around his neck. She opened her lips in invitation.

Cam wrapped his arms around her, pulling her hips tight against him. There was no use pretending he didn't want her. He was hard as the wood in his headboard. "Mandy, Mandy."

Her name was lost as he pressed his mouth to hers. The feel of her tongue probing, welcoming his, made his pulse pound.

"Oh, Mandy, sweetheart, you're driving me crazy."

He lifted her hair off her neck and blew softly. He felt her shudder of delight as he outlined her ear with his tongue.

"Now you're driving me crazy," she murmured.

"I know, sweetheart." As soon as the words were out of his mouth, he stepped back. He did know. He knew every inch of her body, exactly what she liked. Five aces, hell. He had a royal flush, natural.

"Mandy, we need to talk." He held her hands together in front of him to keep her from unbuttoning his shirt. She'd already unbuttoned the top two.

She sighed. "You're right, Cam. We'll talk. Let me freshen up in the guest bathroom. I'll be back in a minute."

As she left the master bedroom, she picked up the fancy shopping bag she'd brought.

He had a really bad—*really good*—really bad thought. Had she brought a seductive nightgown? Man, he'd have to stay ten feet away from her in order to say the things he had to say. Ten feet away with a fire hose at hand. Somehow, he had to make her understand that this "new" attraction she felt for him was not what she thought. Well, it was and, then again, it wasn't. Oh, hell. This was going to be a mess.

He'd never wanted a woman as much as he wanted Mandy tonight. Oh, wait—yes he had.

And that was Mandy, too.

Images blazed in his mind, images of her lying beneath him, shooting stars all around them and stardust sprinkling down like magic. Mandy crying out as she came, him following her an instant later. He moaned.

He went back inside and closed the glass door and the full-length curtains. In his bathroom, he washed up and put a cold washcloth on the back of his neck. Did he have time for a cold shower? He'd have to shower with his clothes on, because if he got naked now, heaven help him.

"Cam?"

He hung the washcloth back on the rack and turned off the light. He'd rather face a wall of fire than the look he was going to see on Mandy's face in about five minutes.

He took a deep breath and opened the door.

"Mandy—where did you...? That's the dress you wore in the picture at the country club."

"I found it in the back of my closet." She stood on her toes and twirled around. "It's too long. But my feet hurt too much tonight to wear high heels."

"You look beautiful in it. Mandy..."

"Shhh." She moved quickly and closed the distance between them.

His ten feet of firebreak became ten inches in a heartbeat. Then nothing. Where was a fire hose when he needed one?

"Mandy, I never thought I would say these words, but here it is. Don't kiss me. Don't put your arms around me." He looked at the shape of her breasts in a lacy bra clearly visible through the slinky silver material and stifled a moan. "Don't even breathe like that."

"Like what?"

"With your lungs."

To his surprise, she smiled. "Cam, it's all right. I know why you're trying to keep me at arm's length."

"You do? Then you should tell me, because right now I'm having a lot of trouble remembering it."

"You, my dear, are a gentleman. You're not a man who would ever take advantage of a woman."

"That, uh, that's right. I wouldn't. I would never deal myself four aces and a wild one-eyed jack. Off the bottom of the deck."

"What?"

"Nothing. Go on. I'm a gentleman."

She eased the zipper down on the side of her dress. "Cam," she said softly, "I remember."

She lifted the dress over her head and dropped it

on the floor. In the soft light of the lamp, shadows played over the hills and valleys of her slender body. Her nipples strained against the bra.

Had one night gone by since they first made love that he didn't remember her in his dreams?

"Aren't you going to say anything?" she asked.

"It'll take a defibrillator to re-start my heart."

She grinned. "That, or a kiss. Is that right?"

"You—" His voice was scarcely a whisper. "You do remember!"

"Yes, Cam. I do."

"Mandy!" He clutched her like a drowning man would a life preserver. Before either of them could say another word—too many words, too much talking—he claimed her mouth and probed deep with his tongue.

She didn't have to guide his hand to her breast this time. He cupped one and kissed down her neck to her chest and delved inside the lacy edge of her bra with his tongue. He teased the pebble of her nipple and moved to her other breast.

"Cam, I want more!" With one quick movement, she unhooked her bra and dropped it on the floor.

He bent to take one breast in his mouth while he stroked the other one. Again she asked for more, more. She was breathing hard and quivering as if her knees would buckle.

"Easy, now. No need to rush." Dropping slowly to his knees, he kissed her mound through the fabric of her bikini panties. The whimpering sound she made and her whispered plea for *more, more* made him chuckle. Gently he tugged the delicate silk down, all the way to the floor. When she moved slightly to step out of them, he kissed her curls and parted her with his tongue, touching her hot wet center.

The shock of Cam's tongue sent skyrockets through Mandy's body and her knees couldn't hold her anymore. She grabbed at his shoulders and cried out his name. His hands tightened at the back of her thighs and he held her up, still teasing her with his tongue.

She rocked against him, moaning softly and breathing faster, panting. It had been so long since she felt such need. "Cam, I'm so close." She twisted his hair in her hands and gasped as the wave of her orgasm broke over her.

"That's the way," he murmured, "that's my girl." He kissed her belly and her navel and rose to his feet, kissing her all the way up and ending with her mouth.

She nipped at his bottom lip and broke the kiss to ask a question.

"How come only one of us is naked?"

"Because, as you pointed out, I'm a gentleman. And a gentleman always puts the lady first. You want to help me?"

"You mean with this?" She cupped her hand around his erection as it strained against his jeans.

"Oh, my stars. Yeah, that's what I need help with." He flipped her up into his arms and carried her to the bed. He sat on the edge and in two seconds he had his boots off.

"Stop right there, mister," she said. "I got hired for this job and I don't want no interference." She pressed his shoulders down on the bed with his legs off the edge. "You hold still and I won't have to hurt you."

She unsnapped his jeans and lowered the zipper. "Looks like you got some kind of a growth there."

"Are you some kind of doctor?"

"Trust me. I know what to do. It's a delicate operation, and you have to hold ever so still." She tugged his jeans and briefs down his legs and dropped them on the floor. He scooted further onto the bed.

"Ah, ah, ah! I said don't move. You do not want to make me angry."

"Is this where you say we can do this the easy way or the hard way? Because I want the hard way."

She stretched out beside him and stroked the length of his erection. "You shouldn't have asked for the hard way, 'cause now I'm going to give you the easy way."

"You vixen! Well, I can take it. Have your way with me."

She cupped him and leaned down to kiss him on the end of his throbbing organ. His eyes went wide. She laughed and rolled away, scooting up on the bed until her head was on a pillow. "Well, that was a lot of fun. You want to watch TV now, or what?"

He got on his hands and knees and moved up the bed. "Has anybody ever told you that you talk too much?"

"Well, there was this cowboy in Montana. Good lookin' and whoo-ee did he know it! He used to tell me that. He used to shut me up by kissing me until I begged for mercy."

"Did he ever give you any mercy?" He loomed over her and she fought to keep from giggling.

"Never." She opened her mouth and caught her breath when he plunged his tongue into her mouth. She reached between them with her right hand and grasped his erection. When he moved his mouth to her breasts, she moved beneath him and grabbed his hips with both hands.

"Not yet," he said.

Again he trailed his tongue through the valley and sucked gently at her twin crests. His right hand was tangled in her hair and his left hand drifted down through her curls. He parted her and rubbed his thumb on her tender spot.

"Oh, Cam!" She rocked forward, looking for more

contact. He kept his thumb circling her and gently plunged a finger inside to heighten the sensation. In less than a minute, she was panting, helpless with wanting release.

For the second time the orgasm overwhelmed her. "Cam, please, please, be inside me, please. Now."

"In a minute." He moved a few inches and she heard the drawer of the bedside table open. "There," he said. "We're both ready now."

She parted her legs and looked up at him. Her eyes locked on his. "I remember."

Gently—he was always, always gentle—he entered her. At first, she gasped at the size of him, then relaxed and took more. With each stroke in and out her core seemed to swell, welcoming him home. Each stroke of his shaft built tension in her center until she was close to another orgasm.

Cam was torn between wanting the pleasure to last and wanting the sweet release of coming inside her, torn between wanting to understand what it all meant and wanting to soar mindlessly in sensation.

The taste of her skin fired his imagination; the sound in her throat drove him exquisitely crazy. If she kept moving like she was, he would lose control. He broke off their kiss and inhaled like a whale getting ready for a deep dive.

"Cam, Cam!" She called out and her body tensed.

The muscles inside her gripped him in rhythmic contractions and he couldn't wait any longer.

"Mandy!" One word, then he was over the crest, laughing and hugging her, riding the sensation that ripped through every part of his body.

"Oh, Mandy, my Mandy." He lowered himself onto his forearms to keep his weight off her but still reach her mouth with his. He kissed her lips, her eyes, her cheeks. In the dim light of the single lamp, her eyes were darker blue than he'd ever seen them before. Her smile was lazy, satisfied, satiated. He laughed.

"What's so funny, mister?"

"I know how the crazy guy at the circus feels when he's shot out of a cannon. A hell of a ride!" He kissed her again and slowly lifted his hips. He could feel her deliberately holding him in. He laughed again.

"All right," she said, "You can have your handy tool back, but I might want it later."

"I'll be right beside you all night."

"Ummm, that sounds so nice. Sneaking around was fun when I was eighteen, but sleeping together is a lot more appealing at my age." She opened her eyes wide. "I meant to say at *your* age."

"I'll be right back." He went into the bathroom; when he returned she was under the sheet and duvet. He slipped in beside her.

She snuggled against him. "I missed you."

"I was only gone a minute."

"You were gone twelve years." She rested her head on his shoulder. "Okay, okay," she yawned. "Technically I was gone twelve years. But any which way you slice the salami, I missed you." She sighed and settled closer against his side.

"I missed you, too, Mandy. Every day, no matter how hard I tried to tell myself that I didn't."

"I don't know..."

Had she dozed off? He smiled. His life had been good for a long time, but now it was perfect. The silence seemed to settle around them like fog in a valley. He closed his eyes and his breathing slowed.

"Cam?" she said softly, "are you awake?" Pause. "Cam?"

"Yes, I'm awake. Mostly."

She laughed. "I remember the two of us making love. The first time, and after that. A lot of times after that. We were embarrassingly like bunnies, weren't we?"

"I prefer to think of it as two healthy people madly in love. Two exceptionally healthy and extremely imaginative people."

"True. Yes, but something is nagging at me." She yawned.

"What's that, sweetheart?" He was so close to sleep, completely relaxed. She yawned again, and he thought she'd fallen asleep. But her half-asleep, mid-yawn question woke him up like a gong.

"If we were so much in love, why did we break up?"

Chapter 15

Mandy woke up and reached across the bed for Cam. He wasn't there.

She could tell from the light coming in the skylight that she'd slept late. After making love three times in one night, she needed sleep. But so did Cam, so why wasn't he in bed?

She lifted her head and saw that the bathroom door was open. Still groggy, she inched to the side of the big bed and went to the window. Pulling it aside a couple inches, she could see that the ranch was in full operation. The cowboys she knew who worked for Cam, including Joey Dix, were all out there. Two heavy-duty trucks, each attached to a horse trailer, were parked in a flat area by the barn. Four men she hadn't seen before walked back and forth behind the closed trailer doors.

She heard a door close downstairs and saw the top of Cam's hat come into view outside. He strode across the dusty driveway and shook hands with each of the visitors. She crawled back into bed and picked up the phone. D'Ann answered on the fifth ring.

"It's me. I need a ride. In fact, I need a way to disappear." Mandy explained how many men were outside and how busy Cam was.

"I'd like to make a graceful exit," she added. "Cowboys are notorious gossips."

D'Ann yawned. "I see your problem. Let me think a minute."

Mandy waited. And waited. She slipped open the drawer under the phone and took out the pack of condoms. Twenty condoms, three gone, seventeen left. What a delightful thought. She put them back and closed the drawer.

"D'Ann! Did you go back to sleep?"

"Huh? Of course not." Another yawn. "I was planning a reputation-saving campaign. And I think I have it. Where are all the men?"

She told her.

"So if I drove in toward the ranch house but took that fork that loops around the pond and came up to the other side of the house, nobody would get a good look at me. Am I right?"

"I think so."

"You come out that side door and hop in the truck. We'll park by the kitchen and walk around and say, 'Hello, there, what a surprise. We came to see the puppies!'"

"The grand puppy caper! Do you secretly work for the FBI?"

"The FBI is not smart enough to come up with a plan like this. Be ready in—" she paused and groaned. "Be ready in an hour. I'm not going to see Joey looking like this. And I don't care how much jeopardy your reputation is in, I'm having a cup of coffee."

"All right. An hour, but please bring a mug of coffee for me, too." She spotted her bra on the back of a chair and thought of the filmy top she'd worn last night. "Uh, better bring me a pair of jeans and a shirt. And my canvas shoes."

She hung up, sighed heavily, and flopped back against the pillow. What a glorious night! She hugged herself and giggled. Of course it was "just" a fling. Sure, sure, sure, she was teetering dangerously close to falling in love with Cam, but the best way to scare away a bachelor—any woman knows—is to say the C word. Commitment. Or, heaven forbid, the L word.

Besides, she was still recovering from a serious injury to her think tank. What man in his right mind would believe she knew how she felt about anything? She wasn't sure she believed it.

But, oh, it had been fantastic. He was the best lover she'd ever had or heard about or read about. The best. She hummed the tune to "I Hope You Dance" to herself and relived the sensation of swaying against him.

It was a crazy paradox, but it seemed like once she'd remembered Cam's tender lovemaking she forgot every other man she'd ever been with. Her "love life," a list of affairs so salaciously reported in the tabloids, had in real life been seldom and boring. Because not one of the men who tried to bed her was half the lover Cam was. It had been easy to say no. It had been easy, too, to let people think whatever they wanted.

The truth about her fun-filled life was not what it appeared. The first couple of years were a whirl and she believed she was having as much fun as the tabloids said she was. Then gradually the smile was harder to freeze into place. That was the thing; it was gradual, like helium leaking ever so slowly out of a balloon. When that pathetic lonely man kidnapped her and shot her, he took away everything that mattered to her and left her with the one thing she didn't want. Fame.

She would always be "that TV actress, what's her name? The one with the bullet in her head."

God saw fit, by what miraculous medical intervention she couldn't begin to understand, to give her a second chance. She had a lot of thinking to do about what she would do with that chance.

The first thing she needed to do today was revert to her days as an actress and make people think she'd arrived with D'Ann.

She headed into the shower and adjusted the showerhead so it wouldn't get her hair wet. Ah, there was that luscious scent. Rainwater soap. She lathered her body, wishing Cam was there, doing it for her. Next time, yes.

****

"Good morning!" Joey called. Cam turned his head to see who he was talking to.

What the hell? How did she pull this off?

"Hi, Joey, Cam," Mandy called. "I hope we won't be in the way. We came over to see the puppies."

"You didn't tell me the place would be so busy," D'Ann said to Joey. "We could have come another time."

"You're always welcome here," Cam said. "Did you bring us anything to eat? Something right out of the oven?"

"Not yet," Mandy said with a big smile. "Cookies this afternoon. Now don't pay us any mind. We'll take a look at Polo and her pups and be out of here."

"You know the way," Cam said.

He called to the men waiting to load a pregnant mare into the maroon and white trailer. They were to deliver her to a new owner in Idaho. "Okay, let's get her settled."

About twenty minutes later, he saw the sly sisters come out of the barn. Joey strolled over to walk them to their car. A few words, a laugh, and then he waved goodbye.

When Cam saw them drive away, he told Joey he was going inside for a few minutes to get a cup of coffee.

Joey nodded. "I told D'Ann I can't get away before two."

"Before two?" Cam's mind was overflowing with concern about Mandy, and about the Japanese visitors, plus other ranch business.

"Today's the day we're going to ride. You know, to the arch. D'Ann's going on Mustang Sally."

Cam almost swore but stopped himself. He'd been tuning Joey out too effectively. When the visitors moved up their visit by one day, and Hussy starting showing signs of being ready to breed, he'd called the veterinarian to come out and give her a flush of antibiotics. There were so many details to keep track of that he'd forgotten it was Joey's first day off in over a month.

He could keep from swearing, but he couldn't hide the look of dismay on his face.

"There'll be plenty of other days to ride," Joey said with a shrug. "I'll call her."

"No, it's your day off. God knows you've earned it. And it's time Douglas got more responsibility. Two o'clock is fine."

He strode to the back door and kicked the dust off his boots. Inside, he spooned coffee into the filter and poured in water. As it brewed he leaned against the cooking island. Something caught his eye by the stairs.

Mandy's sandals, the ones she'd worn because her boots had rubbed blisters. He grinned. Unlike Cinderella, she'd left them both behind.

Seeing her this morning made him ache with longing. He'd been telling himself it was a good thing they'd acted on their powerful attraction. Now they could move on, get better acquainted. Like go out to dinner, go to a movie. Go on dates.

Ha. Who was he trying to kid? All the ways he thought of getting better acquainted with Mandy McCay involved piles of clothes on the floor.

The big problem that loomed like a giant devil's-head piñata above his Stetson wasn't going to go away simply because he wished it would.

And the damn thing wasn't filled with candy.

Oh, no. It held all the pain and rejection and

blame of that last day with Mandy. The day she drove away from Bitter Falls Farm in a cloud of dust. The day he told her no, that he wouldn't marry her.

The honorable thing.

He could still taste the dust left by her Thunderbird's spinning tires.

He slumped down on a stool and rested his head in his hands. And moaned.

"Good Lord, what a mess I've made," he muttered. He'd made love to Mandy the night before—thinking she remembered everything.

Yeah, the first time.

He told himself to quit pretending he was such a fine upstanding gentleman, that he hadn't taken advantage of her.

He'd lain awake long, long past midnight after her half-asleep question shot an arrow into his heart.

If we were so much in love, why did we break up?

She had remembered the best of times, not the worst of times. He'd lain in the dark, listening to her breathe, smelling the heady combination of Mandy's scent and her favorite perfume, the same one she used to wear, White Linen. The taste of her was still on his lips; the sound of her throaty laughter reverberated in his head.

He'd told himself there could be no more love making until she knew the whole story. But then she'd rolled to her side and draped one leg over his. Half asleep she'd kissed his shoulder and giggled.

He'd gone still as a bird dog and his shaft pointed toward the ceiling. If he didn't move, she'd go back to sleep and he could slide out from under her leg. That's what he wanted to happen.

Yeah, that's what he wanted to happen—right after the sun burned up the earth.

But oh, Mandy. Mandy-by-moonlight. She knew

him so well. Her hand strayed to cup him and stroke him.

"How nice," she'd murmured in a husky voice. "Hold that thought."

She moved away and he heard the drawer of his bedside table open. The sound of the foil pack opening was like the first cannon report in the *1812 Overture*. Without a word, she sheathed him and straddled him. They climaxed together and she went back to sleep. That time he slept, too.

And not long before dawn, she'd wakened him with kisses down his neck and nipped tender little bites on his chest. He'd opened another packet and entered her from behind, the two of them spooned together and both his hands on her breasts.

He deserved to be horsewhipped. When Mandy *remembered* why they "broke up," as she phrased it, or when he *told her the truth...*

Oh Lord. Whichever event came first, she'd throw him out of her house, off her farm, and out of her life.

He deserved it.

He loved her. But how could she believe him?

He wanted to go her, *now*. Every hour that he waited only made it worse. Ford McCay's request—demand—that Cam wait until he got home from his trip so he could support his daughter didn't matter. The need for honesty overrode other considerations.

Besides, what was he going to tell her father? That he'd planned to wait, but—*get ready to laugh, sir, this is a good one!*—Mandy and I got naked and went to bed.

All other things being equal—and nothing between Mars and Venus was equal to Mandy urging him to make love to her—she needed to know the truth now. With no delay. No waiting for Dad.

He couldn't leave the ranch now, not with a new stallion having arrived yesterday. And Hussar's

Regimental Lady was going to be bred this morning. Dar-Kanyon was getting light exercise and Joey was getting the breeding shed ready.

The Japanese owners of the champion Arabian mare were arriving at noon to tour the ranch.

He looked at his watch. The soonest he could get to Mandy's house was three. He hoped it would be soon enough.

Chapter 16

At one-thirty, D'Ann strutted into the kitchen. "If you keep cooking like this, I'll have to buy the next size of jeans." She took a cookie out of the open tin and moaned in what could only be ecstasy.

"Take them from the plate," Mandy said. "That tin is for Cam and the guys."

"What do you call these? They're fabulous."

"Black Forest Cookies. They have semi-sweet chocolate chunks and vanilla milk chips, slivered almonds, and candied cherries."

"I'm going to buy a grocery story and get rich selling ingredients to you. Is there no end to your culinary wonders?"

Mandy turned a clear glass bowl upside down, waved her hands over it, and leaned close to peer through. "Hmmm. Not that I can see. Next, I'm going to recreate Mother's blue ribbon King Cobbler using Tompkin's King apples, her favorite tree."

"I haven't been out to the old orchard in years. How is it?"

"Lefty takes good care of it. I'm sure Dad spends time out there, too. If it weren't for those apples, McCay Enterprises wouldn't exist. And you and I would not be wearing top of the line custom-made boots."

D'Ann swung one foot up on a stool and pulled her jeans up to her knee to show off her cowhide boots. "Expensive, but worth it. These will last longer than I will, and they're a perfect fit. By the way, I'm going to buy a horse."

"Won't that be a tight fit in a townhouse? Or is this your way of announcing a change of address?" For D'Ann to talk about moving to Bitter Falls was one thing. Making such a drastic change was another.

"I'm resigning by fax tomorrow and going to work at Bitter Falls Hospital. Nobody, and I mean nobody, is shoving or dragging me out of Montana again."

Mandy sighed. "You've always known what you wanted to do, haven't you?" She ran hot water to rinse her measuring cups and spatula, and set them on a rack to drain. "You wanted to be a nurse and help people, and you charged ahead like a horse toward a barn."

She looked out toward the lush grape arbor and sighed again. "You got your nursing degree and went right to work, while I did nothing that mattered to anybody—myself included."

Memories of the flash-flash-flash of paparazzi cameras made her flinch and shut her eyes. It seemed like the more she tried and failed to remember why she left Montana, the more details of her years in California floated in front of her, words and exclamation marks in headlines on the front pages of tabloids.

Mandy's Turn to Cry!!! bleated above a story about Troy Walden dumping her for his ex-wife's personal assistant. The way they trumpeted her breakup with Errol Kidd, *Mandy Leaves Errol at the Altar!!!*

She scrubbed her hands with antibacterial soap, as if that might remove the sleaze she'd so willingly embraced for more than eleven years.

D'Ann ate another cookie. "I had an advantage over you."

It took Mandy a moment to come back to what

they were talking about. Oh, yes. *That my little sister became a medical professional while I showed my butt crack to adoring fans.*

"An advantage?" She dried off her hands. "What was that?"

"That Dad was so wrapped in you, worrying so much about how you'd turn out, that he gave me more space."

"I don't remember him being so involved. I was on my own a lot. Obviously, too much."

"It wasn't that he was so involved."

D'Ann seemed to be picking her words like wild blackberries, avoiding vicious thorns.

"He was vested."

"I don't follow you." Mandy leaned against the counter and wiped her hands with a towel.

"He wanted a lot for you."

"All parents want a lot for their kids. Are you saying he expected more because I was his 'first-born'?"

D'Ann said something she couldn't hear.

"What? What are you saying?" The timer went off and she took another tray of cookies out of the oven.

D'Ann sighed. "You and Dad fought a lot. A lot. All he had to do was make a rule and you'd be looking for a way to break it."

Tears sprang to Mandy's eyes. She wiped them away and dropped the last of the cookie dough on a sheet. As soon as she put it in the oven and set the timer, she took the hot cookies off the other sheet.

She pressed the towel to her face.

"Oh, Mandy, I'm sorry. I've made you cry and all I want is to see you happy."

D'Ann put arms around her, but Mandy shrugged out of the embrace.

"You're just telling the truth. I know, I have to face everything about the past, the good and the bad, before I can go on. Don't apologize."

"I'll call Joey and say I've changed my mind."

"No! Go on the ride. And take the cookies with you. I promised them to Cam."

"He's crazy about you. I guess you know that."

Mandy wiped a half-moon swath under each eye to clear away her runny mascara then rocked her head from side to side, weighing the statement. "That could be true." She lowered her voice like a conspirator. "I remembered him yesterday. We were, ahem, quite the hot item that summer."

"And you're a hot item again, judging by your need for an exit strategy this morning."

She grinned sheepishly. "Yes. He's so sweet, such a gentleman. Listen to this: he wouldn't come on to me because he said that would be playing poker with marked cards or something. All this time...oh my gosh." She covered her face with the dishtowel.

"What?" D'Ann tugged the towel from her hands. "Come on, spill."

"All this time, while I besieged him with delectable food and did everything but put a banner over Main Street saying 'There's more where that came from,' Cam was hiding the truth—that he remembered me. All of me. And I, witless, thought he was a handsome stranger."

Knowing that he'd remembered her, and that they'd been lovers, put the events of the past week in floodlights. She found herself saying, *No wonder,* and *Well, duh,* over and over.

How did he keep a straight face when she showed up at his door with cookies? And coffee cake, and pie. And that red blouse, with no bra. Coffee, tea, or...me?

"Anyway," she continued, "once I convinced him I'm in full possession of my faculties and perfectly able to give informed consent, well, you know."

"The music swells and the lights go out. I saw that movie. Well, well. I knew some good would come from that first batch of cookies."

"Now get out of here. I have dishes to wash and a college catalog to look at. Thanks for getting it and pretending you might want to take a class or two."

"I wasn't pretending. I need to update what I know about pharmacology." D'Ann grinned. "Joey is starting there in the fall. He went into the Marines right out of high school. He wants to get a bachelor's degree in biology and apply to veterinary school."

A car pulling in front of the house caught Mandy's eye. "Who's that?"

D'Ann joined her at the dining room window. "A woman. I don't recognize her."

"Oh, hell. It's Gerri Melman. Cam said she was acting uncommonly nosy to him yesterday. She manages—and for all I know, owns—the Victorian Inn."

"I'm out of here the back way. Joey's waiting."

"Have fun." She followed D'Ann to the kitchen. "And don't forget the cookies!"

She pressed the lid on the tin and handed it to D'Ann.

"Any message for Campbell West, formerly known as that handsome stranger?"

"No message. He knows where to find me." The doorbell rang and Mandy swore softly. "I'll see you later. Dad should be here in a couple hours."

"Make an excuse for me. I'll be home late. Make that very late."

The screen slapped closed behind D'Ann as Mandy headed for the front door. She wiped her hands on her apron and opened the door.

"Gerri! What a surprise."

****

Cam was on his way into his house when a loud whistle hailed him. He turned and shaded his eyes.

Douglas, the MSU Aggie he counted on almost as much as he did Joey, was waving his hat from the door of the barn.

Cam muttered, "Now what?" and headed back out. "What's up?"

"Colonel Jackson whacked his head against the stall and opened up a cut over his eye. The blood is making him panic even more."

"I'll call Doc Larue. You and Turk cover his face and calm him down until the vet gets here."

Assured by the veterinarian's answering service that either Doc Larue or his new partner would be there as soon as possible, Cam ran out the back door. As he neared the stable, he heard Colonel Jackson snorting and blowing. His companion, the gelding comically named Gift Horse, nickered and whinnied to the stallion, "There, there," in horse language.

He hung his hat on a peg inside the stable that still smelled like new-cut lumber. He began to roll up the sleeves of the good shirt he'd worn to meet the Japanese visitors but, on second thought, took the shirt off and hung it under his hat. His T-shirt could be tossed. This job was certain to get messy.

"Easy, big fella," he murmured as he slowly entered the stall. "Doc Larue will give you something to settle you down. We're going to fix up that nasty cut."

Gift Horse poked his head through the opening and shoved Cam in the shoulder. He turned and stroked the gelding's nose.

"Don't you worry about your buddy. He'll be good as new. You'll see."

Gift Horse nodded his head sharply up and down.

Douglas and Turk stood on either side of Colonel Jackson and held a soft velvet hood in place. Like Cam, they murmured assurance to "big fella" as they stroked his neck and his withers. Douglas softly sang "Home on the Range" twice.

When he stopped, the stallion kicked one back leg and struck hard on the wood between his stall and Gift Horse's.

"I believe he wants another verse," Cam chuckled. "Who knew you'd have such a big fan?"

"The things I do for money," Douglas sighed. "Oh give me a home, where the buffalo roam..."

"Whatever works," Cam muttered, and joined in. "Where the deer and the antelope play..."

The delay in getting to Mandy weighed heavily on him, but it was unavoidable. What was the saying, heaven can wait? Well, so could hell.

And talking to Mandy today was much more likely to be the latter than the former.

Chapter 17

Mandy had the strangest sensation as she sat across the dining room table from Gerri Melman Johnson Woolery.

It's hard to describe. A feeling of lifting, floating. She'd felt this way before. *Sometime—when?* Her head began to ache.

She had a sensation that she was hovering above herself, split into two precise halves. No, not halves; duplicates. Two Mandys. One sat in the chair, sipped tea and nodded slowly; the other Mandy hovered. The sound of Gerri's voice seemed off-kilter somehow, like the delay on the phone line when her dad had called her from China.

Her head hurt more. "Excuse me for a minute, Gerri." She pushed herself to a standing position and returned to the kitchen. From a drawer under the microwave she retrieved a container of ibuprofen and shook out four tablets. Grabbing for the first glass on the shelf, she washed down the pills.

"Are you sure you won't have another cookie?" she said as she sat. The flowers Cam had brought were still vibrant in the blue vase. A flush of warmth cocooned her; memories of lying in his arms made her skin tingle.

Gerri had suggested they sit at the kitchen counter, but Mandy ushered her to the dining room, saying it was better for "company." Truth was, she didn't want her kitchen sanctuary violated. The kitchen where she'd cooked for Cam, an act so intimate it made her blush to think of it. Right there at the sink he'd removed his watch and pitched in to clean up.

How he must have laughed when he saw the aftermath of her manic, tornadic cooking enterprise. He would have laughed that rumbling laugh deep in his chest that resonated when he held her.

No, the kitchen was private, sacrosanct.

She hadn't realized until she saw the flowers that the dining room, too, was full of Cam West. The candlelight had reflected in his eyes.

"Your cookies are terrific, Mandy, but every hundred calories I take in, I mean over the bare minimum, means I have to walk the treadmill twelve minutes. I had liposuction on my butt once and let me tell you, girlfriend, once was enough."

She listened to Gerri, and willed the pills to work. Gerri went on about her time at the University of Washington and her two marriages; Mandy pretended to be interested.

When Gerri went into detail about the prayer groups she'd initiated to pray for Mandy after the shooting, Mandy adopted an attitude of prayer herself. She prayed that her father would come home early and she'd have an excuse to show Gerri out the door.

"How long do you plan to stay?"

She focused her attention on Gerri's mouth. It wasn't moving. Had she asked a question? Yes; she was waiting for an answer. Her mind raced back over what they'd said.

"Oh, uh, to stay in Bitter Falls? I haven't decided yet."

"You'll probably go back to California."

It wasn't a question, so she said nothing.

Gerri tapped her long manicured nails on the polished wood table. "Or maybe not. You probably want to stick around a while, see if anything develops with Campbell West, Esquire."

More nail tapping. She barged ahead without encouragement.

"Cam is rich enough on his own, but his mother is rolling in money. Who would ever guess that Cam West was the son of Arabella Billings West? If I'd known that back in the day, I might have tried to catch his interest myself." She laughed and winked. "Not that it would have done me any good. That cowboy was such a fool for you, I could have pranced around naked while cracking a bullwhip and he wouldn't have turned his head. Of course, I'm not telling you anything you don't know."

The pain of the headache lifted slightly and Mandy could think more clearly.

Cam came from a wealthy family. He'd chartered a private jet to come get his mother when she took ill.

Then why had he been close to broke when she'd known him before?

She needed to know more. Gerri could fill in some of the blanks, but Mandy didn't want her to know she had holes in her memory. She'd have to act blasé about the whole thing.

"So, are the two of you getting back together?" Gerri asked breathlessly. "My stars and little fishes, Mandy, it's like a movie. Poor cowboy refuses to marry heiress, gets rich, and gets a second chance." She sighed dramatically.

Mandy forced a laugh. It sounded as tinny as a handful of flatware dropped in an empty horse trough. *Refuses to marry?* What did she say? Cowboy refuses to marry heiress?

The image of herself in Cam's bed late the night before flashed in front of her eyes and her stomach twisted in a figure eight. Still tingling from her orgasms and tucked up next to his heart, she'd asked Cam a question. She'd fallen asleep, still waiting for the answer.

If we were so much in love, why did we break up?

She didn't ask Gerri anything; instead she shrugged and said, "I was young and headstrong. Honestly, I don't know what I was using for a brain when I took off for California like that."

"You were furious! Absolutely furious! I knew you were in up to your starry eyes with your dad's hired man, heck, I covered for you about ten times."

Mandy smiled. It was getting harder and harder to appear relaxed. To keep from clenching her hands into fists, she held onto her glass of tea with one and flattened the other one on the table. She took a sip of tea; it tasted like vinegar.

"I was looking at my old scrapbook yesterday," she said. "I'll go get it." She stopped in the living room to take deep breaths then picked up the dusty book she'd finally brought in from the mudroom.

She brought it into the dining room and opened it to the picture of the two of them on the porch, Gerri in the red satin gown and herself in the silver and white sheath.

"This was right before we got in your Miata." She set it flat on the applewood table and picked up her glass. The tea had become nothing more than a stage prop to her. If she tried to swallow anything, she'd choke.

"Oh, yes! Your eighteenth birthday party. Next best thing to a debutante party. What a night. I hooked up with a state senator's son. He was all over me and I thought I was hot stuff. Then I found out the jerk was engaged to a girl in Texas."

Gerri ate a second cookie and said they were so good she was willing to do her penance on the treadmill.

"You wanted to get more pictures, but you didn't have the film," Gerri went on. "Cam took this one. That was the night you went to the motel. I, of course, was your alibi. You were 'spending the night at Gerri's house.'" She made quotation marks in the air. "You never did tell me any details, but I could see you'd gone over the moon with Cam West."

"Apparently I didn't want to kiss and tell."

"Kiss? *Kiss?*"

Gerri laughed what they used to call her banshee laugh.

"Girlfriend, I think your only rule with that cowboy was 'Don't do it in the streets and scare the horses'!"

Would a jury convict her if she strangled Gerri with her bare hands? She could use the diminished mental capacity defense. But if she did it now, she might never know what Gerri meant by "cowboy refuses to marry heiress." If only she had D'Ann's skill at getting people to talk without leaving a mark on their bodies.

"I was too young to get married, anyway." She walked to the bay window and looked up the driveway. A few minutes before, she'd hoped to see her dad coming. Now she hoped for the opposite. She needed to extract information from Gerri. She liked that image. Extract. She could take pliers and pull a molar. No anesthesia required.

"Oh, I know. Eighteen is too young. For me, Twenty-two was too young."

Gerri laughed, thoroughly enjoying the bonding she obviously thought was taking place.

"Come to think of it, twenty-seven was too young, too." Banshee laugh again.

"It might not be your age that was the problem," Mandy said. "Could be it was those particular men."

"Well, I like to think so. I also like to think the third time will be the charm. Not that I have anyone in mind."

"What do you think went wrong?"

"With my marriages? Or your near miss?"

"Both." *Liar, liar, pants on fire.*

"It would take too long to talk about mine. I just thank the powers that be every day that I don't have children tying me to Judd Johnson or Billy Ray Woolery. And don't ask me about my ex-in-laws!" She drank her tea and asked for another glass.

Mandy took her glass in the kitchen and refilled it. She hoped Gerri wouldn't change the subject by the time she got back.

She needn't have worried.

"I know you're right that you were awfully young to get married, but you were so much in love. You changed a lot that summer. You were pretty much going to go to college in Virginia to please your father. I was kind of glad when you put your foot down and said you wanted to stay here and go to the community college. Your dad liked to have had a stroke over that, but when he found out you wanted to marry his hired cowboy? Whoa!"

"Pretty wild around here, huh?"

"You were on the phone to me, crying. You wanted to stay here and you wanted a Christmas wedding. I was going to come home from school in Washington and be your bridesmaid."

"Then it all went to hell in a hand basket." Mandy nodded and sighed as if she knew it all so well. The truth was—she was starting to get flashes of it. Like subliminal ads at the movie theater, split-second images of butter dripping into popcorn.

A picture of herself in the grape arbor with Cam. She was crying. Not just crying. Sobbing.

"Once your father put his foot down, no wedding, and Cam refused to elope with you, you drove south to la-la land. You left town so fast you didn't even say goodbye to me."

Mandy rubbed her forehead. "Gerri, I hate to be a lousy hostess, but I'm under strict orders to get more rest. If my father comes home and sees me staggering, he'll lock me in a tower."

"Staggering?" Gerri asked.

"If I overdo it, the muscles in my weak leg fold up and I trip. A headache is usually the first sign, and my head is starting to throb."

"You poor thing! I'm leaving right now, and you go lie down."

"I will." She stood and headed for the front door.

"You take care, now," Gerri said. "I'll call you in a couple days. Hey, I have an idea—you could come over to the Inn and have breakfast."

"That would be nice." She put her hand to her forehead again to make sure Gerri didn't linger.

Mandy closed the door and stood there, leaning on the wood, going over it all in her mind.

A Christmas wedding.

Memories that had trickled into her mind like snow melting in the mountains now tumbled like a spring flood, colliding and turning and swelling. She covered her face with her hands.

Yes, she'd wanted a small church wedding. Cam had told her his plans for the horse ranch on the land his great-grandfather had homesteaded. They were going to live in a trailer on the land until they got their "starter" cabin built. She was going to get a job and go to school part time at the community college.

She lowered her hands and walked to the kitchen. Again she looked out at the grape arbor; again she saw herself and Cam. She'd been crying; tears of anger, sorrow, confusion. She'd slapped him and tried to slap him again but he caught her wrist.

She rubbed it as if the pain was fresh. All their plans, everything had come crashing down around her.

Days before that implosion, Cam had taken her to his land. He'd parked his old pickup right where their cabin would be.

She was surprised now that she hadn't had a flashback the first time she looked out his windows. She'd been too nervous about her first batch of cookies and what to say to the handsome rancher...a man she was attracted to from the first moment she saw him in the feed store.

The handsome stranger.

The *gentleman* who wouldn't take advantage of a lady with a memory gap the size of the Kiger Gorge.

That is, until he did exactly that.

She took off her apron and threw it over a chair. She picked up her car keys and purse. Montana would be buried by glaciers the next time she got in that man's bed!

Chapter 18

Cam stood under the showerhead to rinse off the grime and lathered soap. He'd scrubbed all over with Lava Soap once and now did a quick wash with the fancy soap his mother had given him. The rainwater scent Mandy liked. Not that raindrops on roses or whiskers on kittens would do him any good in the coming domestic drama.

The four of them, Douglas, Turk, Doc Larue, and himself, had the devil of a time getting enough sedative into Colonel Jackson so Larue could stitch the gash over his right eye.

"I should have been a plastic surgeon in Beverly Hills," Larue said. "Now that's real money."

With a good guess of how much he'd owe Larue for this emergency visit, Cam rolled his eyes.

"Money, yeah. But you'd have to work with human prima donnas instead of quality clients like Colonel Jackson. And you couldn't count on hair growing over all the stitches."

His T-shirt was soaked with blood from the stallion and with sweat from both of them. He still might have tried to wash it out if Colonel Jackson hadn't ripped a gaping hole out of it with his big teeth.

Larue had laughed. "Human prima donnas might want to rip a man's clothes off, but they have smaller teeth."

He wiped off his instruments and dropped them in a separate bag to be cleaned and sterilized at his office.

"I heard your foreman has a litter of puppies. How are they doing?"

"Polo is going for mother of the year. Why, you want a puppy?"

"I'll take a look. We had to put down old Shep and my youngest boy is taking it hard."

They strolled into the old stable and Cam gently pulled back a curtain the guys had rigged to give Polo and her pups privacy.

"Hi, Little Mama." Larue sat on his heels. "What a good mama you are. Could I have one of your pups for my boy Travis?"

Polo showed her teeth and growled.

"On second thought, I believe I'll come back when you're more in the mood to talk." Larue laughed and stood. "Six pups. They look to be collie and red heeler cross. Good combination for a family dog."

Family dog. As Cam dropped the curtain, he'd smiled, imagining puppies and toddlers underfoot in his big house, around a Christmas tree, with Mandy in a soft robe, sitting on the big couch with a steaming cup of cocoa.

His smile had vanished, however, when he recalled how slim his chance was now—or ever—to win her love.

He stepped out of the shower and toweled off. In the bedroom, he looked at the bed, the sheets still tangled and the duvet at a crazy angle after a night of lovemaking. If only he could go back to the minutes before midnight, when he'd stood there holding her hands together to keep her from flinging them around his neck. *Don't kiss me,* he'd said. He could have told her the truth—the whole truth—and Cinderella could still have picked up her sandals and left for home before the clock struck twelve.

Mandy might have stayed. Unlikely, but

possible. Or she might have gone home and thought everything through and the two of them could do what he hoped they'd do. Date. Get acquainted. Build their relationship from the ground up the way he'd built this house.

Fall in love. *Fall back in love.*

Instead, she said she remembered him, and he'd wanted so badly to believe it—to believe that she remembered him and *still wanted to make love*—that he left too much unsaid.

He heard a door open downstairs. He stepped into clean briefs and jeans and looked out over the balcony. Beside D'Ann's small pickup was a second vehicle with McCay Enterprises on the door.

He turned around as Mandy walked into the bedroom. He opened his mouth to say her name, but didn't. She walked across the room, picked up the clean T-shirt he'd set on the bed, and threw it at him. He was glad he hadn't left a fire ax on the bed.

"I'll be downstairs," she said.

He pulled on the T-shirt and stopped long enough to put on socks and boots. It was an old western axiom that a cowboy wants to die with his boots on.

"Or live," he muttered under his breath.

All day he'd agonized over their overdue truth session. But he had a different picture in his mind. More like Mandy throwing herself into his arms. Then he'd tell her, and she'd be furious. And, of course, deeply hurt. As bad as that would have been, this was going to be worse.

He knew three words he was certain he wouldn't need to say to her again. *Don't kiss me.*

He listened to the hollow sound of his boots on the wood as he went downstairs. She was in the kitchen, sitting on a stool at the cooking island. He walked to the back door and turned the lock. He didn't need any of his hands coming in to look for him now.

"Can I get you anything?"

"No. Yes. Water."

He filled two tall glasses with ice and filtered water and set one in front of her. Then he pulled a stool to the other side of the island and sat.

I love you, Mandy. I will love you until the day I die.

The words rang so clearly in his mind he thought he must have shouted them aloud, but no. She stared at her hands.

"I'm asking you again, Cam. If we were so much in love, why did we break up?"

"When we made love last night, I swear to God I thought you remembered all of our history."

"My question didn't tip you off that there was less to my data recovery miracle than you first thought? Or did you stay quiet, hoping I'd forget all about that? Mandy and her evaporative memory. Here today, gone tomorrow. Wouldn't that be convenient?"

"You're right, yes. When you asked that question I realized—" He stopped. His mouth was stuffed with alfalfa.

"You realized that while *you* were playing with five aces—isn't that how you put it?—that I wasn't even playing with a full deck!"

Her eyes blazed with fury, her fists clenched so hard her knuckles were white.

"I want to slap you! I want to scream! I want to beat against you with my fists until you bleed!" She put her face in her hands and cried, long ragged sobs and quivering, loud gasps to get more breath.

He battled with himself. He wanted to fold her in his arms, but she didn't want him to touch her. Loving her with all his heart gave him no license to violate her space. He rested his elbows on the hardwood surface and ran his fingers through his damp hair. He had no right to hold her. But a man would have to have a heart harder than granite to keep from trying.

He stood and walked around the island. He stood quietly beside her. Finally, he put out one hand and smoothed her hair.

She lifted her head and showed her face, ravaged by the pain of what he was putting her through. He looked around for a box of tissues and found instead a linen table napkin. He touched it to her hands and she snatched it and pulled it inside the tent of her hands like a chipmunk grabbing a nut.

He smoothed her hair again and bent to kiss it. The aroma of chocolate and vanilla mixed with her perfume.

"Mandy, are you ready to hear the answer?"

She got her shaking under control and wiped her eyes and cheeks. She took a drink of the water. "Yes. And this time, for fun, let's hear the whole truth. I'm sick and tired of playing *Guess what? Oops, now guess what else?* I just went through five rounds of that game with Gerri Melman."

His heart sank. "I wanted to be the one to tell you. I was on my way when I had to deal with a serious injury to my new stallion. I got out of the shower ten minutes ago, getting ready to drive over and face you. I know I'm a coward not to have told you last night."

"Cowardice is not the problem, here, Cam! Two empty condom wrappers hit the floor *after* I asked the question."

"Please forgive me, Mandy. I swear it wasn't just lust. I love you. I'm a jerk, a cad, a butthead, the biggest fool in Montana—"

"In fifty states!"

"You're right. The biggest fool in fifty states. But I love you. Even if you never let me touch one hair on your beautiful head again, please forgive me."

She dabbed her eyes. "Talk!"

"Okay."

"From over there!" She pointed at the stool on the far side of the island.

The island he'd built never seemed so large before. Why had he wanted to put an acre of hardwood in the middle of his kitchen? He sat and took a long drink of water.

"You and I were completely, hopelessly in love," he began. "It started for the wrong reason." He sighed. "Because if your father whispered *black* you shouted *white*. The two of you didn't agree on anything. It wasn't a case of oil and water. More a case of oil and a match. Meeting the hired cowboy in the grape arbor for a kiss was another way for you to rebel."

"You're saying I was a—" She winced as she said the next words. "A cock tease."

"No," he said softly, wishing he could take her hand in his. But even if he reached her physically, she was a hundred miles away from him in her head. "I said you and your father disagreed, but I didn't say you were the one in the wrong. You were funny and charming and full of life. And smart. That was when we sneaked a few kisses. You weren't teasing me. And you weren't acting, well..."

"I think the word you're looking for is slutty."

"No, that word *never* fit you. It was a harmless romance. You kissed me, I kissed you back. Later, when we got to know each other better, our relationship changed. And I'm here to swear on—" He looked around the room, walked over the microwave and took a book off the top. "I'm here to swear on *Betty Crocker's Hostess Cookbook* that Mandy McCay in love was the eighth wonder of the world. Dazzling, audacious, kind, warm, sensuous."

"So, we fooled around, then we had sex."

She sounded as if it was boring, an act of no importance.

"We made love," he said emphatically. "Don't ever think it was less than that, Mandy. You weren't capable of just *having sex*. It meant as much to you as it did to me."

"Go on." She sounded less angry, but it might be wishful thinking. God knows he was doing enough of *that*.

"Your eighteenth birthday was our first time to be together." The image of her in the silver dress— and then in nothing—made his heart race like a runaway truck halfway down a mountain road.

"I made the reservation at the River View on the other side of the pass," he said. "You told your dad you were spending the night with Gerri."

"So she told me. Oh! it was torture to listen to her. By then I'd remembered our first time and a lot more times, so it wasn't all a shock. But I purely hate that she knows anything about it. You said I was smart, but the evidence of that is weak. I certainly had lousy taste in friends. And I'm wondering if my taste in lovers was anything to brag about, either." She took another drink.

Cam said nothing. She was right to be angry. He should have sat bolt upright in bed and answered her question, no matter how painful that would have been for both of them. Lies, whether by statement or omission, ate at them like acid.

He set the cookbook on the island. Instead of returning to his stool, he moved close enough he could touch her if he put out his hand.

"Skip to the end of this soap opera," she said with a dramatic sigh. "The part that had me leaving town like someone had set the law on me."

"We planned a future together." He smiled and twirled a stray curl of her hair between his fingers. She batted his hand away.

"We were going to live close to the bone financially for a couple years, but I wasn't as dumb as people thought. I had excellent land and I knew what I needed to do to build up my ranch. You and I shared a vision of the future, Mandy. Kids someday, but not until we could afford them."

He paused. "Some of the people around you thought you were shallow and spoiled, but they saw what they expected to see. They didn't know the real Mandy McCay. Not like I did. Inside you were...you were a true western woman, as capable and as close to the land as your mother and your grandmother and your great-grandmother. Ford McCay didn't just inherit that land from his *male* ancestors."

"I thought the story was *Johnny* Appleseed." She cracked a smile.

"I think it was really *Jemima* Appleseed but they let a man write it down."

This time she laughed. His heart thumped like a jack rabbit warning fifty cousins that a coyote was on the way.

"So we planned to get married," she said, "a Christmas wedding if Gerri is to be believed, but my father pitched a fit. Is that what happened?"

"Yes. The two of you had an unholy argument."

This was where the story got difficult. He gripped his hands together. He'd said he would tell her the whole truth. But he couldn't.

"So why didn't we elope?" She said it so softly he wasn't sure he heard her.

"I guess I got cold feet."

"You? Try something I can believe," she said.

"We had a terrible row, and I was a horse's ass. That's all I can say."

They sat in silence. She stared at her hands and twisted the napkin. Finally, in a small voice she said, "I think I...I think I told you I never wanted to see you again."

He said nothing. Time dragged by. At last, she raised her eyes to his face. He gave a slight nod of his head.

Tears welled in her eyes and spilled down her cheeks. "In order to hate you less, it looks like I have to hate myself more."

He couldn't stand the distance any more. He swiveled her stool enough that she faced him. Gently, he put his hands on her back and pulled her face to his chest. Her hot wet tears soaked into his T-shirt.

"Don't say that." He kissed her hair and massaged her shoulders. "You were deeply hurt. You felt completely abandoned by me. The fault is mine. I didn't see your anger as a cry of pain. I took it as an assault on my manhood. And I wouldn't give an inch on my pride."

The assault on his character had not been by Mandy alone, but he wouldn't say any more about that. He'd blamed her for a long time, but the fault lay on his doorstep. When she'd lost her temper and slapped him, he easily caught her wrist and held it until she was probably bruised.

Big man, make a woman feel small.

The shame of it burned in him.

She'd said she would leave Montana and he'd never hear from her again. And what did he do? He got up on his high horse and by God he wasn't coming down. *She could beg!*

He had his pride, his righteous character. His precious *manhood,* whatever that meant.

After a month, six months, a year, it was too late. He had his pride, all right. Set firm in the concrete he'd poured around his heart.

Now she pushed him away; not hard, but he got the message and backed up. She used the soggy linen napkin again.

"I'm going home, Cam. I don't like either one of

us much, but at least I can walk away from you. I can't get away from me. I have to...face myself."

She pressed her fingertips to her temples. He ached to hold her.

"Maybe we can see each other sometime. I don't know. I'm not going to run away again, leaving flaming bridges behind me, but I'm not sure I'll stay here either. I mean for the long term."

"I understand," he said. "I hate it all to hell, but I understand. Please let me say something before you go."

She moved toward the door. "I don't think—"

"Please, Mandy. One minute."

She turned, stopped, and nodded.

"I love you, Mandy. You're the only woman in the world for me. If I have to wait until you come to Bitter Falls for your twenty-fifth or thirtieth or fortieth class reunion, with me leaning on a cane and hoping you're single, then that's what I'll do. But I'd much rather spend all those years with you, building a future. Starting a family. Planting a grape arbor and an apple orchard."

She looked at the floor and he held his breath. At last, she looked into his eyes. Hers were brimming over with tears.

"Don't wait for me, Cam. I don't want your loneliness on my conscience." She walked to the door, unlocked it and opened it.

"Mandy—"

"Cam, find someone else."

Chapter 19

Mandy pulled into the driveway. Her dad's silver SUV was in the open garage. She turned off the ignition and sat still in the hope her headache would lift. No such luck. Crying had made it worse.

She stared at the grape arbor. Cam hadn't told her the whole truth; she knew there was more. If he'd loved her, why hadn't he married her? If she'd loved him enough to marry him, why had she fled from Bitter Falls like pronghorn ahead of a prairie fire?

Maybe it was as true about relationships as it was about apples, that one rotten apple spoiled the whole barrel. One glaring, unforgivable act could be a noxious weed that poisoned the ground.

No. People make mistakes; people can be redeemed.

Even me?

She got out and waved to Lefty. He and the man named Springer were doing something with lumber over where the corral used to be.

"What's up?" she called.

He touched a gloved hand to the brim of his hat and walked toward her. "Your sister is buying a horse and we have to get the corral and the old stalls ready. It's going to be good to have stock here again."

"Does one horse qualify as stock?"

"Well, no, I guess not." Then he grinned. "But maybe she'll get a pregnant mare and we can have the pitter patter of little hooves."

"You love horses, don't you?"

"I do. Cam West and I had great times when D'Ann was riding in rodeos. I'm real glad she came home. And you, too, of course."

Please don't talk about Cam. "When the doctor gives me the okay I might look for a nice gentle horse for myself."

"Cam's the one to ask. That man knows horses better than anybody I could name. That's quite a breeding operation he has over there. I stop by from time to time."

She nodded and turned to hide the tears that threatened to flow. "I'd better go in. I see my dad's home."

"Yes, ma'am. He got home about half an hour ago."

She walked into the house and called upstairs to her dad. She should think about fixing him supper. Cookies and milk probably didn't qualify.

No. She'd find something later.

She opened the drawer beneath the microwave, took out the ibuprofen, and stared at the container. This headache was too much for over-the-counter help. She took out a small prescription bottle instead and shook two painkillers into her hand.

She swallowed them with water; then she drank half a glass of iced tea without taking a breath. It didn't slake her thirst. Her bones were as dry as cattle skulls. As dry as tumbleweeds in that movie. She tried to think of the title.

Oh, yes. *The Grapes of Wrath.* She looked again at the arbor and closed her eyes. Eyelids blocked light; they did nothing to block images that were already somewhere in her battered brain.

"Hi, honey. Did you have a good day?" Her father came to the bottom of the stairs and crossed to her to kiss her cheek. "Has it been this hot the whole time I was gone?"

She turned around from the sink and nodded. It had been hot. She watched him tuck the bottom of his golf shirt into his khaki shorts.

"I'd like to talk to you," she said.

"Sure, honey. Is something wrong?"

She didn't answer. Instead, she walked deliberately to the living room and lowered herself carefully onto the sofa. She was back to concentrating on how to walk. Her right knee wasn't quite as firm as it should be.

He followed her into the living room and stood with his hands resting on his hips. "Something is wrong, I can tell. Mandy, talk to me, honey."

She wouldn't go through a recounting of the battering onslaught of memory she'd been facing. It didn't matter how she'd remembered things, or who had told her what and when. Cam last night, D'Ann and Gerri this afternoon, and Cam again for—what did he call it?—their truth session.

Truth.

Was it *all* truth, though? If she believed the bad news, should she believe, too, that he loved her and wanted a future together?

She said nothing. She watched her father take a seat in his favorite chair, the wing chair diagonally across the living room from her.

Her headache was thundering in her skull; she hoped to goodness the painkillers took effect quickly. She needed to get this ugly game of truth and its unintended consequences over with and go to bed. She'd told Cam she needed to think, and that was true. But thinking right now was like driving in a fog so thick she couldn't see the white line on the right side of the road. Stopping was too dangerous, but so was driving on.

"Twelve years ago," she said, "I was very much in love with Cam West. We planned to get married. I remember how angry you were. I remember the big fight you and I had over it."

"Did Cam West tell you this? I warned him not to tell you until I got home!"

"You did what? You *warned* him?"

He shrugged. "Well...warned is probably the wrong word," he said with an unconvincing chuckle. She knew he was backing away from words that upset her.

"When he came for dinner Thursday night we both could see that you didn't remember how, uh, close the two of you had been. You were only eighteen."

She'd heard *that* enough today. At least Cam gave her credit for being rational about their plans and truly capable of love. Everybody else acted like eighteen was her IQ as well as her age.

"I told—I mean, I suggested to Cam, and he agreed—that it would be better for you if I were here when he told you that you'd come close to marrying each other. I was afraid it would put you in an emotional tailspin. And it looks like I was right."

Cam had said she'd had an unholy argument with her father about the Christmas wedding. She'd wanted to elope. He'd been willing to elope, too. Not just willing; it was set. She remembered packing her clothes.

Before they left, though, he went to see her father. He said it was the right thing to do. Something about gentlemen.

It was odd that he didn't mention his visit with dear old dad when he'd agreed to tell her the whole truth today. Instead he'd said he'd refused to elope.

Something was missing. A lie by omission? All this probing for answers was like looking for one slippery meatball in a vat of spaghetti. She couldn't untangle the strands that clumped together, not the way her head hurt.

But details were coming back to her. Not details

of what the two men had said to one another—she hadn't heard any of that. They'd been in her dad's office at the far end of the first floor. She'd been upstairs packing.

No, she'd heard what her father *said* had happened.

It was time to put all the cards on the table. No wild cards. She wasn't letting Ford McCay revise history. Not anymore.

"After Cam had dinner here, you told him not to tell me we almost got married." It wasn't a question; he'd already admitted he'd "suggested" it to Cam to protect her.

Her dad rubbed his face, looked down, and nodded.

"Dad?" She waited until he met her eyes. "You can tell people not to remind me of painful things, but you can't stop me from remembering them."

She let her words reach him like slow, pin-sized darts. She knew he "got it" by the emotions that showed in his face and the way his hands shook. She waited.

"Cam came to see me," he said. "I'm talking about that day, years ago, when he worked here."

She nodded for him to go on.

"It was the day after you and I had a blazing, hot-tempered argument about you doing what I wanted you to do."

"Which was?" she asked.

"I wanted you to go to college in Virginia, to have a career if you wanted it. To marry someone suitable, not a one-hat, no horse cowboy. Once I realized how much influence Cam West had over you, I was determined to get you out of town as fast as possible. I was taking you to Missoula that night to catch a plane."

He massaged his left shoulder, then gripped his hands tightly together and pleaded with his eyes.

"Mandy, honey, I wanted what was best for you."

"By the time Cam came to see you we weren't yelling anymore," she said. She knew how she'd felt, a combination of anger, regret and sadness. Her dad had been blind to her feelings.

"No," he said. "I wasn't yelling. I thought things were better, that you were coming around to a more sensible way of thinking."

"*Your* way of thinking," she snapped. In order to get her on the plane out of Montana, he'd held out the lure—he called it a promise—that she could marry Cam in two years if she still wanted to. But it had been patently obvious he thought that couldn't happen. He didn't believe for a minute that she loved a cowboy more than the lifestyle she enjoyed.

She had plans to leave that night, all right, but not with her father. He could have his Thunderbird convertible and all the things he bought her. It seemed to her as she packed that her father had been trying to buy her agreement to his plans for a long time. Five dollars for every "A" in school had seemed like a harmless bribe, but the pattern had continued, hadn't it?

Cam had seen through the dust storm of the feuding and fighting and seen that McCay needed to know he wasn't losing a daughter. She didn't have to choose one of them; she could have both. That's what he'd told her before he went to see her father.

"I'll talk to him," Cam had said. They'd stood in the grape arbor, clinging tightly to one another. "A man owes that to another man when he's marrying his daughter. Then we'll leave. We'll get married in Libby."

She'd waited in her room while Cam went to her father's office in the suite he'd built onto the old house. She'd waited...but what happened next? She was close to remembering, but then it was gone. Her head pounded with pain.

From where she sat in the living room, she saw Cam's truck pull in front of the house. Her heart leaped with...surprise, yes, but something else. Joy. Time seemed to—no, it can't stand still. As if to declare that fact, the grandfather clock chimed the half hour.

Across the room, her father massaged his shoulder; hunched over, he put his face in his hands.

She rose and opened the front door before Cam knocked. She glanced at his face, then lowered her eyes. He opened the screen and came inside, his hat in both hands.

With the door open, sunshine spilled across the hardwood floor. She left it open and pulled the drapes on two windows as well. It was time to let light into all the dark corners.

She said nothing. Cam hung his hat on the elk-antler hat rack and put his hands in his pockets. As she sat, she observed a look pass between the two men.

Ford McCay sighed. "As you said, Cam came to see me."

She felt Cam's gaze on her but stared at her hands. They were as dry as flour. As dry as her bones. Was she drying up from the outside in, or from the inside out? Did it make any difference?

That night so long ago she hadn't held out any hope that Cam could change her father's mind, but she blessed him for trying. She kept packing. Instead of packing for college, she was covering her fancy dresses with plastic and packing all her new college clothes in boxes, putting her scrapbook and mementoes in a drawer of the old bureau in the attic.

The only things going in a suitcase were her jeans, sweatshirts, flannel pajamas and underwear. And one short, filmy nightgown she'd been saving for her wedding night.

The possibility had never entered her mind that her father would change Cam's mind, that the man she wanted to spend the rest of her life with—for richer, for poorer—would tell her No. That he would refuse to elope.

It must have been in a state of fury and heartbreak that she'd turned her back on both of them.

"Cam went to see you," she repeated, "which took a lot of courage. He told me he had to do it, that it was a requirement to stay in that hoity-toity club men always claim to belong in. *Gentlemen*."

Her father didn't smile. Instead, the line of his lips tightened even as his cheeks sagged. His face had lost its color.

"So this is the only question that remains about who knew what when," she said. Her voice was getting hoarse. It seemed like she'd been talking constantly, for hours and hours. Or gargling with gravel.

The pills still had no effect, and her head hurt more.

"One question remains," she repeated. "Because I wasn't in that room. And yet whatever passed between the two of you changed my life, sent it spinning off in a direction I hadn't even considered before that."

Her father looked away, unwilling to meet her eyes. But she wouldn't back down, not now. She was in a shooting gallery, and all the ducks were stuck in the up position. Suddenly, nothing was hidden. Whatever psychological mechanism suppressed her memory of that awful night, she'd blasted through it like a freight train through drywall.

"Dad, did you or did you not buy him off?"

She saw Cam come closer as if he would barge in and stop her from getting the answer. She glared at him and he stopped.

"I tried," her dad said, then cleared his throat and sat up straight. This time he met her eyes. "I tried, but he wouldn't be bought. I called him a fortune hunter. I said that I knew that's all he was after. He kept insisting that he loved you and he could take care of you, but I laughed in his face. I wrote a check and stuffed it in his shirt pocket and told him to get his sorry ass off my land."

He rubbed his face with both hands and sat forward to rest his elbows on his thighs. "I left the room. When I came back, I saw the check on the floor. Or rather, what used to be the check. He'd torn it into confetti and thrown it down."

"But you didn't tell me that, did you?" Her voice was hardly more than a whisper. She rubbed her forehead. The pain was worse, much worse.

She saw Cam's boots in front of her but couldn't look up into his face. He sat beside her and she felt the heat of his leg beside hers. Still she stared at the floor. Slowly, she raised her eyes to meet her father's.

"You didn't tell me that," she said again.

"No, God forgive me, I didn't."

"You went to my room. You told me you'd bought him off, that you knew all along that he was a fortune hunter. And that he'd admitted that's all he wanted me for."

She took a deep breath and exhaled slowly. "If God forgives you for the lie, I hope God forgives me for believing it."

She looked at Cam. "You left out that part this afternoon, Cam. You said you'd refused to elope. But you left out my accusations and what I called you. You left out how I slapped your face. How my trust in you crumbled so easily."

"Mandy, I should have—"

"I understand, Cam. You were wrong twelve

years ago to let me believe what I did, but I understand. The only way to defend yourself was to call my father a liar. You knew I'd never forgive him, and you didn't want to be responsible for that. So you told me the elopement was off. And I said I never wanted to see you again."

"Mandy," he began, then stopped.

"Three people," she said. She smiled at Cam and then at her father as tears spilled down her cheeks. "Three people with enough self-righteous pride to ruin any chance at happiness for any of them."

"It doesn't have to end that way, Mandy," Cam said. "What I said at my house was absolutely true. I love you. I want to marry you. I want us to spend the rest of our lives together, to have a family."

"I can't answer you now. I'm tired. Too tired. I'm going to lie down. Maybe tomorrow or the next day I'll be able to think more clearly. Please leave, Cam."

"Mandy, forgive me—"

She pressed her fingers to his lips. "I do forgive you. And I'm trying to forgive my dad. But I don't see how I can forgive myself."

He took her wrist, gently, and kissed the fingers already against his lips. Then he opened her hand and kissed the palm and the inside of her wrist. He released her and she slowly pulled her hand away, pressing it against her waist.

Cam had told her this afternoon that people thought she was shallow and spoiled, but that the real Mandy McCay was so much better. How had he put it? That she was a true western woman, capable and close to the land.

All those summer nights so long ago, he'd believed her to be worthy of his love.

Well, she'd proved him wrong, hadn't she? If slapping his face and driving away at eighty miles an hour didn't prove it, then throwing herself into Hollywood and in front of every camera—for eleven years and four months of barren, empty uselessness—well, she'd surely made her point.

It took a near-death experience to bring her home to Montana. But she couldn't forgive herself enough to come all the way home to Cam.

He opened his mouth, probably to state his position again, but he closed it and nodded. She watched him step slowly out the front door. Time crawled by as she listened for the sound of his truck leaving.

Ford McCay sat motionless, his face in his hands once again. If she felt better, physically, she would go to him, get him to stand up so she could hug him. They loved each other. They simply hadn't shown it the right way, either of them.

As it was, she only had enough energy left to get to bed. She stood and shuffled to the stairs.

Away from the windows, the stairwell was dark. Holding the banister as she had the first day she got home, she climbed up the polished hardwood stairs. Left foot up, firm. Drag the weaker foot up and get it on the stair. Lock the knee. Do it again. Don't let go of the banister. Use the strength in her arm to compensate for the weakness in her right knee and foot. She was nearly to the top. One more step.

Without warning, her left knee buckled. Her hand slipped off the banister and she lurched to her right—but her right leg collapsed.

"Dad!" She cried out as she fell. The last thing she saw was the floor, far below her.

"Mandy! Oh, my God! Honey!" Her dad's voice seemed far away. Then it faded completely.

Chapter 20

Cam stood outside the curtain in the emergency room.

"Excuse me, sir. Could you step back, please?"

He stepped back reluctantly, getting only a quick look at Mandy's pale face as the technician shoved the cart with a balky wheel into the examining space.

Minutes dragged by. A boy in a baseball uniform walked in, holding his arm against his chest. The angle of the elbow wasn't right; the kid's face was as white as Mandy's. Cam could tell he was trying to be brave.

Hell, he knew exactly how the kid felt.

"Excuse me again, sir. We're going to take Ms. McCay to get an MRI."

A nurse snapped the curtain back and pulled the narrow bed on its rollers and its satellite IV cart into the center of the room. While she stopped to pick up a clipboard, Cam took Mandy's right hand. The left arm was immobile, with plastic tubing taped to an IV needle.

"Mandy, I'm right here. They're going to take pictures of your head and then you'll be back. I'll be here."

Before he could say more, the nurse and a technician wheeled the bed and cart out through double doors.

"Cam, why don't you take a seat in the waiting room?" Dr. Vogle put her hand on his arm. "This will take a while, and then you can come back in. I'll come get you."

He nodded; he was in the way. He wouldn't even have been allowed back there if it weren't for Elise Vogle being a personal friend. They'd worked together for a year on a program to let special-needs children learn to ride ponies.

Feeling like a zombie, he thanked her and trudged to the waiting room. More to have something to hold in his hands than because he wanted anything to drink, he poured a cup of coffee. It tasted surprisingly good.

Across the room sat Ford McCay. Bent forward at the waist, he clasped his hands and stared down at them. Over McCay's head, the second hand on the black and white wall clock clicked off the time, but Cam looked at his watch anyway.

He'd been about to turn off the main road into his ranch when he saw the ambulance coming toward him. He pulled off the road to the right and watched it fly past. Something—he couldn't say what—made him pull a U-turn and follow the flashing red lights. His worst fear was proven true when he saw it slow and take the corner into Bitter Falls Farm.

Before the paramedics even got Mandy on the gurney, Cam had been on the phone to Douglas at his place, telling him to take the other truck and drive all the way up the pipeline road toward the arch. Joey and D'Ann were up there in the wilderness and there was no way anyone could phone them.

"Don't baby the truck, Douglas," he'd barked. "Make it climb. Get D'Ann down to the hospital."

As he spoke, he'd watched McCay follow the gurney out the front door. Slow. Measured. Like a pallbearer.

The pale, white-haired man with hunched

shoulders looked nothing like a titan of industry as he stood by the open ambulance. The paramedics folded the legs of the gurney and slid it inside.

Cam gave McCay a hand to step up into the vehicle.

He sat on the narrow bench and called to Cam, "She'll be all right. She's a fighter."

"She'll be all right," Cam had echoed. "Yes, sir." He wondered if he sounded any more convinced of that than McCay did.

He'd followed the ambulance to Bitter Falls Hospital. It wasn't hard to drive that fast. Hell, it was hard for him not to press the accelerator to the floor and pass the ambulance. When the fierce woman guarding the entrance to the ER tried to keep him out because he wasn't "family," Dr. Elise Vogle overrode her veto.

In the examining cubicle, Vogle told Ford McCay and Cam that Mandy's vital signs were good. She wasn't responding to voice commands, however, and they would take her for an MRI of her head in a few minutes.

"I have a call in to Mandy's neurosurgeon and radiologist at UCLA Medical Center," she'd said. "If possible, I want them to look at the MRI in real time. I believe they'll be able to tell if anything has changed."

****

Mandy couldn't open her eyes. She could smell something. How odd; how puzzling. Apple blossoms.

She tried again to open her eyes, but nothing happened. And yet, inexplicably, she could see. She could see a woman on a moving bed, and two women—one a nurse and one a technician, she was certain of that—sliding the patient onto a narrow bench.

The paper cover on the bench crinkled as the woman's bare back moved against it. The woman was shivering, but the other women didn't notice.

Now they were sliding her into a circular hole in the machine. They went away. She was alone in the cold machine. Alone and scared. The machine began a banging noise, like jackhammers. Again and again. Then a pause. Again, bang, bang, bang. Too many to count.

"You're not alone."

The woman heard the voice above the sound of the machine.

"I'm right here. I'm up here, above the machine, watching."

"Am I dying? Am I dying this time?"

The Mandy hovering against the ceiling didn't answer.

The Mandy inside the jackhammer opened her eyes.

****

Cam stood beside the bed in the examining room. Mandy's hand looked small in his. "I'm right here, sweetheart," he murmured. Over and over, like a mantra. *I'm here.*

He hardly knew anyone else existed but Mandy and himself. Regret weighed on him like an anvil.

Now that the truth of their bitter break-up was exposed, the "what ifs" ran through Cam's mind like a hundred gerbils in a hundred cages. What if he'd been up front with her—and her father—about his background? He'd gone to see Ford McCay that day prepared to tell him he wasn't as poor as he appeared to be. He hated to tap into his trust fund; he'd gotten to be quite proud of his vision of himself as an independent man, a self-made man on his way up. But he'd decided to use the money set aside for him to make their life—Mandy's new life—more comfortable.

He never got a chance to say any of that. McCay had been too angry, too certain that Cam was a no-account cowboy out to marry into money. An opportunist. It had all ended in disaster.

Movement at the foot of Mandy's bed caught his eye. Ford McCay had been sitting in a chair out of the way of the nurses. Now he stood, his hands clenched around the metal bar at the foot of the narrow, moveable bed. His knuckles were white. Bloodless.

"Sir?" he said. "Mr. McCay?"

No response. He moved closer and saw that McCay's skin was ash gray and he was sweating profusely. Cam touched Ford's arm and spoke his name again. This time McCay looked toward him, but his eyes showed confusion instead of focusing.

Cam wheeled on his heel and rushed out of the cubicle. Snapping his head one way and the other, he rushed to stop Dr. Vogle in the aisle.

"Ford McCay needs a doctor! Now!"

She gave one look at Cam's face and turned around. "I need assistance here, stat!"

In about two minutes, Mandy's dad was on a gurney with an oxygen mask over his face. They moved him into the examining room next to her and started sticking round electrodes all over his bare chest.

A nurse thumped the inside of his arm. "I've got a good vein here." She paused. "Okay, IV is in."

D'Ann arrived like a dust devil and took charge of her dad, answering all the questions about his health history. It seemed like every third minute someone had a question for her about Mandy. She was cool, unruffled. Clinical. Cam admired her more and more.

While Vogle and the neurosurgeon on staff at Bitter Falls Hospital consulted with doctors in Los Angeles, Cam spent longer periods holding on to Mandy's hand and telling her, over and over, that he loved her. He told her about the house, how the second bedroom would make a perfect nursery, and how he would get plans drawn for an addition in the back.

"I'm thinking three more bedrooms for when the kids get older. And whatever you want to do with the kitchen—name it. I'll fix it any way you want it."

Her eyes fluttered. At first he thought it was involuntary eyelid motion, but they opened. And he was sure—or was it wishful thinking?—that she focused on him.

"Mandy?" he asked. "I'm right here, sweetheart."

"Bright. Copper. Kettles."

D'Ann appeared at his elbow. "Did you say what I think you said? Bright copper kettles?"

"Yes."

Her voice sounded awful, but Cam never heard such a beautiful sound in his life.

D'Ann laughed. "Either she's channeling Julie Andrews and her next words will be 'warm woolen mittens,' or she's telling you to put up a ceiling fixture in your kitchen. Her kitchen."

"What?" He was completely lost.

"She told me the other day that if it were her kitchen she'd want an assortment of copper-bottomed pans over the stove. Easy to reach. I think it might be good to put a TV in the kitchen, too, so she can watch the Food Channel while she pan-sears scallops and sautés beef medallions."

He leaned forward and kissed Mandy's forehead. Her left eye was a shiner. She was going to hate looking in a mirror for a while.

"Mandy," D'Ann said. "Good news. Double good news. You have a concussion, nothing worse. They're keeping you overnight for observation and putting me, Nurse Ratched, in charge of your recuperation at home."

"I thought you said..." Mandy gave a crooked smile. "Thought you said good news."

229

"What's the other good news?" Cam asked.

"Dad had an episode of unstable angina. It looks like he has blockage in one, maybe two, arteries. Not enough oxygen getting to the heart. He needs to be seen by a cardiologist for an angioplasty. All that is state of the art these days, and they have an excellent specialist on his way in. Nothing to worry about. Of course," she grinned, "when they let him go home, he, too, will be taking orders from me. You have a horsewhip I can borrow, don't you, Cam? If things get desperate."

Mandy squeezed his hand and said, "Water."

D'Ann reached over and put ice chips on her lips.

Mandy reached up and took her sister's hand. "Do you want...?"

"Do I want what?" D'Ann, too, kissed her forehead.

"Do you want to be maid of honor?"

"Do I have to wear a flamingo-pink dress with a bow across my butt and butterfly sleeves?"

Mandy nodded and winced.

"For you, yes," D'Ann said. "Does Cam have to wear a tuxedo? The kind with tails?" She leaned closer as if telling Mandy a secret, but spoke loud enough for him to hear. "I think he'll agree to anything right now, so you might want to press your advantage."

Mandy squeezed his forearm. "He can wear jeans."

"So the groom will be in jeans, and the maid of honor will look like something from a cotton candy machine after a power surge. What about the bride? How about a chef's hat?"

Mandy slapped playfully at D'Ann's arm. "Go away."

"All right." She looked at Cam. "Don't tire her out. That's an order!"

"Yes, Nurse."

"And don't call me Nurse. Call me Aunt D'Ann. You might as well get in some practice before I have nieces and nephews to spoil and adore."

She left and closed the curtain all the way.

"Alone at last," he said.

A nurse or doctor outside their curtain chose that precise moment to call out for assistance. "Millie, get me that rectal probe, would you?"

Cam winced. "Not quite as alone as I'd like."

Mandy smiled. "I do love you." She touched her chest above her heart.

"I know that." He touched his chest as she had. "I know it in my head, too. And my liver and my spleen and my large intestine and my bones. Or it could be a sign this place is getting on my nerves."

A male nurse as big as Cam pulled back the curtain. "Time to take your vital signs, Mandy. How you doing? Sir, could you wait outside for a while? We'll be moving Ms. McCay to a private room. You can see her there in about half an hour. I promise."

Cam leaned down to touch his lips to hers, once, softly. It was all the promise either of them needed.

A word about the author...

I live in Sequim, Washington, on the beautiful Olympic Peninsula (northwest of Seattle), with my husband, Bill, and our old, sweet-natured mutt, Laddie. The name of my website, RainshadowRomance, refers to the climate of Sequim, which is located on the Strait of Juan de Fuca in the rain shadow of the Olympic Mountains. My favorite activity (after writing and reading) is downhill skiing, which we usually do in Utah.

My writing background includes time as a newspaper editor in New Mexico and four mystery novels. You can read about them on my website. "Love with a Welcome Stranger" is my first romance novel.

Visit Lynnette at www.rainshadowromance.com

Printed in the United States
212023BV00004B/2/P

9 781601 543141